The Green
Grassy Slopes

W. A. Ballinger

The Green Grassy Slopes

CORGI BOOKS
A DIVISION OF TRANSWORLD PUBLISHERS

THE GREEN GRASSY SLOPES

A CORGI BOOK   552 08219 8

First publication in Great Britain

PRINTING HISTORY
Corgi Edition published 1969

Copyright © W. A. Ballinger 1969

This book is set in 10-11 pt. Baskerville

Corgi Books are published by Transworld Publishers Ltd.,
Bashley Road, London, N.W.10.
Made and printed in Great Britain by
Hunt Barnard & Co., Ltd., Aylesbury, Bucks.

The Green
Grassy Slopes

PART ONE

PART ONE

PROLOGUE

There were heather and bracken beside the road and here and there were green, grassy slopes where cows grazed. In a fenced field before a rough stone-built cottage with a corrugated iron roof that had once been thatched, a big sow rooted desultorily with an earthy snout. A kestrel hung on the wind above the mountain and stooped indecisively on a grouse that rocketed for the cover of a stand of wind-distorted Scots pines. The victim cackled derision as the hawk soared again to its invisible station in the sky.

The road led to the west, a long, undulating road with a fair enough surface for the few cars and buses and lorries that used it.

Next to the road a man was sharpening a scythe. He had been cutting rushes in the field. They grew in clumps about the grass, a sign of dampness and a need for draining. On the Black Mountain there should have been no need for draining but the rushes grew and that proved the sourness of the soil.

The cry of the grouse faded and the song of the whetstone on the scythe blade was the only sound in the land. There was a red, faded kerchief about the whetstone, for a stone laid down in a field is a lost stone without some touch of colour to distinguish it. The blade kissed the stone, this side and that of the edge, and then the man laid down the scythe to light his pipe. It had broken at the stem and it was wrapped with black insulating tape that leaked a little air into the suction. The black, damp tobacco did not light easily.

The cry of the grouse had been loud. The song of the scythe had filled the air. Now there was only the scratch of match on box and the hissing suck of breath at pipe.

The clip-clop of hooves came very clearly from the distance.

The pipe was drawing at last when the strangers came in sight and the man left his scythe where it lay to go and lean on a gate and watch them pass by.

The hooves were a donkey's, a fair-sized, mountainy-looking donkey that could have come from Donegal where they bred donkeys to carry turf and panniers of potatoes and seaweed up from the shore. The countryman's eyes took in the donkey first and then its burden, which was a pair of panniers and a woman.

There would be a turnip or two in those panniers and like enough a bushel of potatoes and maybe a chicken as well, lifted from along the way. Tinkers would lift anything.

And yet this couple did not have the look of tinkers, the woman in a blue, hooded cloak and the man a great, gaunt caricature, six and a half feet high or maybe more; dark rusty clothes and an age-greened bowler hat.

A tinker in a bowler hat was a strange sight and perhaps these were no tinkers, for with a slump laying men idle all across the world anyone could be driven to the roads. His own cousin in the Americas had become what he called a hobo this last year and gasping for a sight of Ulster again. Yet only a year or two back he had been a millionaire in New York and drinking champagne and whisky for his breakfast.

The Wall Street crash they called it and America worse than Ireland now if you could believe it. Anyone at all could be on the road these days.

The man watched the others pass and come up to the crest of the hill beyond and he knew that from where they had halted they were looking down on the city beneath. He puffed his pipe and watched and speculated mildly on whence they had come and where they were going. He also watched that they did not leave the road, for he had a hen laying away in the ditch up there and her eggs were meant for no tinker.

He watched them pause there and look down on the city as if it was the Promised Land.

He heard the man say a single word and that word was 'Belfast.' There was such a strange yearning in the voice; it was so clear, so full of some vital inner force that the memory of it stuck with the man long after he had gone back to his scything, even after he had gone to his bed that night.

Belfast! What was there in the word to stir a man so?

*

From the Black Mountain above Hilltown the whole city was laid out in a great bowl, contained by hills on three sides and Belfast Lough on the fourth. The hills contained also a smoky pall that rose from chimneys and was never quite dispersed even in a gale. The smoke blurred the city's shape, softened its colours, transmuted it into something a little less than real, muted its harshness.

The River Lagan pierced the city and widened out to the lough and the sea. And by the Lagan stood the gantries of the shipyard, rearing high and bleak among the rows of little houses that surrounded it, dominating the city they had created.

Gantries and cranes and long, ugly fabricating shops and machine shops brooded about the river as if in resentful wonder at their own idleness. There were no completing hulls on the ways, no clatter of riveting hammers that would have reached even to the hilltop; there was only that tall, gaunt, structural assembly waiting like Frankenstein's monster to have life breathed into it.

The tall man beside his donkey gazed across the city, taking in the centre with its ornate city hall, its shop buildings and its surrounding slums, viewing the suburbs with their gardens and tree-lined streets, gazing across the city to the rounded hills of County Down.

The city was laid out at his feet and it was as if he surveyed it like an heir coming at last into his own. There was in his face an eager, prescient hunger as he looked down across the city of Belfast shimmering in its smoke haze, waiting for his coming.

Then he plucked lightly on the donkey's rein and they moved forward down the slope.

CHAPTER ONE

"I'll give you that again, dear lady. 'As bloody warfare tonight swept the streets of Belfast...' No, I am not swearing, lady. I never swear in the presence of members of the gentler sex unless they prove so utterly moronic ... No. That is not a part of the story. It is a philosophical reflection."

Tod Milligan was moderately drunk. He considered that he had every reason to be. The hissing and crackling on the line to the Manchester office of *The Daily Post* made conversation no more confused than the thoughts in his head.

"Dear lady, sweet thane of the typewriter and copy-taking pool, I'm going to start again. And this time for Christ's sake try to just take down the story and keep your comments for afterwards. Otherwise I will come zooming down this wire and pull your knickers off and smack your little bottom. Or if it is a big bottom I will smack that ... Go on then, complain. But take this bloody story first – and I was swearing that time."

Milligan took another pull at the whisky, pushed Rafferty's body further into the corner of the telephone kiosk with his foot and began again to dictate.

" 'As bloody warfare tonight swept the streets of Belfast in a new outbreak of sectarian bitterness, troops were being moved into the city from the nearby British army barracks at Holywood, County Down.

"The Northern Ireland Cabinet, in permanent session since rioting began to get out of hand three days ago, has issued appeals to both sides of the community to keep calm.

"The armed Royal Ulster Constabulary, in special armoured cars protected against grenade attacks, have been patrolling the main battle area, between the Falls and Shankill Roads. However, their intervention has not been enough to prevent the bloody warfare which has sent houses flaring, littered the streets with dead and brought terror even into those areas where the conflict between the Orange and the Green, the Protestant and the Catholic does not normally extend.

"As I phone this story from Belfast's swank Royal Avenue, main shopping centre of this red brick, industrial city, a man lies dead at my feet. His name is Rafferty and he had nothing to do with the conflict. He was killed as he talked to me, killed by a bullet which may have been intended for me or may simply have been fired at random by some trigger-happy killer of either persuasion.'"

The copy-talker called for a moment's halt to change slips in her machine. Milligan finished the whisky and dropped the bottle with a soft plop on Rafferty's belly. Tears welled in his eyes. Poor Rafferty. Just a casual passerby – and now he lay dead. He knew his name was Rafferty because this name was stamped in neat gilt lettering inside his bowler hat. Of course the bowler could be stolen, or borrowed.

Poor Rafferty, Tod Milligan thought. He had only come into the kiosk to call a taxi. If he had not stayed, argued whose precedence it was at the phone, he would be alive now. And Tod Milligan would probably be dead.

"Yes?" the girl in Manchester was saying. "Yes? I'm ready . . ."

Over-ready, Milligan thought. You've gone off, dear lady. You sound like a sour old spinster, a real oul' bag.

"Right," he said aloud. "The story goes on: 'In the city tonight they are asking, quote, Is this a return to the days of Civil War, to the twenties which everyone hoped were forgotten? End quote.

"As the bullets sing their deadly way down the main streets and the dull sound of the explosions of the hand

14

grenades echoes in the little back-to-back kitchen houses they wonder if once again the streets will have to run with blood before . . .' "

There was an interruption at the other end of the line.

"Milligan, this is Parkinson, night news editor. Not too much of the colour, old boy. We're a little tight for space tonight, two local by-elections, you know – "

"But, Mr Parkinson – this is practically civil war."

"Quite so. But it's not happening in England; the by-elections are."

"Northern Ireland is an integral part of the United Kingdom."

"I know all that. Good Lord, we have every sympathy with you Catholics, oppressed as you are by these Dublin Protestants – "

Tod Milligan was not quite sure whether or not the Englishman was joking. He had a heavy suspicion that he was not. But a correspondent cannot quarrel with his bread and butter, joking or not.

"Just keep to the facts, Milligan, will you? Casualties, any official statement, that sort of thing."

"Yes, Mr Parkinson."

"And I'll tell you what, Milligan. We'll have room for a nice little think piece the day after tomorrow, a nice background story on how it all started. About eight hundred words. Try to get it on the wire before three in the afternoon. Thank you, Milligan – you can give the girl the rest of your story now."

The sky was reddening in two or three quarters when Tod Milligan fumed out of the kiosk and set off on the unrewarding venture of finding a pub which had not closed.

The English, he thought, would he ever understand the English? Two by-elections and Ulster ceased to be news. War on their own doorstep and they couldn't be less interested.

He thought of the Orange Lodges with their continual affirmations of loyalty to the constitution and their fervent pride in their British nationality – and he thought of England's ignorance of and indifference to them. It would have been funny if it were not also so tragic, if people were not being killed because of it all.

He was challenged by a police patrol as he crossed the Queen's Bridge on the long walk homewards to Knock. He had his curfew pass and for a little he yarned with the men. He was able to give them a little news. They gave him a titbit or two in return.

"The Papishes are getting the shit beat out them," a rawboned Ballymena constable declared. "They'll not want any more for a while after the boys is finished with them."

A morose constable sat in the truck, not joining in the conversation. Milligan deduced that he must himself be a Roman Catholic. Life must be very difficult for him just now. He would be mistrusted by the Protestants and treated as traitor by his own people.

At first, the thirties had seemed to usher in a new decade of understanding in this country. Now, however, it appeared as if everything was back to normal again – if there was a normal in Ireland.

He felt bitter as well as increasingly sober and the bitterness deepened as he remembered Parkinson's request for eight hundred words on how it had all started.

By now he was on the Newtownards Road and on impulse he turned away from the main road, down one of the endless rank of identical side streets that made up the throbbing heart of Ballymacarett.

Behind the curtains he sensed the eyes watching him, a stranger. The rows of red brick terraces, two storeys high, each house like its neighbours even to the coffee-coloured lace curtains in the windows and the white-clayed front doorsteps, were infinitely depressing.

He came to an open space with some evidence of abortive building work on the clay and puddles. There was a mound in the middle which had been levelled off and flagged roughly with paving stones. About the mound there was some evidence that there had once been a garden. A few plants still struggled for life with weeds growing among them.

Also on this muddy patch of ground there were piles of builders' supplies, sacks of cement under a tarpaulin, some bricks stacked up, a clutter of shovels and picks. There was a watchman's hut but the brazier in front of it was unlit. The tools and the cement must take their chance with the petty thieves. No night watchman was liable to be out of his house in these troublous nights.

Besides the bricks there lay incongruously the framework of two children's swings, their heavy iron already beginning to pit with rust though they had not even been erected. Beyond the waste ground there was a gaunt building with a corrugated iron roof on which the rain drummed.

Milligan wished that the whisky had not been finished, that he had enough left for a last bitter toast.

For this was the place.

It had started here, the fighting whose echo still sounded sporadically through the city.

This was the place and the toast would have been to Mungo McMaster whose ghost must surely walk the mud for ever.

CHAPTER TWO

"Unity," Shane Hendrick had said. "The unity of the working class against the capitalist, the unity of the trade union against the employer, the unity of the exploited against the exploiters. This is our purpose. Unity."

He had spoken with heat and conviction. And yet he knew that his message was making no impact at all on the men gathered in the John William Cowen Memorial Hall, Ballymacarett.

Whoever John William Cowan was, thought Hendrick, he could scarcely be very gratified at this particular erection to his memory. The hall, on whose corrugated iron roof – for the memorial money had run out before slates could be put on – the rain was pattering with relentless persistence, contrived to be at the same time both musty and damp, to be both stuffy and chilly.

Though it was not an Orange Hall, a portrait of the King in naval uniform was flanked by two Union Jacks on one wall, while the opposite one was occupied by a large poster of the Prime Minister, Lord Craigavon, with the faded legend 'A Protestant Government for a Protestant People.'

The floor of the hall was occupied by rows of uncomfortable wooden benches which in turn were about half-occupied by Hendrick's audience, a bored audience here only because it was free, because there was nothing better to do and because there would be tea and buns afterwards.

Hendrick continued to speak with a fervour which was in his mind but not his heart as he tried to strike some spark from the grey, unresponsive faces that stared up blankly at him.

It had been a mistake, he was thinking now, to come back to the city of his birth. It had seemed a wonderful opportunity when the Amalgamated Shipbuilding Union sent him to replace Natty Johnson as local organiser. Natty had sold out to the bosses, they said in London. Now a new man was needed, a man with fire in his belly and a tongue to call spirits into life.

Hendrick remembered the Belfast he had left, the city of bustle and laughter and argument, the live city for all its dour ways.

He had come back to a dead city, a city gripped by the thirties Depression as no city in England that he had seen had been affected.

Belfast's eggs had been in one basket, in the shipyard. There was linen too, of course, but the Queen's Island – that was not an island any more – was the heart of the city. When the gantries were still and the riveting hammers silent, Belfast was silent also.

Or, as a plater had put it to him more pithily: "When oul' Rebbeck takes a physic, Belfast shites."

Frederick Rebbeck was chairman of Harland and Wolff Ltd., which in turn was the Queen's Island.

And no one was buying ships that year, not in Belfast, not on the Clyde, not on the Tyne, not anywhere. In America the hopeful emigrants were walking the roads and the out-held hand was the signal of the times. It was 'Buddy, can you spare a dime?' time.

The rest of the world was no concern of Shane Hendrick. Belfast was – and especially its shipyard workers; these grim, grey-faced men with their duncher caps, their mufflers, their threadbare suits and their hopeless eyes. Sometimes a stub of a Woodbine would be extracted from a waistcoat pocket, lit, drawn on for a couple of luxurious puffs and then carefully extinguished and returned to the pocket. These occasions were the only time when any interest was shown by anyone, so far as he could tell.

And yet this gathering was the elite, the men who would be shop stewards, branch secretaries and treasurers. These were the ones who still had enough interest in the Union to attend a meeting, dare to dream of a future that would not be spent on 'the Buroo', on assistance from the State or from private charities. These were the best – so what of the rest?

Thinking of the bright hopes that had been in himself through his Union training course, thinking of the even higher aspirations that had accompanied him to Belfast, he wondered grimly what would become of them.

And yet his Union training had been thorough enough for him to show no sign of his own discouragement in his voice.

"You do not need me, brothers, to tell you what the times are like. We can look out of that window and we can see the rust red on the gantries of the Queen's Island. Weeds grow in the gutters of the engine sheds. On the slipways of the greatest shipyard in the world, the grass is growing green . . ."

A bench grated and a thin, bent man with steel-rimmed glasses rose, hawked and – despite a prohibitory notice – spat on the floor.

"Mister, never mind the grass on the slipway. What about the green, grassy slopes of the Boyne?"

In a thin cracked voice he began to chant:

"On the green grassy slopes of the Boyne,
Where the Orangemen with William did join,
Where we fought for our glorious deliverance,
On the green grassy slopes of the Boyne."

One or two of the others joined in and the rest showed their first sign of interest of the afternoon.

"Good man yourself, Harry . . . Give it till them . . . No surrender."

Hendrick felt a pulse begin to twitch beneath his left eye. When he left Belfast in 1914, to join the Royal Navy, there had been no violent cleavage between Protestant and Roman Catholic communities. There had been a degree of separation but it was far from complete.

The Easter Rising of 1916, Home Rule and Partition in 1922 had changed all that. He had read about it in the Press, of course, but as he had no close relatives in Belfast since the death of his father during the war, the real facts of the situation, the bitterness which now soured relations, had never really come home to him.

"That's enough," he called now. "This is a Union meeting, not the Twelfth of July. Keep your speeches and your songs for Lodge nights."

"By God, it's coming to it," scowled the singer, "if a man can't express his loyalty to the Crown and His Gracious Majesty without being shut up. John William Cowan would be whirling in his grave if he heard of the like."

"Be as loyal as you like," Hendrick snapped, "but wait till afterwards. Now, I was telling you about the need for unity in the struggle for decent wages and decent conditions – "

"Just a meenute, my mannie. Not so far. Not so fast at all. About this unity, now. Just who's going to be united? Are you maybe talking about the Papishes?"

"I'm talking about working men being exploited by their bosses."

"Yon's no answer. Show us your colours, mister. Where do you stand? Maybe – now maybe you'd happen to be a left-footer yourself. Come on, mister. Where d'you hang your hat of a Sunday? What foot do you dig with?"

Quietly, with an inner sadness, Hendrick answered: "I was baptised in the Presbyterian church. And as for your other question – "

Hendrick was about to say that the Union had no interest in men's religion or lack of it. But he was saved from this disastrous revelation by a cry from the window:

"Hey, boys. C'mon here. Come and see this . . . Jeez!"

*

The coming of the Reverend Mungo McMaster was not an event that any who saw it would ever forget. It had a carefully stage-managed visual impact that an impressario would have envied, though Mungo McMaster would certainly have visited a brothel sooner than a theatre.

Out of the rain and across the muddy puddles of the waste ground there strode with slow, deliberate ploughman's steps an immensely tall, grotesquely thin man in an ill-fitting suit of dark, respectable tweed and a bowler hat that was green with age.

His head was a little bowed and his shoulders seemed to jut obstinately into the wind that pressed against him.

Behind him, led by a rope halter, there followed a piebald donkey with two wicker panniers slung across its back. And on the animal's rump a figure squatted which could have been male or female, so swathed was it in a thick, blue, hooded cloak.

The man led his donkey across the waste ground to a mound of rubble and rubbish which rose above the mud in the centre. This was all that remained of Gonagal's bakery, which had stood there until 1925, when an explosion, followed by a fire, had destroyed it utterly.

There were two views about that explosion. One indicated that because Gonagal had sacked a Catholic workman the Fenians had made the place a target for terrorism. The other view was that Gonagal was two steps out of the bankruptcy courts and might have had something to do with the fire himself. Certainly he had taken his insurance money very smartly out of Ulster and now ran a moderately elegant little hotel in Brighton.

Whatever the view, the ground lay waste, 'Gonagal's Piece', mud in the rain, dust in the dry, the rubble mount a monument to either desperation or destruction.

On the mound the donkey was halted. The tall man helped down from the donkey's rump the figure, which could be recognised now as a woman.

22

"Yon's a funny sort of tinkers," someone commented in the hall.

Hendrick sighed and himself came to the window. A side-long smirk greeted him: "Aye, man. You'll not can fart against thunder."

The two figures on the mound were motionless now, heads bowed.

"Would they be praying, do you suppose?"

"They'd hardly be looking for sixpences there, anyway."

Briskly now the big man unloaded the panniers from the donkey, together with some long sticks that were thrust under the straps. The animal was freed to find what fodder it could in the weeds about Gonagal's Piecè.

The man and the woman began to erect a tent and they carried the panniers with their remaining contents within. It was a stained, patched tent but not so raggedly impromptu as a tinker's tent. It looked as if once it had belonged to the British Army. Some of the men in the hall who had fought in France and Flanders felt a little, painful pang of recognition. Mud and a tent . . . it was very familiar.

Hendrick's occasional summonses to his class were ignored. They watched, with the fascination that any break in the order of monotony has, while the man went in again to the tent – in which the woman had remained from its erection – and came out with a small wooden stand which he set up before the tent entrance.

Onto it he now fastened a folding placard of hardboard or plywood, on which was written in large red letters:

'MINE EYES HAVE SEEN THE GLORY OF THE COMING OF THE LORD'

In the hall the message was read slowly. Comment came at last.

"Ach, sure he's only an oul' preacher.'

It was not the sort of assessment they would soon be making.

CHAPTER THREE

"How d'you feel it's going, Mr Hendrick?"

It was the time when the cinema had just begun to exploit the drama potential of the newspaper world.

"Hold the front page. I'm coming in with a big story," was become cliché. So were battered hats on the back of the head and stained trench coats. As usual, nature was imitating art to the best of its ability.

No one could have mistaken Tod Milligan for anything but a young journalist, even without the notebook in his hand and the poised pencil.

Tod Milligan spoke in what was called locally a 'Malone Road accent', which is to say with a clarity and refinement not general in this city. But whereas most of his contemporaries wore the neat lounge suit of the aspiring solicitor or doctor, Tod was clad in the inevitable trench coat and his hat was more battered than most.

"Oh, not too badly. A little progress . . ."

Hendrick stiffened in suspicion, stared at Tod now that he saw him properly.

"Who the hell are you?" he demanded. "How did you get in?"

"Tod Milligan. *Northern Standfast*", the reporter answered. "And my news editor thinks I could write something horrible to discredit you and the union."

Hendrick stared, not sure whether or not to be angry.

"I got in through the door," Milligan went on. "With the others."

He gave his most engaging smile and since he had very white, even teeth and eyes that crinkled a little at the corners, the effect was disarming.

"This was not a public meeting," Hendrick observed heavily.

Big Jim Jarvey, who had trained him, would not have been so quiet, Hendrick thought. He would have thrown the reporter out. The boot might have gone in. But he was not Big Jim.

"Your news editor is a fool," Hendrick went on quietly enough.

"Now, sir, you are talking with the tongues of eloquence and truth. Mr Grant is a fool. Furthermore he is a Scotch fool and I don't know if there is a worse kind. But if you have noticed anything, Mr Hendrick, you will have observed that in Belfast it is a great deal better to be Scotch than good. Belfast is Glasgow's poor relation, the recipient of all her castoffs. Go into any newspaper and ask for the editor and the uncouth accents of the Scottish Lowlands will greet you. Seek the manager of most enterprises – and if he is not a Scotchman then his father was."

Hendrick pursed his lips.

"You talk a lot, Mr Milligan."

"A real oul' gabshite," Milligan agreed cheerfully. "That's what they call me in the office. Now about this almost libellous and certainly denigratory piece that my editor wants me to write before the Red shadow is cast across the Queen's Island and the slipways run blood . . ."

"I'd just as soon you went away," Hendrick answered. "I don't think your newspaper would be very much interested in what we're doing here."

Tod Milligan had no chance to protest or coax further.

The sound of an explosion rocked the flimsy building.

*

25

Milligan picked himself from the floor where he had judiciously thrown himself, the 'Troubles' being still sufficiently fresh in his mind, and ran after Hendrick to the small ante-room just within the outside door. It was used as a Committee Room and also as a kitchen. In it there was a sink and a gas geyser.

It was from the geyser that the explosion had come. A pile of unwashed mugs lay beside the sink. There was a table in the middle of the room and sprawled across this there was a pair of blue panties. There was a girl inside the panties but it was the garment that caught the eye first, for the girl had been blown across the table and her torso dangled upside down out of sight.

Tod Milligan's introduction to Pamela Hendrick was thus a good deal more intimate than was usual at the time.

"Pamela!" her father cried and helped the girl upright.

She had dark, curly, now tousled hair and her mouth kept opening and shutting without any sound coming out, like a fish's, or a man's who has been struck in the stomach.

"Head between her knees," Tod Milligan ordered. "Pump her, get some air into her lungs – "

He hurried over to the small window and opened it after a struggle, for fresh air was never craved greatly in that area. He turned off the gas and went back to the table.

Hendrick was bending the girl from the waist and straightening her again, forcing the air into her lungs. Some colour had begun to return to her cheeks and she tugged her skirt down over legs that were both long and shapely.

"S-stop it, Dad," she managed to say. "I'm all right now."

Still seated on the table she took a few more breaths and then slid to the floor. She gave a questioning look at the reporter.

"A Mr Milligan, Pamela, a reporter. From the *Standfast*. My daughter Pamela . . . I think I'd better get you home now."

"I'm all right. I'm perfectly all right."

She spoke with a Londonish accent, Milligan thought.

Not quite a Cockney but not far off it.

"You're not all right. You're going home. What happened, anyway?"

"The geyser. It must have blown out with the draught. When I went to light it – "

"Boom!" said Milligan brightly. "Your father's quite right, Miss Hendrick. You should go home. Being blown up is well known to have an enervating effect on the constitution."

She snorted contemptuously and rather entrancingly.

"It's easy to talk. If you knew the trouble we had getting this hall . . . And if the caretaker finds all these cups left dirty – "

"I'll do them," said her father. "You just go home."

"Dad, I'm perfectly all right. Now will you let me get on with my work?"

And there was sufficient determination in her face and voice to quell any further argument.

"Unless you plan writing a supplement on dish-washing," said Hendrick sarcastically, "I would suggest you return to your newspaper."

"I can take a hint." Milligan smiled brightly and left the hall.

*

The rain had almost stopped by now and came under the heading of a 'grand soft day'. Tod Milligan did not even turn up his collar as he fumbled through his pockets for a cigarette. The lighter did not work in the breeze and he had to pause in the lee of the hall and shelter the flame with his coat before the smoke began to draw.

But for this delay he would not have seen the Reverend Mungo McMaster come out of his tent once again. He would not have heard him speak.

There was no doubt that this was an impressive man; so tall, so gaunt, with a blazing fire in his deep-set eyes.

McMaster now wore a clerical collar and his bowler hat had been left within the tent.

With his head a little bowed he walked slowly to the frame that held the stiff placard. The top of the frame was a tiny lectern and on it he set the Bible that he carried in one huge hand.

For a few moments he seemed to pray and then he threw back his head, hair tossing like a lion's mane.

"Dearly beloved brethren. We are gathered this day to hear God's promise. Verily, verily I say unto you: Harken to His promise and surely ye shall be saved. But harken not and have not faith and behold the Lord has digged traps for thine feet and hath prepared in the nethermost pits of Hell such a bed for thy bones as . . ."

Tod Milligan had heard preachers before. Both the orthodox in their pulpits and the alfresco at the street corners and the Custom House steps. But he had never heard anyone quite like Mungo McMaster.

His invocation to a non-existent congregation should have been either absurd or pathetic. It was neither. There was in that all-embracing, reverberating bass-baritone voice, some quality that saved it from either ridicule or pity.

And, after all, he was not entirely alone. Here and there in the houses round Gonagal's Piece windows edged open a fraction. One or two doors did open. The booming voice carried loudly above the distant rumble of traffic on the Newtownards Road, the clank of tramcars and the desultory rattle of a pneumatic hammer digging up a road somewhere.

Tod Milligan was a nominal Christian. He had been baptised in the Church of Ireland: the Irish branch of the Anglican Communion. When friends were marrying or members of the family being buried he went to church. Occasionally his mother succeeded in getting him out on Sunday – for he still lived at home – but for the most part he had the journalist's apathy towards religion and the religious.

But his religion had not hitherto encountered anyone like Mungo McMaster before.

It was not so much the words of the tall man that made the impression as their delivery. The words were the words they all used. But the delivery was another matter. That rich, rolling voice with its implication of utter conviction, the deep-set eyes that blazed with sincerity, even the controlled, furious gestures that suggested still greater power simmering below the surface, all combined in an almost hypnotic spell.

Tod Milligan lingered, eyes roaming to glance at the increasing though still distant congregation, snotty-nosed children with their thumbs in their mouths, housewives leaning against their doorposts, yawning unemployed scratching at their beards and murmuring softly among themselves.

Milligan was both amused and impressed. There could be a story perhaps in this gaunt mountebank. He wondered if the fact of the donkey was altogether adventitious or whether the man sought to establish a Biblical parallel in the people's minds. Joseph and Mary perhaps . . .

There might even be a very good story in this man – but not for the *Standfast*. This would be one for one of the highbrow reviews, something with a small flavour of Dos Passos, perhaps, or Saroyan. He thought in terms of American writers then. Most of the would-be's in Belfast at that time did.

"I now end my first speaking to you, friends, brethren, sisters. Tomorrow I will speak for a longer time when the rain shall have ended and the sun shall shine. At this time then, be here also to hear my words which are the words of God."

McMaster stood for another moment in silent prayer then turned and went to the tent again. The rain began to fall harder once more as if it had been waiting for this moment. The windows closed, the streets cleared.

Tod Milligan thought that he was certainly going to learn more about this tall, strange, arrogant preacher.

CHAPTER FOUR

"Mungo McMaster met God in a potato field called the Goat's Bit," Tod Milligan wrote, pecking out the letters with two-fingered care on his very old Remington typewriter. "It is not known who was the more surprised by the encounter."

He read the words over, chuckled at them. Then he pulled out the sheet of paper and threw it to join the others in the wastepaper basket. It was not proving so easy to transcribe on to paper what he wanted as he had expected.

"Tod – tea!" his mother called and he felt a faint relief that he would have to postpone the task.

Going down the reasonably luxuriously carpeted stairs, inhaling the comfortable hot scones and bacon odours from the kitchen, he made a mental contrast with the bare, tattered tent in the midst of the mud. Did a man have to be a saint to live like that?

*

Hendrick thought also of Mungo McMaster when he returned with his daughter to the furnished house they had taken at Ballyhackamore, a mile or so further from the city centre.

"You know, Pamela, it's pathetic. They preferred to listen to that wandering antique than try to get themselves properly organised."

"Our Dad is properly vexed, isn't he?" Pamela laughed. "They wouldn't listen. Maybe our Dad should learn to play the flute."

He was in no mood for persiflage. Usually he looked younger than his age, an earnest, studious, youngish man. But he was middleaged tonight.

"I never really thought it would be like this," he said. "I don't mean just that preacher. It's Belfast. It's changed a lot. When I was at school some of my best friends were Catholics. We all got on the best. Now the Protestants seem more interested in keeping the Catholics down than in getting on themselves. They're cutting their own throats. What employment will ever come to a place where the work force are at each other's throats? Not that it's any way one-sided. I know well enough that in the South, in the Irish Free State, the Catholic majority give the small Protestant minority a hot time. It can be very uncomfortable to be a Protestant in Southern Ireland. Very uncomfortable indeed. I'm glad I'm not one of the poor devils. Because, while the Catholics in the North are a large minority, the Protestants in the South are a small minority – a tiny minority – so they have no chance at all.

"But to revert to our own problems here – look at it another way. If the Protestant workmen doesn't join hands with his Catholic brother the Bosses will set one against the other, keep the rates down with the sure knowledge that if one crowd won't play the other will."

Pamela looked at him with sympathy and some understanding. It was not really the men, she thought, it was not because they were divided. Our Dad was downcast because his audience had preferred to watch a mountebank preacher than listen to him.

And having heard most of his lectures in preparation she did not entirely blame them. She felt a great longing for some brighter, less consciously virtuous way of life than this.

The bright lights, the pop of champagne corks, the tinkle of exotic music . . . If only she could have devised some way of staying in London, alone if needs be. Or in fact even if needs didn't be. Did Our Dad really need her here? Did she need him? Maybe even they would both be better off alone.

Our Dad might pick up with someone which he would certainly be too embarrassed to do while she was around. And she would certainly pick up someone in London.

There was life in London. People weren't afraid to enjoy themselves. They even talked to strangers. She smiled to herself and thought of some of the strangers she had met.

"I think I'll go to the pictures after tea," she declared, as she turned the sausages.

*

"And what has the good Lord provided for our sustenance this day?"

Mungo McMaster seated himself on the folding bed, head bowed not in prayer but to avoid coming in contact with the dripping side wall of the tent.

Dulcie McMaster knelt over a roaring Primus stove on a small wooden box and stirred a much-blackened stewpan. She had taken off her blue cloak now and it hung from a metal spider on the tent pole, dripping slowly into a little pool on the floor, or rather the muddy rubble of the ground.

"There is stew, Mr McMaster," she said quietly. "There is stew of carrot and turnip and dandelion leaf and a little cabbage and the knuckle of a sheep's shank which the flesher in Glengormley gave us yestreen. It is not rich faring."

"Better a dish of herbs where love is," McMaster pulled at his great bony fingers, making them click noisily in their knuckles. "Than a stalled ox . . . Och, I can never remember the words."

His hand ran over her small drenched head in the kind of gesture a man might make to a dog. Her eyes shone the brighter for it in a thin, wasted face. They were very beautiful eyes, large and lustrous and of a light, clear blue; not faded like the colour of her cloak but with a crystalline life like amethyst or sapphire. They were memorable eyes as the rest of her face was unmemorable – a tired face, though lacking in any lines of discontent or malice or envy or despair.

"There should be more to a stew, Mr McMaster, than a few potherbs. A man needs meat and I am ashamed there is no meat."

"Wheesht, lass! It will do very well. If the good Lord wished his servant to feed upon the fat of the land He would have set his steps in other paths. It smells very fine."

He smiled at her and the great white tombstones of his teeth brightened the tent for the woman.

"You do very fine, Dulcie. You're a grand wee manager. How I could get on without you I do not know. With the Lord and you at my either hand . . ."

He shook his head in wonder at his good fortune.

"Will I serve then, Mr McMaster? Will you say the grace?"

McMaster pulled from under the bed the small leather pillow which did duty on these occasions and protected the knees of his suit from the mud.

"Lord, for thy bountiful mercies, for food and shelter given to us this day, make us truly grateful. Lord, thou knowest that when I heard thy call in the Goat's Bit at Glengarnoch I cared neither for hearth nor for home, neither for my raiment nor for that which I might put intil my mouth to eat, saying that since thou hadst seen fit for to send me out to save thy people from the ever-burning bonfire so wouldst thou also see that the poor instrument thou hadst chosen was fed fit to thy needs and likewise clad with decency in the sight of the people. Therefore when I cried out in the wilderness against the iniquities I beheld and also against the privations that were thrust upon me, this was not to be taken, I assure you Lord, as any criticism of thine own divine foresight and providence but only as did Ephanish cry out amidst the groves of the abominations and was not to be taken personally.

"Nevertheless, Lord, if it should suit thy purpose in the days to come that a little kitchen should be provided with our provender there would be a still greater strength to our prayers. You will understand that this is by no means a request but only an indication of the need of the physical body we have to carry around with us. If needs must, we can manage fine on porridge and champ and a wheen carrots and turnips. But a wee bit of meat, whiles, would lift the body as prayer lifts the heart.

"Now do we thank you, Lord, for thou hast set a table in the wilderness and provendered it withal . . ."

Dulcie had coughed twice during the grace. The first cough indicated, though she would never have put this in words, that she was dishing up the stew. The second cough stated that it would shortly be cold and that while a grace was a sweet and seemly thing in the eyes of the Lord, it would indicate a certain lack of gratitude to let the viands the Lord had provided grow cold.

With the relish of hunger they sat to a meal as meagre as anything that was being eaten in the city of Belfast that day.

*

It would have been inconceivable for Dulcie McMaster to complain to her husband about the extreme poverty of their way of life. It would have been inconceivable for her to complain to him about anything at all, whatever devices she might have contrived to introduce a modicum of order into their ways.

In the fullest meaning of the marriage service, Dulcie loved, honoured and obeyed Mungo McMaster. No other way of thought was possible to her. She had loved him even before the Lord spoke to him in the Goat's Bit in the midst of the seventeen stony acres which he husbanded for his cranky father.

Dulcie McMinn had been twenty-nine and plainly a destined old maid when Mungo McMaster came courting across the hill. In the Glens of Antrim they married young. Old maids began at twenty, for the age of marriage was then fourteen, though by a typical Irish paradox the age of consent was sixteen, thus making it technically feasible for a man to be prosecuted for the rape of his wife.

Why Dulcie should have remained so long on the shelf was not obvious. Her father was one reason, to be sure. No one was anxious to have Thomas McMinn as father-in-law for he was a cantankerous and scandal-minded man with a memory for peccadilloes that extended back through the generations. As well he was poor and was offering no more than a cow as dowry for his daughter.

And yet Dulcie was an attractive enough girl and a well-endowed woman. In a more accessible place she would probably have had swains enough. But the Stony Mountain was four miles off the county road and church on Sunday was the only chance Dulcie had to display her wares in the marriage market.

They were a small community of Presbyterians there, an enclave in the midst of a larger Roman Catholic group. There were very few single men of anywhere near her own age. Therefore she had accepted though not grown resigned to the idea of spinsterhood, to the care of her father's declining years and increasing work on the farm.

Mungo could have come in the shape of a toad and he would still have been Prince Charming – if Dulcie had ever heard of such un-Christian fables.

In the generality, Presbyterians are not the dour, cheerless race which caricatures make them seem. About the Stony Mountain, though, the caricature had become the stereotype. In the days of the Plantation their forefathers had come to Ulster, the McMinns, the McMasters, the McCoshums and the Campbells, four or five families who had settled in this bleak area because this was the land allotted to them and because they lacked either the wit or the influence to get something better when the rich land was being apportioned.

Others of their kind had gone to the Americas and had been duped similarly into the hills of Kentucky to eke out a life of very similar poverty and misery. About the Stony Mountain there was one difference from Kentucky. The sun was rarer and the drink was scarcer.

Mungo's father had been an adept once at the making of potheen and had been the last man in the district with this particular art. He gave it up, or rather renounced it, when his wife died of puerperal fever at a time when he was tending the still.

Her death was generally regarded as a judgment on him and he concurred in this opinion. The Bible took whisky's place and was Mungo's sole intellectual fodder.

It was a strange, bleak existence on the Stony Mountain. The tiny fields scarcely justified the use of a plough and in fact there was only one plough and one horse fit to draw it among the six farms on the mountain. Its services were shared in a splendidly communal way, as were any other items of equipment whose cost would run more than a pound or so.

Turnip choppers, hay rakes, even scythes were passed around and as the tools were shared, so was the work. Harvesting, potato picking, all the jobs that needed man-power were carried out in co-operation; first on one farm and then on another – that is, among this Presbyterian enclave. They did not seek help from nor offer it to their Catholic neighbours, though they lived on friendly enough terms with them, except where matters of fences, strayed animals or sheep-chasing dogs rose in dispute.

There were frustrations for a growing lad in this life; for a young adult too. There were few enough girls among the Presbyterians, though families were large. On the other side of the fence, Catholic families seemed to have a preponder-ance of females. Inter-marriage would have been the obvious answer for both communities. But inter-marriage was inconceivable – for both sides.

Yet there could be dalliance of a sort for youth was always stronger than the interdicts of age. To an extent there would even be a blind eye turned to this dalliance so long as it was sufficiently discreet.

There were Presbyterians who took a sardonic pleasure in the thought that here and there among their rivals their own good stock flourished unacknowledged. And for the Catholic girls there was the pleasure of a sin to remember as the years passed, and to confess with increasing frequency in age. The priest did not care greatly who sowed the seed as long as he had its cultivation under his control.

Mungo, named after the founder of Glasgow (despite his being a Catholic saint), was a man who always drew the girls' eyes. Height, strength and an individual animal magnetism, combined with the extraordinary quality of his voice, gave him something that stood out among all the others of his age on the Stony Mountain. There were plenty to notice and a good many from the lower slopes of the Stony Mountain.

McMaster senior certainly heard the whispers about his son. He was intended to.

". . . and his hand up her skirt as far as ever it would go . . . The two of them there in the wee wood and fair throng intil each other . . . I see them, I tell yez, her near bare naked and him as stooky as an Ayrshire bull . . ."

The remarks were just loud enough and the way voices dropped when he appeared at Lodge meeting or kirk session were indication enough about who was the subject.

Mr McMaster heard but took no action, having perhaps a vicarious pride in the lusty prowess of the lad. Apart from which Mungo was bigger than himself and scarcely liable to accept any corporal punishment. As well, the boy was a good worker and he had no mind to drive him away.

There was also the possibility that the rumours were not true. Gossip was almost the only relaxation of those people and a hint expanded into a fact with frightening speed.

But a rumour started at last which could not be ignored and McMaster senior called his tall son to him out of the field where he was earthing up the potatoes with a spade.

"Mungo, 'tis time you were wed," he announced brusquely. "Thomas McMinn's Dulcie is not yet spoken for."

"I have no great notion of her, Father."

"I know fine who you've the notion for."

The father's face darkened at last in anger.

"Oh, ye're the great gowk, the big soft fool. Have you no mind of the oath you took in Lodge about your brethren's wife and your brethren's daughter? What sort of a name is it you'd bring on the McMasters and me a past worshipful Master of the Lodge? It's an end to the fornicating for you, my lad. You'll go over the hill and you'll pay court to Dulcie McMinn . . . And mind he doesn't try to fob you off with their wee cow for her piece. Yon one drops her calves."

*

There were no novels on the Stony Mountain and Dulcie McMinn had no exaggerated ideas of what to expect from a suitor. Just so long as she had one was enough. And to get Mungo McMaster had been beyond her dreams, even if he had been sent by his father and was not there entirely of his own will or desire.

For the period of the wedding, which was rarely lively with a fiddler, whisky and crates of stout filling the house with unaccustomed sounds and smells, Dulcie lived in a delirium of incredulous delight that never entirely died within her.

She had been a drudge on her father's farm and she remained a drudge but though there was a little more work it was made easier by the fact of the McMasters' drinking-well being in the yard instead of half a mile up the mountain.

Happiness eased every toil, from the hand-scrubbing of mired clothes to the sanding of the flagged floor every day.

The farm building was no more than a cottage with a kitchen and a by-room which now became Magnus's bed-room. The young couple had the built-in box-bed in the kitchen. They bedded long, these two, and not only for the saving of the lamp oil.

Unfortunately their exertions were not rewarded. Dulcie had one miscarriage and then a second. Then the doctor was called in – for the folk of the Stony Mountain did not squander their resources lightly. His verdict was grim and technical. Magnus McMaster summarised it.

'She's as bad as yon wee cow her Da' tried to palm off. She'll aye drop her calf."

There would be no heir to the McMaster acres.

What Mungo thought about it no one knew, for he was in any case a man of few words. He took to long silences in the fields and to even more extensive reading of the Bible. And yet he was never unkind to Dulcie, never reproached her with her barrenness. Perhaps indeed he did not want children.

Of more concern to the woman was the fact that after her second miscarriage she found it more difficult and increasingly painful – though this she tried to conceal – to give her husband any pleasure in bed. An infection which might well have come from the rustic doctor who examined her had started a growth which grew steadily through the years.

Probably it would have been operable if the folk of the Stony Mountain had not considered that hospital was a place only for dying in. Dulcie suffered on and felt an increasing burden of guilt at her own uselessness.

Old McMaster died and was buried and his funeral was again the occasion for whisky, spirits made by himself, McMinn related tearfully, a keg he had put by for just this time.

After the funeral Mungo was not seen for two days and it seemed to Dulcie that there were strange scents about him when he returned. She said nothing.

But anxiously she watched him grow steadily more silent, more introspective. His moods she could not and would not interrupt. But she had a foreboding that change was on its way and change is always frightening.

There had been two bad years on the farm when Mungo McMaster heard the Lord in the Goat's Bit. The rural council bailiffs were due the next day to distrain on what they could for non-payment of rates. When they had taken what they could there would be nothing of value left, neither livestock nor furniture nor anything else.

Mungo came in from the Goat's Bit and announced without preamble: "I am to go intil the world and preach the Lord. I am to be as a scourge to they that believe not and a succour to they that are unjustly struck down. In the market place I am to cry the Lord's wares. He has told me."

He looked at Dulcie but did not see her.

"We'll take the ass and the ass-cart and what we can carry in the turf creels and we will be about our Father's business."

"It's as you say, Mr McMaster," Dulcie agreed and began to pack.

CHAPTER FIVE

Mungo McMaster came out of the tent and smiled a little as he gazed at the sky. As he had promised, the sun was shining. The donkey was begging its way along the street, getting a crust here and there, a slice of bread, a lick at a porridge pan or a few cold potatoes.

The donkey never starved no matter where they went. The donkey had no pride and was not ashamed to beg. Watching it, McMaster felt a parable taking shape in his mind.

Some of the bigger children patted the animal, stroked its long ears, began to speculate inwardly if they could ride it. McMaster knew the thoughts in their minds. In his wanderings he had seen the same reactions over and over again.

While he might not have admitted this to himself the donkey served the function of an ice-breaker. It was almost a huckster's device, an advertisement, an attention-getter. And, since others fed it, it was of course free transport. The donkey had no name, for it was a farmer's donkey and farmers do not name their animals any more than city dwellers name their various articles of domestic machinery. It was, simply, the donkey.

Certainly it was a good donkey – strong, willing, not inclined to stray save when it encountered an ass in season. It no longer pulled the cart, for the cart was the badge of the tinker and Mungo McMaster had no mind to be mistaken for one of that other band of travellers. As well, the cart had been almost done and he had been glad enough to exchange it for the tent and other equipment.

The two panniers made a heavy enough load for the animal and Dulcie did not as a rule ride on it, but on this last stage of their journey a twisted ankle had begun to irk her. And there may have been something in McMaster's mind of the effect they would have, arriving as they had done. Since he was a man who acted as a rule rather by instinct than conscious design, the real purposes in his mind were always obscure.

Now he stood at his lectern and made a little sign with his right hand. Dulcie saw the signal through the tent flap and three deep drum notes echoed across Gonagal's Piece. The drum was a parchment stretched across the top of one of the panniers and the note it gave was curiously compelling.

Mungo McMaster held up his arms in a silent benediction. "Let us praise God," he called. "Let us sing his praise."

His vibrant voice echoed from the sooted red brick of the houses about.

"Mine eyes have seen the glory of the coming of the Lord . . ."

Curtains twitched. Doors began to open. People came out into the streets. McMaster's voice was echoed by others.

*

Shane Hendrick was not himself a violent man. He had seen enough and more than enough of violence in the war. It was the memory of mangled bodies in a mess deck that more than anything else had turned him to trade unionism. The memory of dead comrades could be honoured best by helping the living; improving wages, ensuring employment, 'using the head instead of the boot.' The voice of reason meant everything to him and for passions of any kind he had little use.

Nevertheless he felt it would be very easy for him to come to hate the Reverend Mungo McMaster. He felt it as soon as the voice filled the air with its hymn and the attention of his class began to wander.

McMaster's success as an attention-getter was a living reproach to his own failure.

"I want you now to consider the role of the shop steward in the local organisation of the union," he said heavily. "You will find that there are two views on the shop steward, or rather three views; there is management's view, the union's view – and the view of the workmen on the shop floor.

"Nothing is easier than for a shop steward to gain the popularity of his fellow-workers by continually defying the processes of management and also of his own union organisation. Nothing is easier and nothing is more deadly to union discipline . . ."

His voice tailed off. Not even to himself could he make any pretence that anyone was listening. If Big Jim had been there –

But Big Jim was not there. Nor was anyone else so far as audience went. They were crowded at the windows, gazing out.

"Boys, there'll be some sport now!" a voice remarked in almost awed delight. "It's the McNulty Street gang."

*

Mungo McMaster was gratified at first when the little cluster of men came onto Gonagal's Piece. Then, behind them, he saw the women drawing back their children into the houses. He saw doors close, and from a corner of his eye he saw the massed, eager faces at the windows of the John William Cowan Memorial Hall.

Covertly he studied the faces of this new congregation who now stared at him impudently, mockingly.

They were all about twenty, he judged, give or take a year or two. For the most part their clothes were quite new, flashily cut, cheap, not very clean – but new. There was no headwear among them but each had his hair plastered down with haircream in the Rudolph Valentino manner so that they seemed to wear shining skull caps.

They were not related but their faces had an expression in common; a watchful yet indolent insolence, a vicious confidence in their own amoral strength.

McMaster had had nothing to do with gangs before this but he recognised by instinct the presence of the wolf pack.

He finished his hymn and launched into prayer. The gang's jaws moved almost in unison as they chewed gum in close imitation of the gangster heroes who were just beginning to reach the cinema screens.

"Hey, boy!" said one suddenly. "D'you have a licence for that?"

McMaster broke off and eyed the group. He said nothing and his silence was assumed to be a mark of fear.

"I said, d'you have a licence? You can't preach without a licence."

There were giggles and the group moved in a little closer. None of them in his life had done any honest work. It would be a long day before they would.

"What's wrong then? The cat got your tongue? You were gabbing plenty a minute ago."

Mungo McMaster continued to be silent, staring down at them from the advantage of his height and the mound of rubble.

"Look, I'm talking to you, long fellah. And when Herby Vignoles talks, others listen."

Vignoles had a round, red, shiny face and very small, grey-green eyes. Though his face was round his lips were very thin. Now he swaggered the few steps to the mound to stand beside McMaster at his lectern.

He grabbed up the Bible and affected to read it.

"The first lesson is from the First Epistle to the pisshouse," he declaimed, to the delight of his followers. "'Verily, verily, I say unto you that more skirts shall come up and more knickers shall come down . . .'"

He broke off, astonished. McMaster's hand had come down and pulled the Bible from his grasp.

"God is not mocked," said Mungo McMaster with a

44

esperate calm in his voice.

Vignole's thin lips vanished altogether.

"Why, you great long streak of shite," he screamed. "I'll do you for that!"

He struck out, a swinging blow that took the preacher on he jaw. McMaster rocked a little.

"I am commanded that I shall turn the other cheek," he aid.

Vignoles accepted the invitation as it was given and another blow rocked McMaster.

A third hit him in the pit of the belly.

"Behold, Lord," cried Mungo McMaster in a great voice, "For inasmuch as it is written 'Thou shalt turn the other cheek' so have I obeyed. And it is written also 'the wicked shall be chastised and beaten as it were with whips of scorpions and they shall be made humble.'"

So saying he gripped Herby Vignole's wrist, twisted it up his back and thereby forced the gang-leader's face almost into the mud.

With swift precision McMaster snatched one of the uprights from his lectern and began to belabour the other's tightly-stretched bottom.

It was long seconds before the gang took in their leader's ignominy and realised that he was shouting at them.

Then in a group they swarmed up the mound and there was a great confusion of arms and legs, of shouts and gasps and groans. It was not a prayerful meeting.

*

"They'll kill him. They'll bloody well murder him. Those McNulty Street boys don't give a damn for anyone."

Hendrick heard the comments while he himself watched the conflict from the window, torn between his knowledge that it was his clear duty to call the police or get some other aid for the beset preacher and the equal knowledge that to do so must inevitably mean forfeiting what little respect these

45

men had for him. For to go to the police in a working community is the ultimate confession of weakness. It would stamp him as a boss's man though he more than any of them was dedicated to the fight against capitalism.

Torn internally, cursing his own weakness of will, he continued to watch the battle.

And it was far from one-sided as yet.

Mungo McMaster had a countryman's strength. He had worked like an animal in the fields. He had the muscles of an animal.

His long arms swung and punched. His stamping boots sent one after another reeling out of the fight, clutching at feet and ankles.

And above the gang's oaths and shouts, McMaster's voice rose clearly, a terrible elation in it as he sang:

"Mine eyes have seen the glory of the coming of the Lord,
   Thwack! . . . thud! . . . crunch!
He is trampling out the vintage where the grapes of wrath
   are stored.
Thud . . . thud . . . thump! Whack!
He has loosed the fateful lightning of his terrible swift
   sword,
Thump, thump!
His Truth is marching on . . ."

As befitted a gang leader, Herby Vignoles had withdrawn from the actual skirmish and hovered on the outskirts of the maelstrom of whirling bodies, rubbing his bruises, shouting advice and thinking hard.

From the corner of his eye he saw Dulcie McMaster's pale, frightened face peering from the tent opening. He drew a clasp and ran round the tent, slashing at the guy ropes.

Dulcie gave a thin scream of terror as the tent collapsed on her.

"Be of good cheer!" roared her husband. "Inasmuch as these sons of Belial shall soon be castigated even as the sons of Ephaniah and the evil ones of Misbech . . ."

His fists did still greater execution.

But Herby Vignoles was far from finished.

*

"By God, I'm not standing for that! Hey, d'ye see what he's at now . . ."

Shane Hendrick smiled pallidly within himself. The men had watched, interested but unmoved, while McMaster was attacked. They had seen his tent cut down and his terrified wife enveloped in its folds. They had not thought of intervening.

But now in a furious flood they poured out onto Gonagal's Piece.

Herby Vignoles had just begun to hack at the donkey's tail with his clasp knife, intent on a trophy and on causing pain, when the Islandmen engulfed him. And having started they turned their attention to the rest of the gang.

Boots were going in, sogging home into helpless ribs. The McNulty Street crowd were squealing like pigs.

And Mungo McMaster was brandishing his arms amid the confusion.

"Peace!" he roared. "Let there be peace. Or do I have to knock your heads together?"

47

CHAPTER SIX

"You have to remember, Miss Hendrick, that this is a country devoted to war, to fighting and conflict in all its aspects. The whole history of Ireland is tied up with fighting of one kind or another. We esteem fighters above all others, even above the religious. In fact, you could say that at bottom we only like religion because it gives an excuse for fighting."

Tod Milligan had called at the hall on his way into the city, to his day's work which would be, he had a gloomy suspicion, in the Houses of Parliament at Stormont, noting down endless speeches which he could almost certainly have written in advance, since each side of the House had a stereo-type speech which could not normally be deviated from.

"They're not fighting now," Pamela Hendrick pointed out sourly. "In fact they should be in here, listening to Dad."

She was more attractive than Milligan had remembered, though granting that he had seen her in scarcely the best circumstances. Her hair had a natural wave and her face had a lively piquancy that had not been apparent while she still suffered from the after-effects of the explosions. Her clothes were dowdy – a twin set and sensible skirt, both showing signs of careful darning.

On the other hand, Tod Milligan inclined from preference to the flashier type of girl, to plenty of make-up, high heels and jazzy clothes.

"I'm sorry I missed the fight all the same," he commented. "That's another Irish characteristic. Next to having a fight

48

is watching one."

"They watched all right," Pamela snapped indignantly. "They saw that poor man being attacked and his tent knocked down – and it was only when they tried to cut off the donkey's tail that the men interfered."

"A love of animals is another interesting aspect of the local character," Milligan informed her. "I would say they're even worse than the English as far as that goes. A man can beat his wife and children, but let him harm a dog and he's in trouble. Of course, they kill animals too. Shooting, hunting – it's a very sporting country altogether. But I must say I'm sorry I missed the fight. I'd like to have seen Herby Vignoles getting his bottom smacked. He's a real nasty specimen and it's time he got his comeuppance."

He chuckled softly. "The scourge of Ballymacarret gets his bottom smacked like a naughty boy! I wonder if I could get a little piece into the paper about it. Ridicule is one thing that kind of lout can't stand."

He lit a cigarette with a flourish after offering the girl one and having it refused.

"What do they do, that gang, apart from being a nuisance?"

"That's about their limit, nuisance value. They'll break windows, upset shopkeepers' stalls, drive off cars, get into fights . . . I think they levy some sort of tribute on anyone weak enough to pay it. Probably that's what they were after with the preacher. Their 'licence money' as they call it."

"And people let them get away with it? Why don't they go to the police?"

"In this country no one goes to the police. It's an odd thing. The Nationalists accuse the Royal Ulster Constabulary of being the tools of the Protestants – but they'll go to them quicker than the Protestants will, either for protection or with information. I've always thought it odd . . . I suppose your father is pretty cross about the preacher?"

"It's not his fault. The men should pay more attention to Dad. But they don't. They're. . . . I don't understand them."

"Nobody understands an Irishman, not even another Irishman. All that fighting and praying hath made us mad. It's a pity they won't listen all the same. This country needs trade union unity."

"Your paper doesn't think so."

"My paper doesn't approve of the twentieth century. It doesn't want Ulster to know it's actually arrived. It prefers us all to stay snugly in the nineteenth, or is it the eighteenth? It's odd when you think of it, for Ulster and Belfast especially was almost the most radical part of Ireland. If you look into the Rebellions of the past – except the last one – they were nearly always led by Ulstermen, and Protestants at that."

"People like Wolfe Tone and Henry Joy McCracken. No need to be surprised – Dad's an Ulsterman after all . . ."

"I'd forgotten that. Look, would you like to come to a dance tonight?"

Tod Milligan was almost as startled at giving the invitation as the girl was to receive it. The idea had flashed onto his tongue before his mind had fully envisioned it. To his annoyance he felt himself flush a little, and he hastened to add: "The Plaza, not at all a bad sort of place – new, big, jolly good floor and all that sort of stuff. They get the very best bands from London. And even better, as a gentleman of the Press, I get in free."

"How very gallant!" she chuckled and Milligan realised that when she gave that impish smile she was really very attractive indeed. Instinct, he told himself, was justified for it had been instinct surely that issued the invitation.

"We silver-tongued Gaels can always produce the Blarney at the right time," he said. "Or at any rate, you can rely on us to put our feet where our tongues should be. Will you come?"

"Let me consult my engagement book. My social secretary is on holiday . . . Yes, I do believe tonight is free and since you are so very pressing – and it's not costing you anything . . ."

They laughed together and Pamela Hendrick felt in herself something of the same surprise Milligan had known. She had not consciously decided to go and yet her tongue had accepted the invitation. A part of her mind prepared itself for disappointment, since surely there could be nothing in this drab city to stir her. And yet already she felt a little excitement moving in her, a faint echo of a thrill she had supposed she would never experience again.

Irrationally she wondered then how much her father had known or suspected about those nights in Streatham. Had he guessed about the Locarno? Did that perhaps lie behind his decision to come to Belfast? It was absurd, of course, and yet – No, he had come because the Union sent him. He could never have known about the local Palais or his 'little girl's' nights there.

Leaving, Milligan had no idea of the tumult he had stirred in the girl; a tumult of memory and perhaps hope.

*

The Locarno – and Streatham Common. In Pamela's mind the two would always be linked. Saturday night at the local hop, invitation to Fairyland. To think of a dance was to remember that gaudy pleasure, rich with colour, bright with lights that could darken mysteriously and fabricate a new world without substance, without relation to the drab reality of life.

It was a palace and they were all princes and princesses who tripped so lightly across the maple flooring to the echoing, amplified throb of that wonderful music that satisfied almost as materially as food. The exotic and erotic suggestions of the tables under the balconies, the heady mixture of girls' scent, men's brilliantine – Ashes of Roses had dominated – floor polish and sweat, the suave manager and his assistants who were mainly bouncers, even the champagne taste of a bottle of lemonade – they all combined in a rich pot pourri of sensual attack.

On those Saturdays when Pamela went to the dance hall

she was ostensibly staying with Alexandra Grey, her school friend. Alexandra's parents went to the country on Saturday nights to visit relations somewhere down in Kent. It pleased them too that the girl had a companion. And Shane Hendrick was glad to have one night free in the week, to go out for a few hours, have a few pints with his friends, not feel the urgent need to return to a lonely girl.

Sometimes Alexandra came to the dance, but when she did they parted as soon as they had paid at the door, for though girls may be glad of company, the presence of a second one can be an inhibiting factor. It was noteworthy that the better men dancers came alone and those who came with friends were as likely to be shy as they were to be bad dancers.

Pamela rarely had to wait long for a partner. She always dressed quietly, though in good style, for again she had noticed that while men liked to look at the gaudy girls they were reluctant to be associated closely with them. Only flashy men liked flashy girls; the kind who themselves came to be seen rather than actually to dance. Like the girls they chose, they rarely danced well.

And Pamela liked to dance well. It was important to her, a justification for coming. To dance well with a good partner was to move a little off the earthly plane, to be swept by music and rhythm into another, sensual world which scarcely related at all to sooty windows, leaking taps and the tedium of forty-eight hour days.

For good dancers Pamela had an instinct, recognising them as they came towards her with the brief formality of the dance floor. It was in their step, in their eyes, in the way they looked at a girl. Good dancers were rarely fancy dressers. Not for them the Oxford 'bags' or whatever else might be the fashion aberration of the moment. They wore practical clothes as a rule, with shirt collars that were on the large side. They never wore new shoes, for no one can dance well in new shoes. When they looked at a girl it was not so much her face or her clothes or her make-up or her hair that drew them, but the legs and feet, as if one pair of legs recognised another's kinship.

Sometimes there were no words spoken at all, an enquiring smile was answered by a brief nod and the two would sway away into the crowd. Quite often there was no talking at all during the dance, not even a 'Come here often?', 'Good band', or 'Great floor, in'tit?' There was only this strange, abstract physical unity in the dance, anonymous and as impersonal as buying a railway ticket and yet also as intimate as any physical relationship could be.

There was a partner who must have been a sailor, for he had tattoos on each wrist, just showing under his cuffs, an anchor on one wrist and on the other what looked like a pair of ankles which were no doubt joined to legs and a body. Dark curling hairs overran the tattoos and the sailor had about him some strange scent that matched nothing Pamela had known before. She thought of it as the scent of the sea.

The sailor she would never forget. The sailor was perfect, on the floor and afterwards. On his feet he was very light, poised correctly for every step, controlling her delicately so that she moved with him as easily as if they had been partners for years. Best of all, he did not talk. There were no banal words to break the spell of this wonderful unity.

Only between dances when they clapped perfunctorily did he look down at her and smile, a smile that was not quite shy, rather confiding. He had white, even teeth and though his face was a boy's face he must have been ten years older than she was, a curious maturity shading his eyes.

No words when they danced, no words when they sat between dances. He went without asking and brought coffee for them both but he did not speak.

There were the smiles and the pressure of a hard, trained body against hers but no words at all, no need for words. It was some time before she realised that there were no words because he knew no English. He might have been a Frenchman or a Dane or a German or from any nation at all. Then it was sufficient that he was silent and his silence had a miraculous sympathy that made him for ever the partner she would always remember.

Afterwards there were no words either, afterwards when they walked out across the Common.

The sailor tucked her hand firmly under his arm and they walked from the heat and the sound of the dance hall into the chill, improbable purity of the night. A little mist lay at ground level, the warm earth sweating after the heat of the day. In the hollows the mist was waist-high, dense enough to make them seem to swim through it.

Among some trees, old beeches with starlings muttering in the branches, the sailor turned her to him and kissed her. This she had waited for, the climax to the night and she came easily, willing, into his arms, lips parting under the pressure of his, teeth yielding to the intrusion of his tongue, body quivering with its eagerness.

The kiss lasted and lasted and she felt this sailor's hand slide down her back, cup about her buttock and force her still closer to his own urgency.

That kiss ended and there was another one and then a nuzzling into her neck, a nibbling at her ear. He broke apart a little and for a moment she thought the night was ended, but he sought only a little room to manoeuvre, to bring his hand to the front and thrust boldly up beneath her skirt.

Now he kissed her again and she felt the unevenness of his breathing, the tremors of his body while one hand fumbled in his pocket and the other explored with expert touch the most delicate centres of her being. She knew what he sought and could spare a moment's thought of relief that he knew enough to think of contraception, for now her own body was responding with such convulsive eagerness to his touch that she could not have held back even without any precautions.

The roots of the tree spread out from the base so that she was on higher ground than he, so that there were no physical problems of height to master.

The rough bark abraded the delicate skin of her buttocks as now at last he thrust forward in real earnest, joining with her in a sweet, overpowering unity that seemed to make the music of the dance hall echo again in her mind, to recreate the rhythm they had known before and to pulse towards a ground-heaving, mind-dissolving climax that was surely a justification for all existence.

And when they had parted they had still not exchanged a single word. There had been no need for words and if she met him again there should be no need for words. But Pamela Hendrick never did meet the sailor again, if he was a sailor. Perhaps his ship had sailed, if he had a ship. He was a memory only, who would never quite be forgotten.

CHAPTER SEVEN

Mungo McMaster had felt a swelling pride at the sight of his new congregation and it was hard to keep the exultation from his voice as he led the men in prayer. Humility had never beset him greatly and he felt as he thought a justifiable pride, gazing from his heap of rubble at the earnest faces beneath.

"For behold," he declared, "ye are as brands for the burning. And yet ye shall be snatched forth from that great fire that rageth forever and is not satisfied. Yes, though the muckle-horned clootie himself shall take ye by the hand, yet will I snatch ye to salvation whereof the savour is as sweet as myrrh and frankincense. And behold in all the broad avenues of Heaven there will be rejoicing. The angels shall sing their hymns and the saints shall echo their hallelujahs, the one to another."

Exalted, he cried: "Yea, surely we shall drum the Devil from the land and make his ears dirl with the cry of our hearts. Hell hath its places but they shall not be for you . . ."

There was a psalm then in which many of the men joined and Mungo McMaster announced the text of his sermon, from the 101st Psalm, the last verse.

"I will early destroy all the wicked of the land, that I may cut off all wicked doers from the city of the Lord."

But before he could start there came an interruption.

"What about the Papishes?"

McMaster stared across the heads of the others to the thin, fanatical face at the rear. The man wore steel-rimmed glasses

56

and there was a choker about his neck.

"What about the Papishes?" he repeated. "Will ye destroy them early? Will ye cut off all the wicked doers and their chapels and their graven images? Will ye cast them out?"

There was an imperceptible erosion of McMaster's control over his audience. Interest was divided between him and the man at the rear. In another few moments the meeting could degenerate into chaos.

McMaster knew he must instantly recapture their attention or lose it perhaps for ever. He signalled surreptitiously to Dulcie and the drum strokes boomed again. McMaster's voice was louder than before.

"I answer you from the Book of Revelation: 'Come hither, I will show unto thee the judgement of the great whore that sitteth upon many waters: with whom the kings of the earth have committed fornication and the inhabitants of the earth have been made drunk with the wine of her fornication . . .'"

As he roared out the declamation he knew he had his audience again. And whether or not he accepted his own words, that was what mattered – that he should be heard.

*

Shane Hendrick felt a sort of helplessness when he looked at the men as they drifted back into the hall. What had he to offer them but the voice of social reason? He could give them no fireworks, not even the rabble-rousing, heart-warming speeches of Big John.

He could not even call a strike since no one was working. He remained convinced of the rightness of his cause but even less convinced of his own ability to forward it.

"I was dealing with the role of the shop steward," he said wearily. "Now, in all consultations with management – "

There had been fire in the men's eyes when they came in, animation in their faces. But he watched it die and he knew that he was himself the grey, wet blanket that was damping the flames.

Question time came.

"Mister, it's fine to be told how he should hannel the bosses. But we don't have any bosses. What's the good of a union when there's no work?"

"There'll be work all right."

"Aye – but when? Next Juloon?"

A titter of laughter.

"The general position is starting to improve. I have had reports that work is starting on the Clyde soon. Cunard and P. & O. are both thinking of ordering ships."

There was a momentary buzz of interest.

"Oh, aye. Thinking. Talking. That's all we get. We don't get much doing. You don't keep a family too long on thinking and talking."

He could feel their resentment washing over him in a cold tide. And it was useless for him to say that he was not the proper target for their hate, that his only purpose was to help them. In their minds he and the union were as much to blame as the management, as the Government, as the world that denied them a living.

"The role of the shop steward . . ." he began again, helplessly.

*

The last train to Bangor was thundering on its way down the coast as Tod Milligan and Pamela Hendrick started up the long slope from the Hollywood Arches to Ballyhackamore. The area was still residential but not quite so desirable as it had been when the large terrace houses were first built.

The creeping poverty of the city's heart was stretching out along the arteries. There was honest respectability here but the paintwork was growing shabbier. Only the gardens were still neat. It costs little to mow a lawn or tidy a flower-bed.

It was Pamela who had suggested walking, not Milligan.

And romance had not been in her mind, but the wish for fresh air and exercise. She had enjoyed the dance and Tod Milligan's lively, disrespectful company. She needed to get out more, she thought.

"Of course, your father's main trouble is that he's too serious," Tod told her. "And then again, Pamela, he's not serious enough. If you're going to hold an Ulster audience you have to be either a Harry Lauder or – well, a Mungo McMaster. Comic or dramatic."

Pamela gave a vague sound that could have been agreement. She knew all about her father's seriousness, she thought. She knew altogether too much about it. The trouble with Shane Hendrick was virtue. He was the most patient, kind and virtuous man she had ever known. He was almost intolerably kind and serious. Her mother's death had been due, according to the death certificate to pneumonia, but Pamela was certain she had been bored to death.

"This is a country that loves the big gesture. Love me or hate me – but don't bloody well ignore me, if you'll pardon the French. Now that McMaster – he's capable of almost anything to grip his audience. He's really an actor deep down; in fact, if you ask me, most clergymen are. They love to get up there and spout – and know damn fine no one's going to have the nerve to walk out. I did once but I was drunk at the time and it wasn't my own church anyway."

He shot sidelong glances to see how these revelations of depravity were received. Pamela was unimpressed apparently. But then, he thought, outright atheism and agnosticism were common enough in England.

"Did you hear," he asked irrelevantly, "about the two atheists in court for disturbing the peace. The magistrate asked them why two people of like mind couldn't agree. 'Ach sure, y'r Honour, isn't he a Papish atheist and amn't I a good Protestant atheist.' "

Pamela did not laugh very much and Milligan chided her. "Dear Pamela, you're like the Belfast audience in the Empire Theatre when Harry Lauder was over here. He was in great form – but never a laugh could he get out of them. Afterwards the Lord Mayor went backstage. 'Man dear, Sir Harry, you were great, just great. You were that funny I could hardly keep from laughing.' "

Pamela continued not to laugh very much.

"I'll tell you what – I'll stand on my head," said Milligan. "Maybe that'll bring a smile to those ruby lips."

"Oh, you are an idiot, an absolutely priceless idiot!"

The house Shane Hendrick had taken was in a street leading off the main road, not far enough from it for the sound of traffic to be subdued. The faint strains of song came from some public house nearby with every now and then the barman's anguished, urgent cries: "Will yez have a titter of wit? It's long after closing and if the peelers come in . . ."

"That," said Milligan profoundly, "is the supreme expression of the Ulster character."

"Drinking after hours?"

"Oh, that as well. No, I meant that we still call policemen 'peelers' a century or so after the term went out of fashion in England. Oh, we're very, very conservative in some ways here."

Milligan did not go into the house. It was almost time for the last tram and he had no intention of spoiling his evening by a long walk home.

It was as he waited for the tram that he realised there had been something to spoil. Pamela was not especially glamorous, nor did she sparkle conversationally. But she did make him feel that he was enjoying himself. So?

"To the Junction," he told the conductor grandiloquently. "Hang the expense, my good fellow. I come from a very wealthy family."

"Oh, aye," said the conductor sourly.

CHAPTER EIGHT

'Why now, Mrs Anderson, that is indeed a most kindly offer, a Christian offer. But I could not accept it. I'm sorry. I'm truly sorry. But I have sworn that yonder tent shall be my home until again the spirit of our Redeemer sweeps the land – aye, and the world itself."

Mungo McMaster was indeed touched by Mrs Anderson's offer to him of a room for himself and his wife, free of charge as she had been at pains to make clear.

And he knew also that his answer was not the whole of the truth. Though he did not put it into words, perhaps could not have done so, the tent and the donkey were part of his mystique, his symbols, his trademarks. Without them he would be in some slight degree diminished.

There were practical issues also. Mrs Anderson would certainly be delighted to have him in her house, he a minister. But against her delight would be the affront felt by all the women who did not have him. He had to remain apart, be beyond the normal – above it perhaps, but certainly beyond.

Mrs Anderson, a dumpy woman with a tight, round face, hair in a bun, and steel-rimmed spectacles on her snub nose, accepted his refusal with dignity.

"If it's so then it must be so," she nodded. "But I was wondering . . ."

Her voice dropped to a whisper and she glanced about her secretively.

"It's my daughter. My wee Janey. I was wondering would you maybe see fit for to say a wee prayer for her?"

Mungo McMaster said nothing, but stood towering over the woman in the midst of Gonagal's Piece.

"She hasn't been right this good while," said the woman. "And forbye it's a lack the money coming in it's a sad thing to see her lying there, just lying ... Do you have the healing gift? Can you pray, Mr McMaster?"

He knew what she meant.

"I can ask a blessing for the laying-on of hands," he said. "That I can surely do."

She led him to her house, on one of the corners that marked the boundaries of the waste ground.

"Will you take a dish of tea?"

She led him into a minute parlour, packed with gimcrack Victorian furniture. A photograph of a heavily moustached man glowered down from above the fireplace. It had a dusty black ribbon draped about it.

"Anderson that was," she declared. "He had the insurance. He was a good man, though he smoked too much."

No one else had smoked in the house from the time of the funeral, McMaster thought. It had a musty, scented, faded smell of middle-aged femininity. The tray with the tea was brought with a celerity that showed she had expected him to come.

McMaster chewed slowly at a slice of rich fruit cake and sipped at tea which had been infused overlong. He put the cup down at last. His heavy eyebrows rose enquiringly.

"You'll want to see her – "

The bedroom was very small with a single bed jammed between door and window. The girl on the bed could look out on the waste ground; she would have been able, McMaster thought, to hear his sermons.

"Janey! See who I've brought til see you. It's the preacher and he's going to do a prayer for you, Janey, isn't that the lovely thing?"

The girl on the bed might have heard the sermons, McMaster thought. But she would not have understood them, it was now plain.

62

She had the translucent skin, the ethereal look of the chronic invalid. Her hair was a little darker than golden, untrimmed, untended. It spread out on the pillow. Her eyes were blue and her features had a soft, blurred outline that might with more flesh have resembled her mother's. She made no comment on the minister's arrival in her bedroom.

"She was that bright as a wee one," whispered Mrs Anderson. "Go, go, go all the time. Asking questions – aye, and answering them too. Such a help in the house. Oh, a lovely light hand with pastry. Then . . ."

McMaster kept silent for silence was as effective a tool as speech.

"She's been in this dwalm two years or more. And not for the lack of doctoring, I can tell you. I've had her at the Royal. The specialists. I never grudged. But not a thing have they done for her. They couldn't even give her a word of hope."

How often had she told the story, McMaster wondered. There was a certain glibness about it. The words came quickly, easily; there were no tears. And yet, after so long, should there be tears?

"She just came home from work the one night – she was a half-timer in the York Street – and she said never a word but walked up the stairs to her bed and hardly a word has she said from that day to this. Hardly a word. Even when her father died. The doctors said it was shock. But what sort of a shock? What sort of a shock, Mr McMaster?"

She looked at him directly. "I never tried a preacher, for to tell truth our own minister is not the sort you could go to. Would the prayer help? The laying-on of hands?"

"All things are possible to a bountiful and merciful God. I will pray for her."

"Aye. Aye. Well, I'll leave you till it. You'll not want me by you."

He heard her feet clump down the steps and he knelt beside the girl's bed, face in his hands.

In sonorous terms he began to invoke Divine assistance

63

and compassion for the stricken girl. His words rolled out to fill the room with their fervour. Intensely he tried to will the girl better, to give her some of his own vast fount of energy.

None who could have overheard him then would have doubted his sincerity, for here there was no audience to be impressed save a crazed girl of eighteen or twenty.

Yet it was this girl who interrupted his prayer, interrupted it so abruptly and shockingly that he doubted the evidence of his ears.

"Piss," she said.

McMaster's head jerked up and he stared at the ethereal little face. The pretty lips formed the word again.

"Piss," said the girl, a little impatiently.

And then, while he still stared, she swung her pale, thin limbs from the bed, got to her feet and with the chamber pot from beneath the bed demonstrated that she meant the word literally.

When she had finished she swung back into the bed smiled gently at the preacher and in explanation smiled again.

"Piss," she said.

*

Wee Hughie Macatammany was moving quietly through the crowd on the waste ground while they waited for McMaster to come out from the tent.

Wee Hughie was as small as his name implied, about seven stone in weight, a shoulder hunched from an accident when he fell off a staging – for he was a riveter's holder-on – and he wore very thick, steel-rimmed glasses. His coat hung nearly to the ground, for he bought his clothes from the secondhand barrows round Smithfield Market and he rarely found anything from anyone of his own small stature. His trousers would have been as incongruously long if his mother had not cut off the bottoms. Coats were beyond her, though, and in any case the length of the coat meant more warmth. He had his cap in his hand and his brown eyes bulged with sentiment as he went through the crowd.

"Lookit," he pleaded in his husky, deferential voice, "Hasn't your man been here a week and never took a collection yet? Give's a make ... Give's a make ..."

And here and there a penny or a halfpenny did clink into the sweaty old cap.

Hughie heard the service through with his eyes misting and his fingers counting and re-counting the greasy coins in his cap. There was one shilling and tenpence there and he wondered how he could ever bring himself to offer such a piddling little amount to the emissary of God.

For certainly Mungo McMaster spoke with God's tongue. Wee Hughie had known that the very first time he heard him. That great, ranting, booming voice had evoked ecstatic, sympathetic echoes all the way through the little man's body, down to the inner depths of his soul.

He would have rushed forward crying that he was saved except that he did not care to make an eejit of himself before them all.

Now the service ended and the crowd dispersed into little groups, edging gradually back towards the hall and Hendrick waiting sourly for his pupils.

"Minister!"

Was it because McMaster was so tall and he was so small that Wee Hughie had this silent devotion?

"Minister, I took up a wee collection."

And from his great height, Mungo McMaster gazed down unsmilingly on the minute, cringing figure. His first disciple, he thought. The first of the faithful. The first brand culled from the burning.

The heart of Mungo McMaster swelled with a great pride, for where there was one there would be others. Every flock must have its nucleus and here was a start. On this rock, on this minuscule pebble, rather, would he build. In his mind trumpets sounded and banners flew as Mungo McMaster led the faithful into the Promised Land.

"Will I be saved, Minister?"

A frown gathered thunder on McMaster's brows and whether that frown was directed as Macatamanny or inwards at himself no man could have said. For it might have been that he chid his own vanity for that brief vision of the procession of triumph and his own position at its head. The words, though; the brief, brutal words were directed at Wee Hughie.

"Salvation is not for sale," said Mungo McMaster and turned on his heel to walk into the tent.

Wee Hughie stood there with his hand held out and the coppers still resting in a greasy heap in his palm. He looked utterly crushed, woebegone, forlorn. His mouth hung half open, showing the stained teeth.

And yet in his heart there was a bright glow.

"Whatna man," he breathed, eyes shining their devotion. "Oh, whatna man!"

CHAPTER NINE

"Mr McMaster! Could ye come, Reverend? Could you come this minute?"

Mrs Anderson was standing outside the tent, hopping uneasily from one foot to the other like a farmyard fowl. There was a curious note in her voice which Mungo McMaster could not interpret, as he rose with stooped head and murmured to Dulcie: "I will see what she wishes."

But outside Mrs Anderson simply clutched his sleeve and dragged him almost at a run across Gonagal's Piece to her house.

"It's Janey," she said, and McMaster knew how great must be the urgency for the woman to make such an exhibition of herself before all the watching, hidden eyes behind the tattered lace curtains.

He clattered up the stairs after her, big boots like thunder on the polished linoleum.

What had happened to the girl? Had her illness taken a turn for the worse? Would he be blamed?

In the bedroom Janey Anderson was sitting up and in her eyes there came at once a bright light of recognition.

"It's the minister . . ."

In triumph Mrs Anderson turned to McMaster. "See!" she panted. "See! She knows you. And she knew me. Spoke sensible this day for the first time. Oh, it's God's mercy! God's mercy. You've wrought a miracle, Mr McMaster – a miracle!"

Mungo McMaster was almost choking with pride as he stepped to the bedside and looked down on the frail, shy figure of the girl.

"So you're better, Janey," he smiled. "You're better."

"Aye. I'm better. Oh yes. Oh, I'm fine now, fine."

"You've wrought a miracle, minister," Mrs Anderson was saying again and again.

McMaster turned to frown at her.

"Not I, Mrs Anderson, not I. But He whose servant I am. Now let us give thanks to Him for His mercy to this His child."

And as they knelt in prayer beside the little bed and McMaster's voice boomed out in the room there was a tumult of emotion in the big man's heart. His prayers had been answered for this sick child. The Lord had answered His servant. He had set the seal of His approval on Mungo McMaster.

And yet when the prayers were over and Mrs Anderson was again babbling her thanks, talking of the miracle he had brought about, McMaster halted her.

"Madame, there must be no more of such talk. I wrought no miracles. This was God's own mercy."

She could not restrain herself.

"Aye, well. I didn't see God handing down too much mercy till you came. And there's others 'll think the same when they hear."

"Mrs Anderson! This is almost blasphemy. And I must insist – not one single word of this outside the house. Tell no one. You hear me?"

"But . . . it's a miracle. Everyone should know."

"Not a word, I conjure you, madame. Not one word. You promise?"

Reluctantly she nodded.

And neither then nor later did Mungo McMaster know in his own mind that the woman would never keep the promise and that even if she did, the neighbours were sure to associate the girl's recovery with his own visits to the house.

Who could know how real was his modesty?

*

The directors of the shipyard were not concerned solely with their dividends and fees when they gazed out from the Boardroom on the desolation of their business. Here was the heart of Belfast and it had ceased to beat. The whole province suffered with the Queen's Island and when they drove in their big cars to the silent yard they were conscious of the silent streets, of the loungers on the corners who should have been at work.

Not only in their pockets were they hurt, for every man has a conscience and above all the Ulster mind, with its strong Scots influence, abhors waste. This, their shipyard, was being wasted and those their people beyond the gates were wasted also. They had a fierce, strong pride in their yard, knowing it for the biggest in the world and certain that it was the best.

Beyond their desire even to see the dividends flow again was their need to hear life, to know that the monster could breathe again.

The chairman's face showed the bad news before they heard it. There were minutes to read and be approved, minutes of the last meeting which had little enough of cheer in them. Then:

"I'm afraid, gentlemen, that Brown's have dished us. It's not official, of course. But they've got the Cunarder."

So the ship which was to be the Queen Mary would enter the Clyde instead of the River Lagan. The work which could have been adrenalin to Belfast's heart would revivify instead the sister city across the North Channel. Belfast's loss was Glasgow's gain. And those of the directors who had shares also in John Brown and Co. Ltd., had some small solatium for their gloom.

"Not that I see them making anything on it," said the

chairman. "You know our own tender. We would have been lucky to break even. And no one can undercut us. No one."

He spoke with a sombre pride.

"So far as the rest goes, our subsidiary plans. The banks . . ."

The banks had never heard of credit these days, not even credit for the Island to set up other subsidiaries, to devote its machinery and skill to making motor bodies or carpet-sweepers or anything else that could be wrought from steel. The banks did not believe there would be a market for them either. When no one had any money anywhere, where was the point in making anything? Where could the consumers be found?

But the chairman did not wish them to go altogether without hope.

"I will tell you nothing definite," he said, "but there is one possibility for a ship – a long shot. But we still have hopes." He would say no more than this to satisfy their curiosity.

"Perhaps we could help," someone said. "Push the idea. Help it along . . ."

The chairman smiled grimly. He knew the dangers of a crowd. The negotiations ahead would be delicate in the extreme. The bargaining would be hard. And if there was to be a margin of profit it would be minimal. The tiniest interference from his colleagues could be ruinous.

"I think the only way you could help would be to pray," he suggested. "And now, gentlemen, unless anyone else has something to raise . . ."

*

Smithfield Market lay only a hundred yards or so from Royal Avenue, Belfast's principal shopping centre, but the gap was one of time rather than space, for this ancient, covered market was a relic of the past.

Here, under one long, rusty girdered roof was a microcosm of commerce, stalls selling everything from second-hand clothes and books to the latest gadget.

Tod Milligan did a lot of browsing there amid the book-stalls, where any amount of reading matter could be picked up for a shilling or so. Books could be sold here as well, and since he had contrived his way on to the paper's reviewing panel he usually had books to dispose of. It was not hard to get on to that panel, for the paper did not pay for its reviews, esteeming the honour of print sufficient recompense.

As well as buying and selling, Milligan liked to stroll about, listening, watching, gathering material for a column which he hoped to sell to one of the papers about the market.

Certainly the place was full of characters, from the old woman on the delft stall who wore three coats summer and winter, to the alleged unfrocked priest who presided over a stall displaying nudist magazines and mild pornography. Most of the gossip of the city could be heard here by those with ears to hear, and Milligan was a good listener when he was by himself.

Now he was watching The Bogeyman trundling up and down the alleyways between the stalls. The Bogeyman had either been born without legs or had lost them in some long ago accident. Below the hips he did not exist. He was mounted on a little four-wheeled trolley or bogey and he propelled himself by means of a short stick in each hand.

He was a man in his middle age with a big, bald head and rather fine eyes. His mother ran a hardware stall and he did her errands, wheeling his way up and down the alleys, thrusting impatiently at the calves of those who would not give way and shouting occasionally: "Ting-ling!" in the manner of a cycle bell. (His other nickname was inevitably 'Ting-Ling'.) Milligan had never heard him speak and did not know whether, in addition to his physical impediment, he was also mentally retarded.

"The Bogeyman Cometh," thought Milligan with relish.

A title for a play? A novel? Was the little man himself too much of the nature of Grand Guignol (he felt innocently pleased at remembering the words) to be used? Libel?

I BUY ANYTHING said the legend over Joe Kavanagh's stall at the end of the market and, glancing towards it, Milligan abandoned for the moment the thoughts of the Bogeyman, for he had recognised a familiar face.

He prowled up behind a dapper figure in dark overcoat and Homburg hat, eyeing the miscellany that almost seemed to make good Kavanagh's boast.

"How's Sid the Yid?" Milligan demanded in the other's ear.

Sidney Levine reacted well. He jumped about a foot and spun round.

"Oh, hullo, Tod."

Levine was not in fact a Jew. His Huguenot ancestors had been named Le Vin when they came first to Ulster to flight from French Catholic terrorism and the revocation of the Edict of Nantes centuries before. They had brought the linen industry with them, their knowledge of the growing and manufacture of flax. They had done well by their hosts and had no complaint if the French accent could not quite be compassed by the Ulster tongue. Le Vin . . . Levine . . . Leveen . . . Levin. A name was a name.

Sidney had been at school with Milligan, though a couple of years the senior. Now he was a solicitor building his own practice. Most of his clients thought he was Jewish and he was content to let them think so, for thus they also endowed him with the legendary shrewdness of that race. He did however conceal with the greatest fervour another secret which was known to Milligan and a few others. He was also a poet.

Under the name of 'Barney McGill' he had already published two columns which had sold well enough for his publishers to want a third – a rare phenomenon indeed in those days, when most publishers put out a little verse now and then by way of an oblation to the Arts and in the sure knowledge that they would lose money.

"How go the torts and misfeesances?"

"Oh . . . they go. And the great, throbbing, tumultous

world of the Press? Exposed any crooked Lord Mayors ecently?"

"Not this week. A drink?"

"Why not. I've only got three clients waiting. I'll wait for another two to gather. Teaches them respect, you know."

They went to one of the nearby inns, Kelly's Cellars, which was perhaps the oldest in the city and made every effort to look it. Walls and shelves were covered with assorted eighteenth and nineteenth century junk – warming pans, brass jugs and the like. There were old and yellowed theatre posters on the wall and everything was covered in dust and cobwebs.

It was not consciously picturesque, but the owners, about to start spring-cleaning at the turn of the century, had been afflicted with ennui and a prescience that the untidiness lent atmosphere. They decided to concentrate on the quality of the drink and let the dirt look after itself.

The bar was very low, not much above knee-height and the seats at it were cut-down barrels. Milligan and Levine took their drinks to the snugs at the far end and seated themselves warily on benches whose only polish had come from the seats of many trousers and which were ever ready to raise a piercing splinter.

"I'm glad I saw you, Tod," Levine mused after the first round and before he had gone for another. "You might be able to help me."

"At your service as ever, my dear Sidney. A paragraph in the paper perhaps? 'For cut-rate conveyancing, try Sid the Yid, Belfast's best and brightest solicitor.' Did you know that in America a solicitor can mean a tart? Come to think of it – No, skip it."

"As well," Levine answered. "Don't trifle with the law, Tod. Don't forget that, humble as I am, I am still an officer of the court. No, what I wanted to see you about was a piece of yours a few days back. At least, I presume it was yours. About a preacher fellow."

Tod Milligan felt that glow which comes to any writer

73

meeting someone who has actually read something of his.

"Mungo McMaster," he said. "The New Revivalist? Yes
How did you know it was mine."

"By the trail of split infinitives . . . No. But seriously. Thi
fellow set an idea stirring in my mind and I'd like to have a
look at him, hear him preach."

"And idea for a poem?" Tod was impressed. He was a
quite genuine admirer of Levine's verse and had even
bought both his books. He had a suspicion that they migh
very well be Literature and he was somewhat awed by the
thought that he himself might have aided at the birth of a
poem.

"It's only an idea," Levine said, "but I felt it boiling
away. I'd need to see the man, though, to know if my idea
was right – "

"Say no more. Leave it to Tod Milligan. He's a great little
fixer."

He felt really quite important as they left Kelly's Cellar
and parted.

CHAPTER TEN

The champagne corks were popping in the Earl of Dail's brake at Downpatrick races. It was a gaily bibulous occasion, his little race meeting in the town which sheltered the grave of Ireland's patron saint. It had about it much of the flavour of a family gathering. The little grandstand, the tiny paddock, the faintly unkempt grass and untidy rails and jumps; these all differentiated it from an English meeting.

There were bookmakers, certainly; a Tote even. Under the stand there were bars and a few tipsters plied their trade in the public enclosure. But generally speaking this was not a commercial occasion but a reunion party of the County's blue blood and its sporting fraternity.

The champagne was popping because the Earl had won a race.

"What sort of dope did you feed him, Tony?" demanded the Hon John Merrilees. "That old plug of yours never even got round the course before – let alone winning."

In his voice there was a faint edge. He had failed to back Dail's horse.

"My dear fellah, the details bore me. I leave these matters to my trainer. Some slosh, old chap?"

They were drinking the champagne from silver tankards which bore the Dail family crest and, inevitably, the date 1690, the year of the Battle of the Boyne. Protestant William's victory over Catholic James in that year had cemented the Dail's grip of their estates.

Dail had a jovial, red, countryman's face which could have

75

been taken for a farm labourer's. Nonetheless he was not the proto-typical mindless aristocrat he liked to appear. His thoughts branched out in a good many directions though currently they were as rustic as possible. He was in fact wondering if Lady Estelle Grantford on the seat opposite was wearing any knickers. She was a hoydenish sort of girl and at present her legs were tucked up on the seat, showing a good deal of her thigh but not the answer to the ultimate question.

Dail liked to think about sex. Sometimes he wondered if he preferred the thought to the reality. The thought at least could be as esoteric as he wished, whereas reality was restricted so very much by the wishes and indeed the capabilities of the partner. Somewhere long ago his ancestors had indeed possessed the complete *droit de seigneur*, and had no need to let their imaginations wait on reality. Those days were gone though his grandfather, it was said, used often enough to send down for the third gardener's daughter.

There was a soft explosion and a champagne cork took him in the right ear from behind. The missile came from an adjacent brake bearing the coat-of-arms of the Londonderry family, though Dail recognised none of its occupants.

"Cheeky devils," Merrilees growled. "Give me that bottle."

He fired a reply shot and followed up by shaking the bottle vigorously to produce a thin, violent stream of wine which wavered over the opposition.

Morning coats and ladies' dresses began to reek of champagne and a crowd gathered to watch the battle, cheering either brake with a fine impartiality, according to which was winning.

Dail contrived dexterously to have half a bottle of champagne foam up under Estella Grantford's skirt and found the answer to his surmise was in the negative.

In the background a worried policeman struggled with his conscience. Undoubtedly this party was creating a disturbance. On the other hand, they were who they were and he had no wish to finish his career in the wilds of Fermanagh. And there was the matter of his legal standing. Was the enclosure a public place within the meaning of the Act?

He strolled behind the stand and smoked a cigarette.

*

"The aristocracy at play," said Sid Levine. "I hope your photographer has a picture or two. And that we'll see them in the *Standfast* instead of the usual elegant hats and groups of bank managers' uncles."

"The People's flag is deepest red," Tod Milligan chanted cheerfully. "You should have backed his lordship's horse, then you wouldn't feel so sour."

"It's the waste. Think of the hangover we could accumulate on all that spilled champagne . . ."

"If the Law is in such sad straits I'll buy the Law a Guinness."

The bar was a mean and gloomy place beneath the stand which looked and smelled as if in other times it had been used as a stable. Perhaps it had, for the course was in use only a few days a year for racing.

"*Ad hoc*," considered Levine. "Very much an *ad hoc* bar. As transitory as life itself. And just about as nasty. I suppose they overcharge for the stout?"

"What else. Barmen have to live. I did a piece for the *Express* last week. I may get in there."

"Lord Beaverbrook will be gratified. Seriously though, didn't you think that display of top-drawer ebullience disgusting?"

Milligan sipped his stout and put it down with a look of disgust.

"It's off," he declared. "Definitely off. Is yours all right?"

"Curate's egg, no more. But what on earth could you expect in a stable but horse piss. Shall we complain?"

"We'd have to wait till the next race starts and empties

the bar. Just break the glasses in protest."

Outside, the air was at least refreshing. The battle of the brakes had ended, and Milligan had a thought.

"Perhaps I should go and do an interview with the Earl of Dail. The least he could do then would be to offer us a drink."

"In the servants' hall, no doubt. Thank you, Tod, but no. I have my pride. It forbids me to nob and nob with dissolute aristocrats. Anyway, what would you interview him about?"

"The Hunt Club. Did you know it was the oldest in the world – and right here in Downpatrick?"

"There is no Downpatrick Hunt. I do know that. There's an East Down Foxhounds and a County Down Staghounds, but a Downpatrick Hunt, no. What would they hunt in Downpatrick anyway? Papishes?"

"My dear, ignorant legal pillar, the gents who belong to the Hunt Club wouldn't be so vulgar as to go out with any common Hunt. Each of them has his own private pack – or at any rate, used to. The Club is a sort of . . . well, they have an annual dinner at least."

"You astound me. Just like an Orange Lodge or the local branch of the Transport and General Workers' Union."

"Have you lost some uncommonly important case or something, Sid? You're full of acid today."

"I'm full of acid every day. Today it just happens to get out. All right then. Go and do your beastly interview. But don't blame me if you get snubbed."

"Reporters are always getting snubbed. It's like water off a duck's back."

Which was not absolutely true. Tod Milligan resented every snub which came, whether from some official source or from people like the Earl of Dail. Not that he had had many dealings with the Ulster peerage other than Lord Craigavon, the Prime Minister who scarcely counted since he was a newcomer. The peerage on the whole kept very much to themselves, not descending into the arena of politics, not in fact doing anything very much – and of course doing it very well.

Dail was a case in point. With his land holdings and the capital he had invested in various industries, he must be in a quiet way one of the most influential men in Ireland. Yet his name was scarcely mentioned in the papers, his picture rarely seen. Whatever he did he did without the aid of publicity. Which seemed inconceivable to a newspaper man.

The champagne battle had petered out as Milligan trolled towards the brakes. That Dail should have been involved in it was in its way baffling. Milligan had a picture of the man of power operating in remote cacuua, protected by hordes of retainers. Yet there was no denying that Dail had seemed like any other drunk. If Guinness had been thrown instead of champagne no doubt he would have been appearing in court in the morning.

"Excuse me, my Lord," he said, annoyed that he should sound so obsequious. "I'm from the *Standfast*. I wonder if I might have a few words with you."

The eyes narrowed a little in the countryman's face gazing down from the brake.

"A reporter, eh? And what do you hope to worm from my store of secret knowledge?"

"A reporter!" Lady Estella Grantford lurched forward impetuously. "You go and tell that bloody editor that if he prints another picture of me like the last one I'll sue him. I'll sue him for thousands. He made me look like a tart, in that rag of yours."

"Darling," said Merrilees, "it wasn't the editor who made you look like a tart. Nature did that."

Dail looked at the other two, shrugged and then swung himself to the ground and beckoned Milligan a little way apart.

"What exactly were you after?" he demanded.

Milligan felt the blue eyes search him shrewdly as he explained his interest in the Hunt Club.

"I doubt if you'll be able to write much about it. Try the secretary . . ." The Earl scribbled on a card. "It's more or less moribund now, you know – just an occasional booze-up.

Surely you can find something better to write about than that. What *do* you write about, anyway?"

Tod Milligan found that the roles had been reversed. Dail was interviewing him. And doing it rather well, he reflected afterwards. He had learned a good deal about Tod Milligan before he finished. But Tod had learned very little more about the Earl of Dail.

As he told Levine afterwards: "There's a bit more to that fellow than shows on the surface. He seems – interested."

CHAPTER ELEVEN

Dulcie McMaster was afraid and the root of her fear she did not know, save that it lay very deep. It would be impious, she knew, to entertain premonitions. The Lord's will must be done. The Lord's servants must obey and certainly it was not for her to question the actions of Mr McMaster.

But though it took a great burden from her own shoulders she did wish that the women would stop sending food. The platters were left outside the tent and there was rarely a clue as to who had left the stirabout or the stew or the sausages sizzling amid the onions or the dish of sago pudding. Outside a child might be seen scudding back to the houses. But even the door he entered would be no clue as to his name or as to who had sent him.

When it came to running messages children were almost communal property in these mean streets.

It was meant in a kindly way, she knew. But what woman could relish seeing others feed her husband?

"I wish they wouldn't do it," she said aloud to McMaster. "It is not fitting that you should be fed from the leavings of another's table."

Mungo McMaster set down his tin plate, still with a sausage on it and a potato, and patted his wife's head gently.

"Oh, my Dulcie," he chided. "We must terribly beware of pride. Our Lord did not scruple to take alms or to be fed wheresoever he wandered . . ."

"But you won't even take the alms," she cried and then

felt stricken. "Oh, Mr McMaster, I should never have said that!"

"Now, Dulcie, now," he smiled. "What's in the heart should out on the tongue. You were right to speak. And it may be that I should have taken the alms offered for they were offered in a kindly way. My heart grieves me sometimes that that small man Macatammany may have been hurt. I think I might answer him differently now."

He forked up the last sausage and ate it slowly.

"I have some mind," he said at last, "that you were praying there would be more kitchen to my meals. Now the good Lord has opened the hearts of these people and we are feeding well. Therefore the Lord has answered your prayers and answered them fairly – aye, as he will always answer the pure and true of heart. Therefore let us give thanks and mind not that we are as poor as any sparrow in the hedges."

Dulcie felt a sort of claustrophobia press in on her from all sides and yet she joined McMaster in his prayer.

*

"He's a saint," breathed Wee Hughie Macatammany. "Yon man is just a living saint."

"I'm surprised to hear a good Presbyterian like you talk of saints," said the man at his side, for they were seated in the John William Cowan Memorial Hall, taking a break after Hendrick's first lecture of the day on 'Economic Processes and Bargaining Procedures.'

"Saints! D'ye think the Papishes have all the saints. What about Psalm 16 then – 'The saints that are in the earth and the excellent in whom is all my delight.' "

"God, man, you should be preaching yourself, Hughie!"

"No, listen now. Wait. Hear me a bit. Yon man – I toul' ye he wouldn't take the money. But he's done more." His voice dropped to a whisper. "Yez know Nita Anderson and thon girl that was took with the dwalm . . ."

*

There were even more today, Mungo McMaster thought as he looked down on his disjointed congregation. The men were scattered in little knots about Gonagal's Bit, some of them close by the mound where he stood, the devout these, with Wee Hughie Macatammany at the forefront but others further off, some even leaning against the walls of the hall.

Those nearest had taken their caps off but the greater the distance away the more caps were worn and at the back some of the men were smoking. McMaster did not mind. It was better for them to be there and smoking than not to be there at all.

The smokers, he thought, would also be the scoffers. And the scoffers were the coughers. Was there a parable there, he wondered, as the first hymn rang about the waste land. Scoffers . . . coughers. The words rang nicely together. There was a point to be made . . .

"My text comes today from the Epistle of James, Chapter Five, verse sixteen: 'The effectual fervent prayer of a righteous man availeth much . . .' "

And from the back, from beneath one of the flat check caps came the first words of dissent Mungo McMaster had heard since the debacle of the McNulty Street gang.

"Prayer, yer granny," came the cry and it was followed by an uneasy titter from the outskirts, angry cranings of necks in the front ranks of the faithful.

"It's that Tommy Kane," muttered Wee Hughie. "Full as a po this time of the day. It's a bloody disgrace and this a religious ceremony. It's not Christian talking like that to the Minister. Come on and we'll do him."

But McMaster was still in command of the situation.

"Indeed, my friend, I can assure you that my Granny did pray – both night and morning."

Kane was in fact drunk, with the best part of a bottle of cheap, port-style wine inside him given by a bookie for a few jobs he had done. It was Kane's nature to get angrily drunk. He was a plater with a family and he resented not being able to keep them properly. He even resented being drunk.

"Aye," he shouted, "My Granny prayed too. And where did it get her? Six feet of clay. On the Parish. Not even the money to be buried decent. That's what prayer did for her. It's all it ever did for anyone. You and yer oul' prayer."

It was not the first challenge McMaster had met.

"I'm sure your granny was a very fine woman. And I know the comfort that her prayer brought her as it brings to all of us. Pray and let the sweet spirit of our Lord enter you and comfort you."

"I know how He could comfort me!" Kane shouted. "He could bloody well get me a job. If he'd bring a ship to the yard there'd be some point til your prayer. But he's as like to do that as he is to drop pennies out the sky on our heads . . ."

He turned his eyes skyward and held out mocking hands.

"I'm not getting rich that quick, you'll see. Maybe if I lived up the Malone Road he'd hear me easier . . ."

"God hears us wherever we are," McMaster answered calmly. "That you must know, friend. Wherever we are and whoever we are . . . 'the fervent prayer of a righteous man availeth much.' "

Kane's voice had a drunken cunning when he answered: "Would there be any righteous men here?"

"Many," said McMaster steadfastly.

"All right then. Put it til the test. Let's see what the fervent prayers of all these righteous men avail to get us a ship to work on. Pray away, my mannies, and see if you can get us a ship – for this time next week, say. We'll see what yer oul' prayers is worth then."

*

"They'll crucify him," Sidney Levine murmured. "Christ of the shipyard. He's right out on a limb and he's sawn himself off. It'll be the end of him."

With Tod Milligan he stood at the back of the crowd and they both listened to the rolling, impassioned, sonorous plea of the man on the mound, the rich entreaty of a desperate prayer.

"Lord, send us a ship!"

"Don't be too sure," Tod Milligan answered. "He did say there were always two answers to a prayer – yes and no."

"Semantics won't get him out of this. As they say in America, he's laid it on the line. No ship will mean no McMaster . . . But I certainly got a great feeling from him. I'm glad I came. I'll dedicate my next book to you . . . God on the gantry, eh? Come on, Tod, I'll buy you a drink."

Meanwhile, McMaster's prayer for a ship continued. He could be heard the length and the breadth of the Goat's Bit – and beyond.

*

"What's happened to your reporter then?" Shane Hendrick smiled at his daughter and patted her on the shoulder as she stirred the stew on the gas cooker in the tiny back kitchen of their house. "Not good enough for you, eh?"

"For a start," Pamela answered, flushing faintly, "He's not *my* reporter. Just because I went to a dance with him once – "

"I saw him today."

"Oh, where?"

She replied so eagerly that he smiled.

"He was hanging around listening to that preacher of ours. I don't think we'll have him much longer, either."

Pamela did not then question the 'either.'

"What's wrong?"

Hendrick told her of the challenge.

"In other words, if there's no ship one week from today he can pack up shop, mount his donkey and peddle himself elsewhere – and let me get on with my job."

"But suppose there is a ship?"

"Suppose the sky falls or we go back on the gold standard."

85

"No, but just supposing . . ."

"In that case maybe we'd better start packing. Certainly no one would listen to me . . . Not that they do, anyway. But I told you – there's no chance at all. I showed you that letter from London this morning. They see no possibility of a ship in the next six months, if then."

"They could be wrong."

"Union headquarters have the best information service in the country. With them it's not a matter of guessing. They know. They knew John Brown's were getting the Cunarder long before it was published. If they say there's no hope of a ship Mr Mungo McMaster can pray till he's blue in the face – there won't *be* a ship."

"I don't know why you should sound so pleased about it."

Shane Hendrick was taken aback and almost denied the charge. But his own innate honesty made him face the facts.

"I suppose I want to see that cocky preacher taken down a peg. And then – well, organisation is so slack here. The men aren't ready for work. It would be back to the old, slip-shod ways if work started in the morning, no organisation, no solidarity, group against group, cut-throat competition, the sweat-shop . . . Pamela, seeing your reporter isn't here, how about your old Dad taking you out for the night?"

CHAPTER TWELVE

A week had passed when Mrs Anderson peeped out through her curtains at the tumult below.

"There was never such a crowd here before, Janey."

"There's an awful lot there, right enough."

She stood behind her mother, gazing out onto the crowded waste land. Already she had put on a little weight since she had left her bed. Her skin had lost its transparency. There was a suggestion of a sparkle in her eyes.

"What'll happen, Mammy? The week's up and there isn't a ship . . ."

Mrs Anderson turned indignantly on her daughter.

"How can you stand there and say that? Mr McMaster prayed you well. Have you no faith?"

Janey Anderson tossed her golden hair.

"Aye . . . but there still isn't a ship."

Wee Hughie Macatammany's face was taut, lower lip thrust out belligerently.

"It's not time yet. It's not time. It was later'n this when he prayed. It's not time."

Tommy Kane could afford to be magnanimous.

"We're in no hurry. We've damn all else to do."

Someone took him up on that and began to sing:

"Oh, we're marching on the Broo,
For we've damn all else to do,
So we're marching on the Broo for Ulster's glory . . ."

The crowd swirled as little angry knots of men argued and wrangled.

In his tent Mungo McMaster was seated, almost slumped, face in his hands. Dulcie was tempted to stretch out a hand in comfort, but restrained herself. This was no time for comforting or even wondering what thoughts were in her man's mind: My God, why hast Thou forsaken me?

They could hear the mounting tumult outside, the tumult that surely spelled defeat for his mission.

"Mr McMaster," she ventured timidly, "you always said that no prayer went unanswered but there could be two answers til it."

His eyes blazed at her as he dropped his hands and it was the last time she ever ventured an opinion to him.

"Oh ye of little faith!" he raged.

*

"Why doesn't he come out?" Was Hughie Macatammany was asking of himself. "Why doesn't he come out?"

"Because he's feard."

Herby Vignoles and the McNulty Street gang were there. In force. Revenge had been postponed but it would be none the less sweet.

"Feard! Run away, boy, before he smacks your bum again."

Vignoles flicked a finger and one of his men kicked Wee Hughie in the stomach. He hit the ground writhing and of his own mates no one stepped forward to protest, to intervene.

"He's kept us long enough. C'mon men. Get that big lanky Creeping Jesus out here."

Gonagal's Bit had begun already to clear. Kane and his crowd were making for the nearest pub. Hendrick's class were drifting back to the hall. The few of the faithful like Wee Hughie were milling indecisively round the tent.

The idol had fallen and the worshippers were going.

McMaster was still inside the tent when it fell and he

urled himself on top of Dulcie to protect her as he heard the
houts of the McNulty Street gang about him and felt the
irst boot slam into his own body.

In her front room Mrs Anderson was screaming quietly:
"They'll kill him! They'll kill him! Get the peelers! Get
he peelers . . ."

Janey Anderson said nothing at first, staring out over her
mother's shoulder at the savagery. Her eyes were very wide
nd perhaps they did not see clearly.

"We should pray," she said suddenly. "We should pray.
Like what he does."

And her lips began to move soundlessly.

In the Cowan Memorial Hall Shane Hendrick stared in
amazement and contempt at the men of his union.

"You mean you'll stand there and see him kicked to death?
And the wife? What sort of men are you?"

Stubbornly they avoided his gaze until someone blurted:
"He shouldn't have promised – "

Hendrick started for the door.

"If none of you are doing anything – "

Afterwards he asked himself if he should have intervened
personally or run to fetch the police. He did not know.

At the tent the McMasters's cooking apparatus had been
uncovered.

"Dear-oh dear," said Herby Vignoles with mock concern.
"It looks as if someone has upset the oil. Now watch you
don't drop a lighted match, anyone . . ."

And then suddenly there was a great surge of men into the
waste ground, men who had come running from the main
road, men who brandished a special edition of the evening
paper.

The McNulty Street gang saw the rush and thought
themselves the target. The matches were never struck.

And the wind caught one paper and blew it towards the
tent so that the first thing Mungo McMaster saw when he
disentangled himself from the folds of the canvas was a blar-
ing headline across the whole page:

'SHIP ORDER FOR QUEEN'S ISLAND'

*

Mungo McMaster had not wished to lead the procession towards the river, towards the gates of the Queen's Island. He had no option in the matter for he was not travelling on his own long legs. He was borne aloft on the shoulders of an everchanging crowd of men while before him Wee Hughie and another man carried the placard which normally stood below McMaster's pulpit.

"Mine eyes have seen the Glory of the Coming of the Lord."

Behind him the tune of the Battle Hymn of the Republic had been taken up. The whole great host, growing as it moved, was singing. The words, though, were unorthodox:

> *"Mungo McMaster has opened up the Yard.*
> *Mungo McMaster has opened up the Yard.*
> *Mungo McMaster has opened up the Yard*
> *And we'll all get back to work . . ."*

Unashamed tears were on many faces and McMaster could have given any order then and a thousand men would have obeyed.

PART TWO

CHAPTER THIRTEEN

"Christ on a gantry reaching high,
Blood-rust, riveted hands to the girders
And beneath the slipway to what bourne?
Around, what Judas shall tremble and cry
For the caulking hammers of his conscience
And shall the red lead blood be dry?"

Sidney Levine's poem had a considerable success.

"Of course, the field hasn't been touched really over here. Ulster verse is still in the pastoral stage. But like the country, it's nudging its way into the twentieth century . . . What do you think of your preacher now?"

"I told you he was a remarkable man," Tod Milligan smiled.

"Yes. But how genuine do you think he is?"

"How genuine is anyone? How genuine is Jimmy Craig when he stands up on an Orange platform and thumps the Pope? How genuine is De Valera when he wants to send the British Army packing? How genuine are you when you write a wee poem?"

"Goad, Mister," said Levin with a fair imitation of the coarsest Belfast accent. "You're a quare geg, so y'are . . . I asked a simple enough question and I got a sermon. What I mean is, does McMaster believe it was his prayer which brought the ship?"

"Probably," Milligan answered. "I don't know if he's

genuine but I'd say he's sincere. Maybe deluded bu
certainly sincere."

He chuckled abruptly.

"The bosses are just about pissing themselves. You saw
their statement . . . 'Without wishing in any way to detrac
from the powers of prayer we would point out that negotia
tions for the current contract have been in process for severa
months and while we are glad to have the support of any
branch of the Christian Church . . .' In other words they're
saying: 'It was us done it, lads, not thon lanky preacher from
Ballymacarrett.' Are you coming to the Cellars?"

They were seated in the pub, almost deserted at that time
of the day, when the door opened, drawing their gaze as an
opening door inevitably does in a pub.

"When the door opens and no one comes in it's the Bogeyman," said Milligan drily. In fact he was right. There was a
faint rumble of wheels and the stocky figure rolled to the
counter. He said nothing but placed some coins on the
counter. He was served with a half bottle of Jameson's
whisky and he rolled away as silently as he had come.

"A figure of pathos?" mused Levine. "Or do you find him
in some way sinister?"

"Both, I suppose." Milligan was staring at the door. "It's
a terrible handicap. And yet he does give you that – well, not
quite human feeling. Creepy. I could imagine H. G. Wells
writing a book about people like him. It's the wheels, I think.
Part man and part machine . . . And yet I've been told he
does well with the girls."

"Never! I mean, how does he go about it? Jack himself
up? And what sort of girl would?"

"Beauty and the Beast," Milligan answered sententiously.
"Who the hell knows what goes on in a woman's mind – if
anything."

*

In the mind of Dulcie McMaster there was a gnawing dread. To hardship and penury she was inured. To public apathy and to humiliation she was conditioned. And now things had changed, had changed so very swiftly.

She stirred uneasily in her bed. This new comfort was disturbing, alarming almost.

Yet to many the change would not have seemed so very great.

The men had come, a deputation led by Wee Hughie Macatammany, to ask Mungo to come to the yard gates, to read a service of dedication.

And while he was gone others went swiftly to work. Almost ignoring her, they had ripped down the ragged tent, levelled the ground and in the old tent's place set up a new one – or, if not actually new – one which was in a perfect state of repair.

This was a small marquee which belonged to one of the social clubs whose function had died in the years of no work. It was vast and roomy compared with the old tent and as well as setting it up they also levelled the top of the mound and laid duckboards within. The tent was partitioned off so that one part might be a bedroom and one part an open hall.

As well they had brought with them furnishings – a bed, a table, a Victorian washstand, no doubt the discards from their own homes and in terms of cash worthless. Yet these things represented luxury far beyond anything Dulcie had known since her marriage.

And yet, as she watched the transformation, Dulcie had terrible doubts. What would Mr McMaster say when he came back? How great would be his anger?

Suddenly she ran out through the open door.

"Where are you taking the donkey?"

"There's a wee stable, just round the corner. Sure, he'll be better there than wandering. Anyway, you'll not be feeding him much now. You'll hardly be going anywhere."

There was kindness in these men, the best of intentions. But for long moments Dulcie McMaster hated them. For at least they could have asked her permission, her advice.

She was panting desperately as she stood at the door, wild-eyed and afraid. What would Mr McMaster say? What would he say?

But after all he said very little at that time. He came walking slowly across the waste ground with a little gaggle of followers trailing behind and he halted before the new tent.

"It is very grand," he said.

"We gey thought it was only fitting," said Wee Hughie.

"A fine, fair tabernacle in the Lord's eyes," said Mungo McMaster and from this they knew that the gift was acceptable. Also they knew that the tent was to be called the Tabernacle.

When the others had gone, McMaster paced up and down the unaccustomed space of his new home in a brooding silence whose depth Dulcie could not probe. Nor did she dare to try. If McMaster wanted her to know what he thought he would tell her in his own good time.

And indeed he said nothing that night but came at last silently to bed. And silently he lay beside her in the dark, silent but not asleep, stirring restlessly sometimes, impatiently almost as if the night was too long, as if he wished to be out and about his business or the Lord's business.

Dulcie lay very still and wondered helplessly what would become of them.

*

"And have you a cup of tea for a poor but honest gentleman of the Press who has been sweating out his guts writing an article on all the American Presidents who were of Protestant-Scots-Irish descent."

"Oh. It's you," sniffed Pamela Hendrick with a toss of her head.

The tea urn was murmuring gently in the Cowan Memorial Hall and from the main hall itself came the muted sound of Shane Hendrick's voice.

"I wasn't too sure if your father's work would still go on now that work's starting."

"He says it's more important than ever now. This is the time, he says, to get the union really tightly knit. Now they've really got something to organise for. So he says."

"You sound less than convinced, Pamela."

She tossed her head petulantly.

"It's so damned dull!" she cried. "Day after day. Year after year . . . the solidarity of the working classes. It's all I ever hear."

Milligan was startled – not so much at her views as at the 'damn.' Ladies did not swear. But he rose to the occasion.

"Let me, dear Pamela, take a little of the dullness from your life? When do you finish here?"

*

The Duke of York public house, like most of the best hostelries in Belfast, was approached by a 'Presbyterian entrance'; a narrow alley leading from Donegall Street adjacent to the Belfast News-Letter's building.

So a man going to such a pub was not, as he left the main street, necessarily heading to alcoholic perdition. He might be making for a business house or even taking a short cut somewhere.

"So conscience doth make cowards of us all," said Milligan as he took her arm. "As Shakespeare or Tennyson or someone said. All the good, sober, respectable burghers sneak in for their sustenance without being spotted. They can pass round the plate on Sundays without anyone accusing them of being drinking men."

"I don't know why they bother," Pamela answered shortly. "Good Lord, isn't a man entitled to a drink? Or a woman, for that matter?"

"For just those words Mungo McMaster would consign you without a qualm to the everlasting bonfire."

The Duke's was moderately full. It was a newspaper pub

with a steady tide of sub-editors, reporters, compositors and Creed operators flowing in and out according to their duties. They came from the *Standfast*, the *Newsletter* and the *Northern Whig*, the Protestant morning papers. The evening paper men and the staff of the Nationalist *Irish News* frequented McGlade's a good deal further up the street.

"No shame, the Papishes," Milligan murmured in the girl's ear. "Do you know they walk straight in the front door of the pub as if they'd every right to?"

Pamela ordered beer, somewhat to Milligan's surprise and a little to his relief, for his experience of women was that they drank genteelly and expensively, of sherry or gin and lime – that is, those few who did drink.

Here and there along the bar there were a few sidelong glances. Emancipation had hit the Duke's earlier than most of the city centre bars. The broad-minded customers were quite willing for women to frequent bars – so long as they were other bars, especially as emancipation had not reached the point where women stood rounds.

Milligan pointed out a few of the more notable characters present, the two painters, solo novelist and single poet who made the Duke their port of call. Snatches of conversation, bursts of ferocious laughter and occasional curses reached them in the corner.

Pamela, Milligan decided, was bored. She came close to yawning twice and made what may or may not have been intended as cutting remarks about the crowd and the smoke. Then Sidney Levine entered and the evening was saved for Milligan. He greeted them and brought them drinks and edged into the corner seat.

He set himself to sparkle and succeeded. He was also, in front of Pamela, unusually deferential.

"That preacher chap," he put forward after a while. "I'd like to meet him."

"That man! Whatever for?"

"Curiosity, maybe. He's a primal force. Poets should be
98

brought in contact with primal forces, though not too close contact."

"Oh, yes . . ." Her gaze and her mind had both begun to blur a little and Milligan had the feeling that he could have expended his money more pleasurably for her in the Plaza Ballroom.

In the lavatory Levine said: "I'll call you at the office. Or maybe you'll call me when you've fixed it."

"Fixed it?"

"To talk to Mungo McMaster – "

"But, Good Lord, you don't need an appointment or anything. He's just a street corner preacher."

"Now, maybe. But wait and see. Will you do it?"

"I suppose so."

"That's my Tod. Have a good night with the girl. She's asking for it if anyone was."

Tod Milligan blinked. Then he accepted Levine's words as fact. It was well known that Sid the Yid had a deep knowledge of the other sex. He had been famed for it at school. And yet . . . Pamela?

Levine's reputation stood the test, though Milligan did not think of it in quite that way. A note was propped on the mantelpiece, indicating that Shane Hendrick would be late back, that he had gone to see another union official.

"Well, that's one name for it," Pamela laughed throatily.

"What do you mean?"

She looked at him sidelong and laughed again but within herself. About this superficially sophisticated reporter there was a great deal of innocence. She tossed her hair lightly with her fingertips.

"Even fathers are men," she murmured. "Maybe even more."

"Oh, I see. You think . . ." Milligan laughed uneasily and almost blushed. He had a suspicion that the girl was laughing at him.

Within himself he felt a growing warmth.

"You know," he blurted suddenly. "You . . . you really are very pretty."

"I know," she answered pertly. "They're always telling me that."

She moved to the sideboard and wound up the portable gramophone. She put on a record. It was a tango.

"It's not the Plaza," she said, "but . . ."

On the few square feet of vacant, polished linoleum, they began to dance. It was awkward since they cannoned from time to time into the furniture and the dance grew gradually diminished into a rhythmic pressure of body against body with very little movement of the feet at all.

Pamela lay back against the support of Milligan's hand, hips pressing into his hips, churning alowly against him, building up in him an ever-mounting surge of desire.

Eyes half-closed, mouth a little open, tongue darting out occasionally to moisten her bright lips, she swayed and swayed to the music until it scratched suddenly into silence, into the mechanical creak of the needle on the inner grooves.

"I'll put on another," she said a little breathlessly.

And as she straightened he pulled her deliberately to him and kissed her. She felt triumph fill her and her hands went round his neck, tightening his face to hers in an embrace that bruised both their lips.

Tod Milligan had kissed girls before – though not as often as he would have liked to think. He had fumbled with breasts on dark occasions and had even contrived once fleetingly to get a hand up a girl's skirt. But this was as far as the girls he knew would let it go, or at any rate as far as he had dared to go.

This time, however, this time he knew it was going to be different. Diffidently he let his right hand slide down to the girl's bottom, pressed her still closer as his tongue parted her lips and her own tongue came to meet it, the two darting together, wrestling as it were in a dark fury of desire.

Breathlessly they broke apart at last.

"After all, I don't think I'll bother," she said.

"Bother? It's no bother."

"The record, silly, the record."

They fell easily into another kiss and moved, it was not clear by whose volition, to the elderly sofa before the glowing gas fire.

Milligan's heart was thumping as he sprawled half across the girl and found his hand on her thigh. Her legs lay a little parted under him and after an instant's diffidence his hand thrust up along the smooth length of her thigh, up past the stocking's end and onto the touch of bare skin.

The girl's hands drew his face tighter in a kiss that made it almost impossible to breathe. And yet he no longer wanted to breathe. He wanted nothing more than to thrust still higher up the thigh, up under the blue knickers that he remembered to the centre of the matter.

It seemed to him that her body came to meet his questing hand as it searched still higher.

And with a shock he realised suddenly that there was nothing to bar his way, no elastic or cloth, nothing but the urgent reality of the female body waiting for his caress.

Pamela Hendrick sensed the instant's hesitation, the sense of shock as the searching hand found her, as fingers touched hair and soft flesh and almost withdrew on the same instant, and laughter almost bubbled through her kissing lips.

This she had known before, this shock on the male side when a man learned suddenly that she had been ready for him, waiting. It gave her the triumphant sensation of a spider sitting at the centre of its web for its prey to arrive.

It was a delicious moment for her at all times, a moment of a sort of conquest. As well, she liked to walk openly in the street with nothing beneath her dress, to imagine the thoughts which would be in men's minds if they knew. Especially when she was going out with a man she liked thus to be ready, to have no delay imposed by the removal of underwear, no hitch in a smooth progression. And as well she had the feeling that at no time was a woman in a more absurd position than when pulling down her knickers. It was inelegant and uncomfortable.

Now she slid a little further along the couch so that her dress rode up her hips, skin light and gleaming.

Her right hand left Milligan's neck and started off on a message of exploration and caress of its own.

Now Tod Milligan was scarcely conscious of the kiss or the face that pressed against him. His whole being was centred now in his loins, in an urgency that he would not have believed a body could ever know.

Clumsily he started to heave himself across the girl while she clung to him still. They were contorted now awkwardly in the brief length of the sofa, body above body, hands caressing, hips thrusting.

Blood-pressure was making Milligan's ears roar. He had become a single point of sensitised desire. Muscles ached with tension and a crick was starting in his back.

And abruptly, long before he had intended or hoped or known, it was over. His body went limp, crumpled over the girl. She broke the kiss.

"Never mind," she said. "Wait a minute and we'll try again."

And already desire was once more growing in him.

CHAPTER FOURTEEN

Mr McMaster was awake. Dulcie knew this, but she knew also that she could make no acknowledgement of it. She knew the cause of his wakefulness also and this above all she could not mention.

She knew exactly what torments of temptation racked him now, how the gaunt, muscled body hungered for its natural fulfilment and the fulfilment she could not give.

Where had she failed that this should be visited on her? That now she could not be a wife to Mr McMaster when more than ever before he truly needed a wife, when his mind must be clear to do the Lord's work and he undisturbed by the cravings of the body?

She had prayed. The good Lord knew that she had prayed. She had besought the full return of her physical health – not for her own sake. That did not matter. For herself nothing mattered. But if her body was well then it could be used by Mr McMaster and this would ease his mind and bring him sleep.

She had tried. In every way she had tried. And almost in the past she had been cast from her married bed.

"Thou shalt not know these strange ways," he had cried. "For this is an abomination before the Lord."

And it had been as if he thought this was for her pleasure and not his that she racked her imagination, called up faint memories of whispered secrets of her schooldays, used ancient, earthy wiles.

It was as if she had combined Sodom and Gomorrah in

herself, his horror had been so great. And now she scarcel
dared to lay a caressing, comforting hand on his body unti
he was asleep. He so strong, so healthy. It could not be righ
that he should be deprived of what was every man's, eve
the meanest.

Yet what could be done? What could she do?

There had been times when coldly she had considered he
own death, for then he would be free to marry again, ge
himself a fine, young lusty wife who would be to him all tha
he needed and desired, a wife who would pleasure him in bee
and get him sons so that his quiver might be full.

And indeed in this city she had walked carelessly in th
streets, stepping suddenly from the pavement almost in th
hope that a hasty driver might knock her down, kill her. Sh
had heard a good deal of blasphemy and that was all. Plainly
the good Lord had no intention of freeing her so easily – o
perhaps that it was that he wished to try Mr McMaster
tempt him as He was tempted, torture him with the thing
of the flesh.

She could not bring herself to a direct suicide for not only
would that be a sin, it would reflect badly on Mr McMaster

"Whatever did he do to drive her to it?" they would ask
"What kind of monster is he?"

Yet there must be something she could do for her man.
There must be something.

*

"Passing strange," mused the Reverend Roger Simms,
Rector of St Cyril's. "Yes, I'd certainly say it's passing
strange. Wouldn't you, Richard?"

He filled his large, curved stem pipe and lit it. Little frag-
ments of tobacco fell glowing from the top to burn more tiny
holes in his waistcoat.

He was a plump man, Simms, full-complexion, full-bodied;
without his dog collar he could have been mistaken for a
bookmaker or a pork butcher. His curate on the other hand,

Richard St Leger, was of the lean and hungry kind. Simms was fond of quoting in comparison the remark of G. K. Chesterton to George Bernard Shaw: 'People looking at you will think there's a famine in the land.' And the playwright's rejoinder: 'Looking at you they'll know what caused it.' Simms was indeed fond of repeating any quip he heard. A joke, it was his belief, improved with repetition.

"It's certainly strange, Rector." St Leger was a man of great formality. "But the fact is quite undeniable. Our attendances have increased considerably since this preacher came to the district."

"What sort of doctrine is he preaching?"

"Oh, very much the standard evangelism, Rector. There is a somewhat Presbyterian flavour but without any mention of the Thirty Nine Articles."

"Has he had an – er – knock at us?"

"Not to my knowledge. He's left the Church of Ireland alone. But Rome has come in for some unfavourable mention."

They smiled gently, seated at the table in the rectory study, sipping amontillado sherry, for this was their weekly and harmless practice, a glass of sherry, a biscuit and a general discussion. Or as Simms preferred to put it, 'a pow-wow.'

"Quite. Rome . . . He's hardly an emissary of the Cardinal's. But what does he do on Sundays? Doesn't he have a meeting at all then? Most of his people must be from our flock . . ."

"There are quite a lot of Presbyterians and Methodists too – from further up the road, you know. I think he's being rather subtle. He doesn't want to antagonise the churches – yet."

"Yet?"

"Rector, this is a man of very considerable personality. His delivery is most compelling."

St Leger hesitated, unwilling to confess to the way he had

himself been gripped when he attended McMaster's meeting.

"He feels himself a man with a mission, I think."

"And we? Have we no mission?"

St Leger wondered if the Rector was being deliberately obtuse.

"I've listened to a good many of these street preachers, Rector. I've never heard such a degree of conviction . . ."

"Self-conviction, of course. I imagine that the reason he holds no Sunday services is that he knows no one would attend. His meetings are all very well as a free diversion during the week. But our Church of Ireland flock would hardly consider them a substitute for worship. Not even the Presbyterians or Methodists would do that."

St Leger's lean face did not show his disagreement.

"There was the ship, Rector. Answer to prayer . . . We may say it was pure coincidence. But we are dealing with an essentially simple people."

"Quite. The ship . . . And was there not some talk of the healing of a girl? It's very fortunate for himself the fellow's not a Roman. Protestants are not at all fond of miracles which are not hallowed by antiquity."

Roger Simms felt pleased with the phrase and finished his sherry which St Leger accepted as the signal for himself to do the same and make departure noises.

"We'll keep a watching brief, as our legal friends say. But I don't think we need worry unduly about the preacher."

*

Certainly it was good to see Mr McMaster eating so well but Dulcie knew she would never totally conquer her repugnance of the gifts that now came so regularly. It was no matter of left-overs now, not now that a ship was coming and more and more of the men working.

Whole pies were brought to the Tabernacle, pot roasts, dishes of fruit, bowls of pudding, piles of soda and wheaten farls, pounds of butter, packets of tea and sugar. From the even flow of the groceries it was easy to deduce that some sort of an unofficial committee was now at work amongst the housewives around Gonagal's Bit, consultations so that too much was as little likely to be supplied as too little.

A wife would have needed to be a saint not to resent this encroachment on her duties and Dulcie McMaster made no claim to sainthood.

"Don't you see, Mr McMaster, they're as good as saying I'm not fit for to look after you?"

McMaster considered her worn, blurred face, the hurt blue eyes.

"Wheesht now, woman," he answered. " 'And the greatest of these is charity.' We help them by allowing them to help us. And it takes a great burden of worry from your own wee shoulders."

"There are worries a woman should have – and the feeding of her man is one of them," she insisted stubbornly.

"Be thankful for a wee rest from this worry then," he snapped. "Be thankful. It's a world where there is little room for thanks. Be thankful to the Good God who has softened their hearts towards us."

And of course Dulcie was silent, for if it was a matter of God she could not argue. Yet it rankled slowly within her, a subtle corrosion that could never be entirely quenched.

And this corrosion, though still very faintly, began to tinge all her outlook, especially towards the women of the district.

The daytime services were a great attraction for the women. For some maybe they were no more than an excuse to leave their little houses, to gather together and chatter without the accusation of idleness or gossip. No neighbour could criticise a woman for flightiness when the neighbour was at the meeting too.

In the Tabernacle they sang devoutly, listened to the fervent prayers and the long diatribes of the sermons. Afterwards they were always slow to disperse.

"A wonderful man!" breathed Mrs Anderson to Dulcie.

"Oh, he is a wonderful man and talks with many tongues. It is a great privilege to be married to such a man."

A slight lowering of the eyelids indicated to Dulcie that she was certainly not worthy of the privilege – an attitude to which she was growing increasingly accustomed. She was, the wives contrived to convey, a typical example of the real saintliness of the Reverend Mungo McMaster. A man who could suffer her about him was a man surely in whom a god-like compassion must dwell. This was made the more intolerable by Dulcie's own feeling that this was indeed the case.

For Mr McMaster she lived and would die. But she could not abide to see him surrounded by that crowd of 'clucking hens.'

Furthermore, she could guess what strains they put upon him, these chattering women in their best clothes and with hints of scent and even make-up about them. She had a deep longing to be wrapped in her long blue cloak again, to be on the open road with the donkey's little hooves clip-clopping along. She longed for the peace of the countryside even if their life there was little better than a beggar's. And she knew as she longed that it was an utterly vain hope. They had been called here and here they must do their work.

Yet something must be done for Mr McMaster . . . something.

*

"Of course he's against the Papishes," said Wee Hughie Macatammany indignantly. "Of course he is. You'll see. He'll not let a one of them by the Yard gate."

"I hear you," grunted Harry Makins, "But I don't heed you. Does he have the fundamentals is what I want to know. Does any about ever have seen him in Lodge is what I ask. I never heard of anyone that saw him walking on the Twelfth."

"Sure, he wasn't even here the last Twelfth."

Macatammany was indignant at anything that could be construed as the slightest threat to his idol. And Harry Makins, who had not scrupled to question Shane Hendrick about his affiliations, was as dubious about the preacher.

"He doesn't seem til me to have his whole heart in it," he growled, polishing his glasses – the same steel-rimmed glasses that Macatammany wore, "prescription glasses". "There's some of them preachers is altogether too soft with Rome and that's my view. Softness! It wasn't softness that won the Battle of the Boyne and saved King William's crown. Them Papishes is like adders. Gin you hold them slack in your hand they'll turn and rend your bosom."

They were talking in Macari's fish-and-chipper on the Newtownards Road, talking at the top of their voices and not caring at all that Macari himself was a Catholic. For he was also an Italian and that did not count.

They would have been shocked if he had not been a Catholic, for he was an Italian and Italians were Catholics, just as Ulstermen were Protestants and Free Staters were Papishes. Each in his own place was altogether all right. But now they were in the debatable land.

"Look, I fought with them on the Somme," Makins muttered. "The Papishes. In the same battalion. The same platoon. And if you got them away from the priests they weren't that bad. But they're not clear of the priests now and a man has to watch himself. Tell that to your man. Let's see his colours."

They worked their way to the counter ās they talked and with their fish suppers parted and headed for home. Makins was married but Wee Hughie had never so much as taken a girl out. He had never had the confidence before but since Mungo McMaster had come, since he had himself become his first disciple, he had begun to change. He walked straighter now. And he was inclined to give his mother advice, which he had never done before. Not that she heard him, being almost totally deaf.

"Eat up your supper before it gets cold," he told her as

he laid the steaming parcel on the table.

"Yes. But it'll rain before morning," she answered. "Och, Hughie, you've got vinegar again. You know I don't like the vinegar. It makes my bowels turn."

But she ate with a good enough appetite for all that. Watching her, Hughie did not see the sagging skin, the rheumy, greedy eyes. His mind was rather on McMaster and what he had heard in the chip shop.

The men were right, he thought. He knew where the preacher stood, of course. No one could ever suspect the Reverend Mungo McMaster of being a Rome lover. The idea was enough to make a cat laugh. But not everyone knew the preacher as well as Wee Hughie.

"I'll just give him a wee hint," he said. "Make sure that he just tells them. There wouldn't be no harm in that. He would hardly mind."

"Aye," said his mother. "He's using that old oil again. It's desperate hard on the belly."

They ate on in silence.

CHAPTER FIFTEEN

The salmon rose sulkily and eyed the fly with suspicion. It dived and its tail flicked the water in derision. Upstream a kingfisher flickered brilliantly along the bank and vanished beneath the dangling branches of a sally bush.

A reel wound noisily and the long rod whipped in the fading light. It was a greenheart rod, fourteen feet long, wood dark with age and even darker here and there where a starting split had been bound with insulating tape. The fly was a thunder-and-lightning, its colours faded but the hook they shielded honed sharp. Age touched everything about this angler's gear, age and poverty.

The rod whipped and the line shot out smoothly to deposit the fly in a backwater at the far side of the stream. The greased line would lie on the surface and the drag of the current on it would make the fly jerk and dart underwater. The fly would look like an ailing fish or crayfish or maybe a big beetle or whatever else a salmon might think it looked like.

Harry Makins did not care what the salmon actually thought. He knew, for this was his hobby, as close to his heart almost as his religion, that salmon ate nothing once they had obeyed their migrational urge and entered the fresh water to spawn. Their stomachs shrank and indeed could not even absorb nourishment for the long months while they lived on the fat stored in their body cells. They could not eat but they would still take a fly. Harry Makins thought it could be put down to pure bad temper.

"They're like a Papish during Lent," was how he explained it once. "Like maybe a Papish would be off the booze or the fags. And he'd be neither to houl' nor to bind. Wanting a drink or a smoke and not able to take it for fear of the priest. The salmon, he's the same. He'll go for a bit of food just out of annoyance and then he'll spit it out when he has it. Pure annoyance."

Salmon and trout; Harry Makins fished them wherever and whenever he could. There was plenty of good water within a few miles of the city and if a man couldn't get a lift a man could walk to a river. It was a useful enough hobby for a man who was laid-off. A good salmon was worth a pound or two at the back door of any hotel.

But the money was not what really took Makins to the country. Simply, it was the sport. It drew him as it drew millionaires, bank managers, journalists, doctors and all the broad spectrum of the fraternity. And of course it took him out of the house. There were no clacking women on the river banks, no girning about money, about rent and food and clothes for the children and all the other things women girned about. There was peace.

The fly jerked and swooped its way across the current and suddenly the rod point dipped. The reel began to scream and Harry Makins gave the fish the butt, spread a thumb across the running line, began the long, delightful struggle that must end with a silver body flapping out through the shallows at his feet.

His fingers were reaching for the salmon's gills when a voice spoke behind him.

"You're trespassing," it said.

For a moment Makins almost lost his fish. But it was so nearly spent that it failed to seize the instant of his hesitation.

Fingers hooked behind the hard edges of the gill covers and he turned as he rose with the fish kicking as it dangled from his fingers.

It had been a woman's voice and when he turned he saw thankfully that she was alone.

"I'm the Countess of Dail," the woman announced. "Will you explain what you're doing here?"

"I'm fishing," he said. He rubbed a sleeve across his glasses to clear them of the spray the salmon had thrown up. He saw a tall, slim woman in faultless tweeds, face rather cold, eyes withdrawn, hair fair, accent English. "Aye, I'm fishing. That's what I'm doing."

His gaze searched the river bank behind her. There was no sign of a keeper or any man at all. He breathed more easily.

"You've no right to fish here. This is private property – private, do you understand? You were poaching."

"Well then, I was poaching," he agreed.

He restrained the smile that almost started to his craggy mouth as he saw a hint of colour come into her cheeks. She didn't know what to do next, he thought. Probably she was sorry now that she had seen him, that she had stopped, that she had spoken at all.

Deliberately he turned to the fish and twisted the hook from its jaw. With slow, deliberate movements he untied the cast and stowed it inside his cap. He wound the line onto the reel and began to dismantle the rod.

"What are you doing?" Her voice was sharp.

"I'm taking down my rod, your ladyship."

He stowed the joints carefully into the thin bag he had in his pocket. Then with care he strung some twine through the gills and mouth of the salmon.

"You can't get away, you know," said the Countess. "I'll follow you. I'm going to give you in charge. There's too much of this poaching."

"Just so, your ladyship."

Carefully Makins put the rod down beside the fish on the shingle where he stood. He began to fumble at his clothes.

"What are you doing?" Now there was a hint of uncertainty and perhaps even of fear in her voice.

"I'm taking down my trousers, your ladyship."

He looked her full in the face as he undid the buttons and let the garment slip to the ground. The changing expression flitting across her face roused a furious silent laughter within him. He could read the thoughts that passed behind her blue eyes; the fear and perhaps a shade of hope.

Then swiftly he gathered up his trousers, the fish and the rod and waded into the water. It rose over his knees as he crossed the river.

"I thought you were going to follow me," he jeered back over his shoulder.

And as he reached the far bank a memory of the Suez Canal from war-time days came into his head. The countess still stood where she had been. She did not move as he lifted his shirt and waggled his body at her as crudely as ever any of the Egyptian fellaheen had done.

Happily Makins pulled on his trousers and headed for the city.

CHAPTER SIXTEEN

t was signing-on day at last and at the yard gate a vast
throng had gathered, many thousands of platers and riveters,
borers and shipwrights. Hopefully they were in dungarees,
carrying their piece tins and their tea cans, each of them
ready to start at once.

In the yard itself work had already begun on a small scale,
making ready for the ship that was to be built. Maintenance
crews had cleared the heavy grease from machinery.
Gantries had been inspected. Great sheets of steel stock from
the Clyde had been unloaded. The draughtsmen had made
their drawings and in the moulding lofts curves had been
laid out which metal frames would be tortured into following.

Now it was time for the real work to begin, for the great
outside to swarm in and over the yard, for the hammering
and the cutting and the burning of metal to make the city
shudder with delicious din.

There were ten thousand men jostling in the approaches
to the gates, ten thousand hungry men, hungry less for food
than for work, hungry to have again a purpose in life. More
than the money, more than relief from all the domestic
pressures, the debts, the sullen children, this was what they
wanted: purpose. A man must feel he has purpose for without purpose why should there be a man?

And if there are no ships to build what good is a ship-
builder?

Within the gates the 'hats' waited; the foremen and the
under-managers whose task it would be to select those who

would work, to select the good and reject the bad, to sort the sheep from the goats.

They were called 'hats' because instead of the caps or even trilbys that some of the men wore, each official head was topped by a black bowler hat. It was a badge of office, distinguished easily at a distance. It was also to some extent a safety precaution. A good bowler hat has a fair resistance to impact. In a shipyard rivets, small tools, bolts are always liable to fall from stagings. The bowler hats were almost as good as helmets.

Among the 'hats' there was as great anxiety as among the men waiting outside. They were staff men, it was true, but even their long service and loyalty to the company had not saved them all from the unemployment of the long depression. Many had been able to stay on in the yard on humble maintenance duties but many more had been as uselessly on the street as the men they now waited to select.

Grim-faced, tense, they awaited the opening of the gates. On what happened now, on the men they chose for this first day's work on this first ship for so long might depend the future of the Yard. Many had known war. All knew the people of their city. Behind them pick handles were lined neatly to hand along the wall of the pay clerks' shed.

*

Outside the gate Shane Hendrick was trying to conduct a union meeting.

"Brothers, this is the time. It is now that we must organise, make the company feel our power. They must build this ship, and without our work it cannot be built. It is at this moment that we can dictate our terms, ensure the management's respect for the forces of organised labour."

Probably no one heard him at all. He stood on an orange box and towered over the men but he would as readily have been heard if he had been standing on the peak of the big hammerhead crane with its five-hundred-ton lift.

Tod Milligan saw him and pitied him as he edged through the throng. He would be worth a paragraph or two in his story.

"Union leader fails to control his men," he phrased it in his mind, or perhaps there might be a gentler way of putting it in deference to Pamela. Yet need he bother? Pamela had little enough love for her father's work. On the whole, it seemed as if she despised Shane.

He tried to put Pamela out of his mind for the thought of the girl brought exciting memories flooding back, the delicious pleasure of her surrender – or had the surrender been his? – and also the vague guilts and anxieties the episode had started in his mind. Somewhere deep in his subconscious was the thought: Suppose I have to marry her?

Therefore it was much better not to think of Pamela Hendrick. In any case there was enough to do here without any extraneous thoughts and worries.

The tensions were greater than any he had ever known in the city, for he had been at school during the 'troubles' of the previous decade. It had been something to talk about in assembly, an exciting background to life. A schoolfellow had even been shot, hit by a stray bullet fired from far away by who knew whom. He had been a hero for at least a week.

School had largely insulated Tod Milligan from the tumult, as it had most of his generation, and tales of the conflict had an unreal quality, legendary, as if it had happened in another age and time. The Great War had more reality for him, for he had seen his father slowly cough his lungs away as a legacy of a gas attack – an attack which had by a typical irony of war been launched by the British. The rolling clouds of phosgene had started for the German trenches and then the wind had changed and blown them back among the British.

From the gaunt, yellow-faced man dying in his chair by the fire, Tod had absorbed a certain cynicism which was fed by his mother's belief that she was not getting a fair share of the profits from the family linen business. Probably the suspicion was unfounded. Linen, like everything else, was at a low ebb.

For the paper Tod had in fact reported on a few sectarian riots in the city, mostly about the Twelfth of July, when the Orangemen paraded their banners and their Protestantism through the streets to the sound of pipe bands, drums and fifes, or on St Patrick's Day when the Nationalist Catholics did the same. But in those riots there had been something of the atmosphere of a Rugby scrum, an almost light-hearted battle in which no one intended to hurt anyone very much but rather to make a demonstration of opinion.

The feeling here in this street by the side of the River Lagan, warehouses looming against the skyline, gantries bleakly red beyond the shipyard gates was very different.

Here there was a good deal more at stake than political or religious principles. This was about work. This was about money. This was real.

Protestants and Catholics had already separated into two loosely-knit groups on either side of the road though in the middle of the road they were mingling to some extent. It was simple enough to distinguish the groups for among the Catholics there were here and there to be seen the little lapel badges of the Pioneers, the Church Abstinence Society. On the other side were Union Jack buttons, Lodge buttons, Masonic badges and rings.

No one who knew Belfast could have been deceived on the affiliations of either segment of the crowd. No one who knew Belfast could have doubted that conflict was imminent.

Across the river, across the city, the dark outline of the Cave Hill could be seen like the profile of a sleeping warrior. It had many names, that vast, recumbent face. It had been ascribed in the past to many a Gaelic warrior. History had halted in the nineteenth century for it. It was 'Napoleon's Neb.' Ominously clouds clung about the central peak, like a handkerchief. Napoleon was blowing his nose.

Tod Milligan worked his way towards the Reverend

Mungo McMaster in the midst of the thickest crowd, tower-ing over most of them, his voice declaiming.

*

A service of thanksgiving was what had been in Mungo McMaster's mind when he came there that morning. The Yard was opening. There would be work again. For his people and all the people of Belfast it was a great day and one which should be marked by a suitable dedication.

But he had not expected there to be so many people. This great, swirling, anxious, hungry crowd was not at all what had been in his mind. That thousands of men worked in the Yard he knew. But in his mind he had never pictured such a multitude.

The thought flashed across him that five loaves and two fishes would not go far at all among this crowd, even with the help of a miracle.

His own people were gathered around him, buffering him to some extent from the mounting pressures of the gathering as the time grew near for the gates to open, for the shuffling throng to edge forward, to be signed on.

There were pressures other than physical on Mungo McMaster then, pressures of whose existence he had known before he came to the city but which he had never really experienced.

"Lookit," Harry Makins was demanding. "Lookit here. Who got this ship? Who prayed for it? All right then, are you going to let the Catholics take our jobs?"

Somewhere nearby someone had begun to wave a Union Jack. Across the street, among the Nationalists, rumour was already seething, aided by certain hastening, furtive men muttering to one group and another: "Sure, it's all a cut-up. They'll never let the one of us in ... It's all fixed in Lodge ... If ye dig with the wrong foot you'll not work in the Yard."

Especially active in this task was a lank, sallow man in a stained coat and a battered felt hat pulled well down.

McMaster was being hard-pressed among his own people.

"Well, where d'ye stand then, Minister? Show's yer colours. What about the Papishes . . ."

And even then, Mungo McMaster understood the situation only partially. Perhaps it would have made no difference if he had known everything, understood everything. A situation was in being and forces were being unleashed that were beyond the control of any individual.

The question, as he analysed it, was whether his followers were to work with the Catholics. And he stood there among them for long seconds before the answer leaped in one swift phrase into his mind.

His hands rose and about him there was a pool of silence.

"You have asked me and I answer you not with my words but with God's words. I answer you from the Second Epistle of the Corinthians. For it is written there: 'Be ye not unequally yoked together with unbelievers for what fellowship hath righteousness with unrighteousness and what communion hath light with darkness?'"

His words were submerged in a rumble of assention as the text was remembered and approved. The word passed swiftly down the crowd.

"There! Now what d'ye think of him? Didn't I tell you he had the fundamentals?"

Wee Hughie was beside himself, prodding Makins with a bony finger, skipping up and down, beaming greatly. Makins nodded sourly.

And McMaster prepared to expatiate on his text, to develop his theme on the lines that now work had come to the city and the future looked bright they should not despise those who thought differently from them but rather seek by love and persuasion to bend them to their own way of thinking.

Whether this view would have been as well received remained academic, for at that moment a great handful of mud and horse dung scooped from the gutter on the other side of the street and aimed at the wielder of a Union Jack splattered across his face.

The effect would probably have been much the same whoever had been struck, but it was perhaps heightened by McMaster's dog collar.

The rumbling, vengeful roar of a crowd become a mob filled the street and the presaged battle was joined.

Mungo McMaster wiped mud and horse dung from his face, and curses were the anthem that welcomed him into his kingdom.

CHAPTER SEVENTEEN

"HOOLIGANISM AT THE SHIPYARD," said Tod Milligan bitterly. "Hooliganism! It was bloody civil war. The Prods were throwing Papishes in the river as far as you could see. It's a bloody wonder there was no one killed. For that matter, maybe there was. I wouldn't be surprised if they're keeping it dark."

Sidney Levine smiled at Milligan's baffled fury and sipped gently at his bottle of stout.

"It was a bit of a party, then?"

"I've never seen anything like it. And I don't want to again. The whole street – the whole Bridgend area – was like a battlefield. They had each other down on the ground, kicking, biting, gouging . . ."

"Like a good Rugby scrum?" Levine smiled artlessly. "What, do you grudge the lower orders a little sport?"

"It was totally terrifying. I don't think I've ever seen people so out of control. Even when the police moved in it seemed to take an hour to get things quiet. And my bloody editor calls it hooliganism. Look at that report. Two and a half columns I wrote, the best report I ever turned in. He cuts it down to a miserable half column."

"Ah, but Jimmy Craig was making an important policy speech at Stormont. You wouldn't have that cut, would you?"

And indeed James, the first Viscount Craigavon who was still better known as Jimmy Craig despite his baronetcy and then his viscountcy, had been making a long statement to

he Ulster House of Commons in which he had reaffirmed
he determination of the Unionist Party to maintain 'a
Protestant Parliament for a Protestant people.'

He had warned also that Ulster would not be coerced and
that he did not intend to yield an inch to popery or violence.

Kelly's Cellars was crowded. The battle at the shipyard
gates was plainly the main topic of conversation. Since this
was largely a Catholic area, feeling was strongly anti-
government.

"Anyway," Levine asked, "What was the end of it all,
apart from people being chucked in the river?"

"Oh, a few arrests, a few hospital cases – "

"In other words, just about what you get after a football
match. Could it be that your editor was right? Maybe a bit
of hooliganism is the best description of it."

"Oh, don't be so damned dispassionate, sitting there like
a judge with a long face. Anyway, there's bound to be after-
effects. For one thing, as far as I know, they didn't take any
Catholics on at the Yard. They won't let it rest there."

"Turned your coat or something?" Levine enquired.
"You sound the regular little convert. Something wrong?"

The Bogeyman had just rolled into the bar. His coming
brought a little hush of respect, or that mixture of respect and
disgust which he trailed among people wherever he went.

"You've seen him before. What's wrong?"

"It's not the Bogeyman. The chap with him – he was down
at the Yard gates this morning."

A lank, sallow man in a stained raincoat was at the
Bogeyman's side.

*

Mungo McMaster turned uneasily in his bed for long
hours, seeking an accommodation with himself. He could
not drive from his mind that fray at the Yard gates nor the
strange elation that had been in him at the knowledge that
he was its progenitor.

He tried to dismiss it all, the shouting, the rage-twisted faces, the eventual blood. But the very violence of the scene had struck an echoing chord in his own being. It had been deplorable, terrible – and yet this was his doing. His prayers had bought the ship. His words had set men against men, had defended the rights of Protestantism against the onslaught of Rome.

And hard though he tried to be humble, humility was now gone from him – and perhaps for ever. In particular there would be no forgiveness in him for the men who had thrown dung in his face.

Many changes were taking place in Mungo McMaster that night, irreversible changes. The man who has tasted power once will always hunger for it, and McMaster had tasted the ultimate power – the power of life and death.

All this was in his mind as he tossed and turned in the creaking bed beneath the canvas of the little marquee and though he prayed for guidance the essence of the prayer was that he should be guided to greater victories.

Beside him Dulcie lay quite still and silent, not knowing what tumults tore her husband and thinking that these were the old agonies of the flesh that gripped him.

Soon, though, she promised him silently, those torments would worry him no more. Dulcie had already begun to contrive for his comfort. She knew what should be done and she knew also, she was sure, how it could be done.

Mungo McMaster was entering into more kingdoms than one.

CHAPTER EIGHTEEN

'What's that quotation: 'Who will rid me of this turbulent priest?' "

The shrewd, heavy features of the Prime Minister swung round in a survey of his Cabinet.

"Is he such a threat?" The Minister of Finance did not rate Mungo McMaster so highly as his colleagues. "A down-at-heel gutter preacher?"

"A description which might have been applied to the founder of our own religion," growled the Prime Minister. "His poverty is in its way his greatest protection. He takes no collections at his services, owns no possessions. He lives totally by charity and if his sermons were as full of the same quality he would be a totally admirable person. Minister of Home Affairs, have you anything further of value to offer?"

"The RUC have McMaster under regular surveillance," the Minister of Home Affairs reported. "It seemed to me at one time that a case might lie against him for falsely purporting to be a Minister of Religion. However, the Attorney General assures me that no offence exists unless he claims to be a duly ordained priest of the Church of Ireland or purports to carry out a wedding ceremony. As the law stands anyone may wear a clerical collar and indeed call himself 'Reverend.' No offence is committed, unless there is intention to defraud. Probably at a later stage he may – "

The Premier turned brusquely to the Minister of Agriculture.

"What do you think?"

"I think we're wasting a lot of time on a nonentity. God knows we've got plenty of gutter preachers in the city. This one seems to be a bit more forceful than the rest. That's all. Anyhow, so far as I can see, everything he has said publicly has been very much what we believe ourselves. He's in favour of the Union with Britain, against Rome, for full employment and prosperity. I don't know what you're worrying about."

The Premier's face became a great, blank, monolithic mask as if there could be no thought behind it.

"Just so," he grunted at last. "Well, I think that concludes the business. Shall we have a drink?"

*

A similarly high level meeting was also concerning itself with Mungo McMaster in surroundings a good deal less impressive than the House of Parliament at Stormont. In a back room of a house beyond Smithfield Market a dozen men and two girls were closely packed though not so closely as to discommode their chairman, seated behind a table by the fire.

So seated in a normal chair, his deformity concealed, the Bogeyman was an impressive figure. Perhaps because most of his life was spent in looking up to other people, physically speaking, his head was permanently tilted back and his jaw thereby prognathously thrust forward like Mussolini's. A further effect was that now his eyes were looking slightly downward and his eyelids were slightly hooded. The result was one of disdain for his company, a disdain that he may very well have felt. His bald head shone a little in the firelight and his big, aristocratic nose wrinkled at the smoke of cheap cigarettes.

"Bogey, we can't go on like this much longer."

The speaker was lank and sallow. His name was Pilette and his nickname inevitably Pontius. He had been a pharmacist and had been discharged for some illegal dis-

pensing of drugs. He preferred to think his dismissal was due
to his religion and his politics.

"The Long Fellow's walking all over us," he complained.
"He's kept us out the Yard. His crowd's all over the city. It's
time we showed him we're not doormats."

"You tried that when the Yard opened," the Bogeyman
said coldly. "What good did it do you?"

He gazed slowly round the room. No one met his gaze for
more than a moment or two.

"My policy is clear," he said. "I thought you would have
understood it by now. McMaster is implementing it as well
as we could do ourselves. Make no mistake. The battle will
not be fought here. It is an Irish battle but Ireland is not the
real battleground. We are fighting in England, in London.

"We all know that the Unionist Government can only
exist so long as it has support from Whitehall. We know also
that a good deal of English sentiment favours our cause. Our
aim must be to strengthen that sentiment. The English have
a saying – 'Justice must not only be done, it must be seen to
be done.'

"We could twist that saying. Injustice is not only being
done, it must be seen to be done. It must be made totally plain
to the English that the overweening Unionist majority in
Belfast is trampling down the aspirations of the minority. Do
I make myself clear?"

The faintest of smiles twitched at the corners of his mouth
as he looked round the puzzled faces of his listeners. Nothing
was plain to them, perhaps nothing ever would be to some.

"But aren't we going to do anything?" Pontius Pilette
demanded. "Never?"

"If you wanted heroics you should have joined the IRA,"
the Bogeyman informed him. "If it's speeches you're after
the Nationalist Party can oblige. But if it's your wish to re-
unite Ireland you'll do as I say. And what I say is – we
continue to wait, we continue to watch. McMaster and the
men like him will give us our opening in due course. That is
all just now."

The men shuffled to their feet.

"As you pass the market, Pontius, tell my mother I won't be down for another hour. The girls and I have some leaflets to get typed."

The two girls remained, Noreen McSweeny, about twenty, dark-haired, hard-mouthed; and the other, Sheelagh Grady, a mousy-haired, plump girl of little more than school age.

"The door's locked?"

"I'll make sure, Bogey."

Noreen ran out into the passage and returned in a moment.

"It's locked, Bogey."

"Good. Come here."

When she stood beside him he did not look at her but his hand proceeded directly to thrust its way up under her skirt. Noreen's eyes had been bright before. Now they glazed a little. Her legs parted. Her tongue moistened her lips.

The Bogeyman did not take his gaze from the other girl. The small, amused smile was on his lips as he saw her face flush violently red and her own gaze stray erratically round the room, from the big, crudely-coloured Sacred Heart of Jesus in an ornate frame above the fireplace to the violin and its bow on a bracket beneath the gas fixture to the varnished brown wallpaper that rolled across the uneven surface of the wall to the linoleum which was worn here and there into bare patches to the bookshelves that covered the walls to a height of three feet but no higher.

Her gaze was everywhere but on the Bogeyman and the other girl, and yet in her eyes too there was a curious brightness.

"Come and stand over here," the Bogeyman ordered. "Take your knickers off if you've got any on."

She did not look at him – but she obeyed.

"Two girls," said the Bogeyman softly. "Two girls are always better than one."

In a little while he released the girls and heaved himself onto the table.

"Who's going to be first?" he demanded as he lay on his back, truncated body now seeming strangely massive, seeming also devoid of humanity as his head fell back.

CHAPTER NINETEEN

"Herrin'!" cried the hawker. "Live herrin' . . ."

There was an obvious mendacity in his words, for the herring on his flat cart, drawn by a weary-looking pony, had a sunken look about their eyes and the water he threw over them from time to time failed to revive the blue and silver of their pristine colouring. But he had always cried 'live herring' as his father had done before him and 'live herring' he would always cry. Tradition had to be maintained.

Mungo McMaster watched the hawker pass and wondered if there might be a text in those long-dead fish being cried as fresh.

"Is this not the epitome of Rome?" he might say. "The herring they try to sell their poor, deceived victims have indeed been long dead . . ."

Into his discourse he could contrive also the story that the Catholic tradition of fish on Friday had been established by a Pope whose brother was a fishmonger. He pulled at his fingers until his knuckles cracked and his big teeth glinted in a smile.

But Mungo McMaster smiled often now. He had much to smile about. There were new comforts in his canvas home, dainties to eat, new clothes – or almost new – gathering luxuries such as the boiler behind the tent that provided hot water round the clock, the new pressure lamps within the tent which allowed him to study through the dark hours when he wished. Also there were many books, great tomes of sermons, dissertations on the Articles, musty theologies which he skimmed through swiftly and perhaps impatiently. Little of what he read impressed him beyond the ordinary text of his battered Bible.

However, it was not the mounting ease of life which pleased Mungo McMaster. He would still have been satisfied in his old tent. The warmth in his heart came from his knowledge of the success of his mission.

He still held his morning service each week-day but the crowds were smaller for them now. More and more the men were going back to work. But they came at night. They filled the marquee and overflowed out on to the waste ground which some of them had begun to pave with slabs of stone. Wee Hughie Macatammany had even planted a garden round the paved space, a broad bed in which wallflowers and Sweet Williams blossomed and a few bushes struggled for existence in the rubble and clay. It was Wee Hughie's first garden and indeed it was the only garden, for close on a mile about. The red brick wilderness of back-to-back houses offered no more horticulture than an occasional window box. Wee Hughie was pleased and Mungo was pleased that his first disciple should be pleased.

For himself, he was indifferent to the garden. On the mean farms of the Stony Mountain plants were grown to feed men or beasts. Otherwise they were weeds. But the Bible spoke well of gardens and Mungo McMaster could not but approve also. Vanities they might be but they were accepted vanities.

It seemed to McMaster as he stood in the sunlight by the tent and heard the distant echoes of the herring hawker's voice that life was very sweet and seemly. His voice was loud in the land and there were ears to hear the words he said.

Across Gonagal's Bit – which was known now more often as 'the Preacher's Bit' – he saw the door of Mrs Anderson's house open. It was always an easy door to identify because there was a shining brass fingerplate just below the lock, a distinction possessed by none of the others.

Dulcie came out and made her way slowly across the waste ground towards him. As always, he felt a surge of tenderness and perhaps pity when he saw her. She looked so frail, so little able to bear the burden of her life. He stepped to meet her.

"My dear." Their hands clasped and hand-in-hand they returned to the tent, unselfconsciously affectionate. And no doubt McMaster was aware somewhere in his mind of the impression this conveyed of marital bliss.

"And how is Mrs Anderson?"

"Oh, she . . . she wasn't in, Mr McMaster. I had a wee chat with Janey. She gave me a cup of tea."

"She would. A kind child, kind. Is she returning to work soon?"

"She'll maybe get a place in a sweetie shop soon."

Dulcie McMaster was just a little flustered. There had been more than tea in her mind in her talk with the girl whom McMaster had prayed back to health.

*

"Oh God, Mrs McMaster," Janey had said. "Oh, I wish there was some wee thing I could do for the Minister. When I was lying it was like I'd never leave my bed again."

"It must have been terrible, right enough." Dulcie sipped delicately at the tea.

"It was like being two people. I could see everything and hear everything but I couldn't make myself do anything. Do you know what I mean? I'd look at myself and there I'd be lying. And me Mam would come in with the food and I'd eat it and take my tea and I'd want to say something and it wouldn't come out. Or I'd hear myself asking for another bit of cake, only it wasn't *me* asking but this other one. Like as if I was seeing it all through a telescope. Me Da' had a telescope and I liked til look down it the wrong end and maybe see my feet that far away they'd be someone else's. And that's what it was like when I was sick. Two people. And the real one inside me doing nothing only remembering."

"Remembering?"

The girl's face coloured and her lip trembled. She was silent for a few moments and her face was averted when she went on:

"I never got to talk about it. I couldn't tell me Mam. She'd kill me. But I can talk til you, Mrs McMaster."

"Of course you can, my dear."

"It was the day . . . the day I got sick."

Dulcie saw emotion struggling in the girl, strong emotion. Her fingers clasped together and writhed as the words abruptly poured out of her in one long flow.

"From the mill, you see, it was a short cut from the mill and I could get the ha'penny stage on the tram if I came down the entry instead of round the road. I came that way every night. Them entries, they're dark. No lights, only what shines in from the end of the road. I'd aye hurry down as quick as I was able with the no lights. Like it was creepy down that way. On'y I saved the ha'penny on the tram with the short cut. And I fair went like the clappers. Oh, I shouldn't have said that!"

"That's all right, Janey – "

The girl hardly heard the reassurance.

"They were there in the very middle of the entry. Two of them. Two fellahs. They were at the gate of a yard. There's a lot of yards at the back there. Pubs. Shops. You know. And the gate was open . . ."

Her tortured eyes seemed to mirror the picture of that narrow, claustrophobic entry, the thin ribbon of sky high above, the faint lights from the street at either end doing no more than outline the entrance to the passage.

"I hardly seen them. I was just past and the one said something and the other clapped his hand over my mouth, just in a flash. And they pulled me through into the yard and pushed shut the gate.

"There was a lot of oul' crates and the like lying and I could see the lights on the windows up above but there was no light on the ground floor.

"The fellah that had his hand over my mouth whispered

in my ear: 'if there's a sound out you I'll strangle you.'

"He gave my neck a brave tight squeeze and I think I said. I'd be quiet. I was that feart I'd have done anything they said. Oh God, Mrs McMaster, I did do anything they said.

"One of them said I had to show myself and I knew fine what he meant though I let on I didn't. He toul' me I had to take my knickers off. Oh, Mrs McMaster, I shouldn't be saying this, you being the minister's wife and all."

Dulcie patted her hand soothingly.

"And that was the worst, Mrs McMaster, him saying to take my knickers off. I hadn't any on. Oh God, that's as if to say I'm a sort of a bad woman but I had a terrible dose of the runs and I had to take them off at work when they was soiled and I threw them in the dustbin.

"When they seen I had none on they began to say all sorts of terrible things about I was a whore and deserved all I got and they'd see I got it. They were feeling me all over then, the two of them at once, up my legs and up me and they had my tits out and all and . . ."

A sob stopped her for a moment and then she was speaking more quickly than ever.

"Like, you're a married woman and it would be different. But the terrible thing was I hated them and – and yet in a terrible funny way I liked it. When the one of them was right up me and doing it, I liked it . . . That was the worst of all, Mrs McMaster. I liked it."

Her face had a tortured anxiety and she kept it averted from Dulcie McMaster as she finished. She was breathing hard as if the recountal of the experience had been like enduring it again.

Dulcie hesitated before she spoke. In her own mind an idea was dimly stirring, an idea that even to herself she did not dare give a concrete form.

"Maybe I shouldn't say as much but I think the good Lord meant us to like it," she said at last. "Otherwise why did he make our bodies in this way?"

"Oh yes. When you want to. But not like that. Oh, surely

not like that! And there's worse, Mrs McMaster. Oh God, but there's far worse."

Dulcie stared, unable to believe that anything could have been worse than the scene of rape the girl had described so graphically.

"They . . . they were Papishes, Mrs McMasters. I seen the Pioneer badge on one of them. It was Papishes done it til me. Papishes."

*

Dulcie McMaster did not reflect consciously on the irony of Janey's attitude. That it was genuine she knew. Rape was in itself bad enough. But rape by the 'others' . . .

"So that was what put you away in the head? Well, well, it's no wonder. It's no wonder at all. Oh dear, you poor child! It would be the shock of it. Aye, it's no wonder you took to your bed. It's no wonder at all."

"You'll not tell me Mam?" Janey was anxious now, maybe even regretful that she had spoken so freely. "Oh God, Mrs McMaster, you'll not tell me Mam?"

"Of course I won't, my dear. Of course I won't. Never a word to a soul will I speak."

They fell silent for a while and then Janey sprang up.

"You cup's out. You'll let me fill it . . . And a bit of cake."

But the girl soon forgot her duties as a hostess.

"What am I do to, Mrs McMaster? What am I to do?"

"I'd say you'd just forget it. That would be the best. Forget it ever happened."

"I could never do that . . . . Supposing some decent fellow was to ask me til marry him? What sort of a girl would I be not til tell him? I was wondering . . . Do you think Mr McMaster could maybe do some sort of a prayer or — "

The thought which Dulcie McMaster had been avoiding came into sudden focus in her mind. And now she was no longer thinking of Janey Anderson's torment but of Mungo McMaster's own sleepless nights, of that gaunt body stretched unfulfilled at her side.

The plan which came to her mind was totally outrageous. It offended every canon by which she lived. And yet she knew that she would implement it. Subtly, deviously, she would contrive. And she would succeed.

"Perhaps," she answered cautiously. "Perhaps there may be a way Mr McMaster could help you. But how it is to be done I do not yet know."

All love demands sacrifice. Dulcie McMaster would willingly have made herself the sacrifice but since that was not possible, the girl must be her deputy. And why should she not be sacrificed? Would she not still be a living cabbage but for Mr McMaster?

CHAPTER TWENTY

'Bogey, there is no doubt whatever that you are the most loathsome specimen of humanity – if you are human – whom I have ever met. Why I continue to know you I do not know."

"Nostalgie de la boue, Tony. You're a shit-eater at heart."

In the oak-panelled study at Castledail, the Bogeyman sat in contented comfort by one side of a log fire while Anthony, fourth Earl of Dail, seventh Baron Fingel and Lord of the Manor of Chumpleigh Minor in Dorsetshire sat at the other.

Seated, the Bogeyman looked far the more aristocratic of the two, for the Earl was a red-faced, untidy man with clumsy hands and feet. He looked like an agricultural labourer and if the malicious gossip which attended his birth was true he might have been the son of one.

They had met in the market where the Earl was replenishing his store of pornography from the stall beside that of the Bogeyman's mother. A totally improbable friendship, or at any rate relationship, had sprung into instant being. Heartfelt insults were exchanged at every meeting and each regarded the other with an almost clinical curiosity.

"I excite your disgust," the Bogeyman declared, smoking one of the Earl's cigarettes and sipping occasionally at a glass of the Earl's excellent brandy. "Physically I excite it because of my lack of lower limbs. On my little cart, a mobile torso, I should be a figure of some pathos. Instead, because I fail to cringe, because I maintain an independence which is itself an affront in a creature from the lower orders, I become

rather a monster. And my monstrousness is heightened because of my invariable success with women."

"Wait. You mean your claimed success with women,
Bogey. Any fool can claim success."

"I've offered to put it to the test. Leave me alone with the
Countess for an hour. I'll be up her."

The Bogeyman laughed throatily. "For all you know I
have been already."

"There! That proves it. How much more loathsome could
you be than make a suggestion like that."

"Much more. I could suggest you stayed and watched.
But you haven't the guts for that. You'd watch through a
keyhole but you wouldn't stay in the room and watch. You'd
be embarrassed."

"You're really filthy . . . filthy . . ."

"And you love it. Let's change the subject for a little till
you cool down. What about the preacher?"

"Preacher?"

"The Reverend Mungo McMaster as he calls himself
though he's never been ordained in any known church.
You're a member of the Unionist Council. You know all the
Cabinet Ministers. Why don't you do something about
him?"

"Why? He's doing no harm."

"If incitement to civil war is no harm then you're right.
Otherwise – don't blame me when the city blows up. My
crowd can only stand so much, you know."

There was an amused smile on the Bogeyman's lips but a
cold purpose lurked at the back of his eyes.

"Think about it," he added. "Get the Inspector General
of the Royal Ulster Constabulary to show you his secret
files. He's had spies watching McMaster for weeks now.
Then come and see me. Meanwhile, I'm bursting for a piss.
The needful, please."

A moment later the Bogeyman was shaking with laughter.

"You think you're pretty fancy, Tony. But you don't have

belted earl to cart away your piss or wipe your arse for you.
So who's on top?"

*

"I've always been on top in this ward, Mr McMaster,"
said Councillor McCullough. "I mean to stay that way. I'm
not saying I won't get in again without your help but you
have a fair old bit of influence here now. The young ones
that are trying to claw me down would think twice if they
knew you were backing me."

McCullough had a steak-red, lumpy face and blue eyes
that watered continually at the corners. He wore an elderly
bowler hat and a raincoat and he walked with a swagger that
was not totally confident. He was a builder and the owner of
a small butcher's shop. He drank heavily and his hands now
had a constant tremor. McMaster found it hard to like him.

"The Lord is not for sale, Mr McCullough," he said,
severely. "Neither am I a dabbler in politics."

Which was certainly not true so far as the second statement
went. Whether he admitted it or not he had already taken
the first steps into the political ring. That evening he would
venture further.

"I can be a damned useful friend, Mr McMaster,"
McCullough scowled then. "I can be the other thing, too."

McMaster stared down at him bleakly. But he made no
comment at all. After a few moments he turned and walked
into the tent. McCullough stamped away angrily, a canker
of resentment already gnawing in him which was eventually
to have the most drastic consequence for the preacher.

Within the tent McMaster made at once for his writing
desk for he had begun now to write his sermons instead of
extemporising them. That is, he wrote out notes which he
memorised and then destroyed.

Dulcie watched him work and after a little brought him a
cup of tea. He nodded abstractedly and continued to write
with a steel-nibbed pen that scratched and spluttered its way

across the pages. His writing was large and angular and h[is]
spelling was as elementary as his grammar. But since he woul[d]
be the only reader of these notes, that did not matter.

At last his notes were completed and he began to rea[d]
them through with satisfaction, occasionally referring to th[e]
Bible at his side to confirm a quotation.

At last he turned to his tea.

"It'll be cold, Mr McMaster. It'll be cold. Let me wet yo[u]
some fresh."

"And whose fault is it that it's cold? My own. So let th[e]
guilty be punished. Anyhow, I have quite a liking for co[ld]
tea . . ."

*

"Like hot brandy after cold tea, that's hearing McMaste[r]
after your ordinary preacher," said Tod Milligan. "There['s]
no doubt about it; the man has something."

"But where's it leading him, I wonder?" mused Si[d]
Levine. "Have you ever wondered that? He seems to have h[is]
eyes set on paths of glory – and the question is how man[y]
others he'll drag with him . . ."

"Here they come now," Tod interrupted.

The procession had swung round the corner from Roy[al]
Avenue into High Street.

A pipe band led the way, playing 'The Bluebells of Sco[t]
land' and behind it there strained in the evening breeze th[e]
banners of three Orange Lodges.

Silken cables steadied the banners, each as big as the sa[il]
of a fair-sized yacht. The leading banner bore a stylise[d]
portrait of King William, mounted on a white horse. Th[e]
Prince of Orange's sword was brandished in a warlike gestur[e]
and behind him a winding strip of blue indicated the Rive[r]
Boyne, scene of the most remembered date in Ulster history[.]

"Did you know, Sid, that William actually rode a blac[k]
horse at the Boyne?" Milligan remarked. "Generations o[f]
bannermakers have had the wrong colour."

Levine did not answer. He was enjoying the spectacle, the strange anomalies of martial music and men in bowler hats – for the Lodges marching behind the bands wore their collarettes and it was not perhaps stretching the analogy too far to see in the bowler hats and the regalia some parallel with men marching to war.

For himself he had never been drawn to the Order and yet he could appreciate its attractions, the solidarity with the group, the music, the sheer pageantry that lent colour to the city's rather drab streets. How many members, he wondered, were drawn to it for these very reasons and not for the ostensible purpose of defending the Protestant religion?

Mungo McMaster walked immediately behind the band, tall, gaunt, impressive beyond any other man there. Levine felt the stirrings of verse within him and wondered if when he went home the feelings would be transmuted into words.

The procession was making its way towards the Albert Clock at the foot of High Street. The Clock gave the appearance of a three-quarter scale duplicate of Big Ben at the Houses of Parliament in Westminster. Was this typical of the Ulster mind that it should set up a copy of a copy in honour of Queen Victoria's consort? Was there something typical in the fact that this should be the first major building to greet the eyes of the cross-Channel visitor – for beyond the clock were the docks, the wharves for the Glasgow and Liverpool and Heysham steamers.

"I wonder," said Tod, "if they've got police permission for this demonstration. The D.I. doesn't look too pleased."

The procession was escorted by a dozen or so members of the Royal Ulster Constabulary in their bottle-green uniforms so dark as to seem black.

The police were armed as they had always been, carrying revolvers in black leather holsters at their sides. The weapons were scarcely ever used but they existed, the visible sanction of force. And yet they were needful also for their opponents did not hesitate to use force.

The District Inspector carried a black, silver-knobbed

cane and he was trying to speak to Mungo McMaster.

Tod Milligan was close enough to overhear them.

"You have no authority for this demonstration, sir."

Mungo McMaster did not pause in his long stride.

"I have the authority. From above."

It would have been absurd but for the frightening sincerit
in the preacher's voice, for the implacable purpose on th
faces behind him. The policeman was not sure what to do
All processions through the city were supposed by law to b
notified in advance, together with details of times and routes
This procession was unauthorised. He would be quit
justified in arresting McMaster and everyone else present.

But to arrest these two hundred or so grim-faced men pre
sented for a start a purely physical problem of cell accom
modation. Half his force would be tied up in the formalitie
afterwards of charging the men – always assuming that th
men came quietly.

A further factor that influenced the D.I. was a degree o
sympathy with the marchers. He came himself from Orang
stock. He believed in the same fundamentals as these people
And though by becoming a policeman he had cut himsel
off from the civilian population, he could not become com
pletely separate.

The practical issues were what finally carried the day wit
him. The time was late evening. There was no great amoun
of traffic on the road. In fact, there was little harm being
done, no obstruction. Weighed against the chaos that migh
follow if he acted, the slight inconvenience to traffic mattered
little.

"I will hold you responsible for any disturbance."

"I am responsible to One only."

The band was playing 'The Sash my Father Wore' as i
swung round the Albert Clock and came to a halt.

"It is oul' but it is beautiful, its colours they are fine,
   It was borne at Derry, Aughrim, Enniskillen and the Boyne,
   My father wore it as a youth, in bygone days of yore . . .'

142

The open square about the blunt pillar of the clock began to fill with Orangemen, casual spectators and another more violent element.

CHAPTER TWENTY-ONE

Of all the people round the Clock that evening Tod Milligan was undoubtedly the best qualified to recall a scene which was as climacteric in its way as the prayer for the ship, but despite his shorthand notes he was never able really to capture the essence of the meeting.

Sid Levine came closest to a description of it as they drank stout in a bar later.

"With people like that it's not actually what they say, it's how they say it. I've told you about that fellow in Italy – Mussolini. And there's a German politician, Hitler – both of them have exactly the same effect. You feel exalted, even when you don't understand the language very well. Literally, you're taken out of yourself. McMaster's in the same tradition. It's the speaker, not the message."

"Yes, but what was the message? I've heard him before. So have you. I'd have said he was preaching the ordinary kind of Evangelism – with a bit of a knock now and then at the Papishes to keep the hard-core Orangemen quiet. That wasn't what he was preaching tonight. I don't know if he was even sure what the message was himself. Did you get that feeling?"

"The message was Socialism. That was plain enough, perhaps an extreme form of Socialism – not quite the same as Hitler and Mussolini are putting out, but on the same lines. Equality, the rich getting a sharp knock or two. And the meek inheriting the earth. That came up several times."

"And it fits in with his way of life – the donkey, the tent . . . but there's more to it than that. There doesn't seem enough in that to stir up the row we saw."

'Row' was an understatement.

*

"Woe to the wicked," McMaster declaimed. "And the unrighteous and they that fornicate for theirs is the kingdom of hell. They shall be cast down and scourged with whips and scorpions, yea even those that fornicate with that great whore which sits on seven hills, they shall be plunged deepest of all save those false priests who have led them into iniquities and abominations before the Lord. For if the shepherd turns his path and knows not the ways of righteousness, how shall his flock be saved?"

The words were familiar enough, pitched a little stronger than was the habit of most preachers, but words that had been heard often enough in this city. Yet there was no doubt that the gathering was strongly affected, more strongly than they had been by the first part of the discourse. There was something about that gaunt figure with its waving arms, like some Old Testament prophet, which had the power to move them deeply.

As the drums of an African tribe can, without the use of reason, whip up the emotions, so could McMaster's resonant voice and the sight of his semaphoring arms. But it was not only his own people who were being stirred.

From the moment when the procession had first formed the messages had been going out across the city. A little tide of men began to drift towards the Clock, moving by alleys and back streets, not an overt progress of an organised body but a drift of small groups, unobtrusive but talking briefly and bitterly among themselves.

Here and there the publicans who catered to the dockside trade noted the signs, began to ease their customers out into the gathering night. Shutters began to go up.

The numbers grew in the side streets and along the quays,

uncertain at first but with their own ire growing ever harsh
within them as McMaster's voice trumpeted across the cit

But they did not interrupt until McMaster's rollin
peroration was in full swing. And it would have been har
to identify the word or phrase that was the detonator or
even there was one. History rather was the detonator th
began the battle, the history of two peoples, two cultur
locked in a tiny space with an infinity of wrongs on bot
sides rankling within men. The same history which gav
Mungo McMaster the earnest attention of the Orangeme
gave the others their bitter fury.

Some missile flew across the cobbled square and a momer
later the battle was joined with fists and pick helves an
bottles and stones.

And inevitably with guns also.

Who fired the first shots was not a matter to be establishe
afterwards. But the hoarse bark of a pistol rang loudly acro
the night and a man slumped back against the clock, han
going to his shoulder.

"Jesus, I'm shot! I'm shot by the Papishes."

It was the final spur to action. Those with sense broke an
ran for the cover of shops and pubs, away down the Hig
Street or Corporation Street, anywhere away from tha
scene of mounting chaos, terror and bloodshed.

Men fought hand-to-hand, clawing for throats, gouging fo
eyes. Others hovered on the outskirts of the battle, skirmish
ing, striking out at any convenient head and caring littl
enough who was the owner.

The police had drawn their truncheons and had begun t
try to drive a wedge between the two sections, an effort tha
was impossible for them, outnumbered as they were, and i
the confusion made the more impossible.

Already the phone calls had been sent for police reinforce
ments. Riot cars were being warmed up. Crews were pilin
into the rears, protected by heavy wire mesh from missiles

Here and there guns popped and barked, the gunme
aiming low so that the ricocheting bullets would strike a

146

many victims as possible. There was the solid whang of old Mausers and Lugers, of the Peter the Painters which had last been used in the days of the big troubles. Other, smaller pistols crackled and snapped among the mob, fired from within a pocket often enough so that no one knew who were the gunmen and who the victims.

A little group smashed in the door of the Albert Clock and swarmed up the steep stairs to the summit where they could drop stones and bottles on the seething mass beneath. This group lasted only a little time. They had nowhere to run to when the police followed them up the steep steps and they surrendered meekly enough but for one man, who hurled himself at the ascending police and crashed his way to the bottom of the flight with a broken collarbone and arm.

Amidst the mob Mungo McMaster was conspicuous for his height and the obvious target for a host of blows.

Tod Milligan saw him twice, his face a red mask of blood as his knobbled fists swung unChristian blows at all around leaving only those sufficiently identified by their collarettes.

Milligan was furiously busy, jotting notes, carrying out brief interviews, noting down names and addresses where he could get them, for to newspapers one name and address is worth a paragraph of anonymous reportage. For Tod Milligan it was an inglorious anti-climax when he was arrested.

Sid Levine had been more discreet. At the first sounds of battle he took to his heels.

Along the side streets the pub windows were being smashed and the pubs and shops looted. Riot and loot are inseparable companions and afterwards there were plenty to say that the looters were the ones who started the riot, had started it for their own aims.

Certainly there were professional looters at work that night; men with cars and vans who used the vehicles to smash open pub and warehouse doors, who heaved out their spoils which were inevitably the highest-priced goods, the easier to dispose of and who were off the scene before the

Battle of the Albert Clock was even at its height.

There were also, of course, the amateurs. For the dockside drabs whose work was mainly pleasuring sailormen at five shillings a time this was bonanza.

There were young women and old among them, but mostly there were not many young. A young whore could still do better than a five shilling stint about the docks.

The middleaged, the diseased, the hopeless, these were the women who swarmed through the broken doors and windows to drink as they had rarely drunk before and to carry off with them in their shawls their petty booty of bottles of whisky or gin or brandy.

The professionals for the most part escaped but the amateurs were littering the streets for hours afterwards sleeping their guilt away until the police could spare the time for gathering them up like so much litter.

More and more police surged into the area together with detachments of the 'B' Special Constabulary armed with rifles. These latter were an auxiliary force, an emergency part-time private army whose presence on the streets was generally enough to clear them. Since they were recruited from Protestants exclusively they had a certain natural bias though since they were also residents of the country their reputation never plumbed the depths of the Black and Tans. Their function was, generally, the protection of rural area and the circumstances were rare indeed which brought them to clear the city streets. The Battle of the Clock provided such circumstances.

*

Pamela Hendrick had known nothing at all about the riot. She had a date in town with Tod Milligan and she had come as far as High Street before the sounds of disturbance began to drown the clatter of the tram's progress.

Someone jumped onto the platform to shout to the passengers: "There's all hell down at the Clock. Yez'd better ll get off. The town's blowing up."

Pamela was last to leave the lurching vehicle, whose driver
had been first to abandon it, omitting to switch off his motor.
The tram continued to inch its way towards the riot and
Pamela was almost engulfed in the fleeing crowds at the
lower end of High Street. Of Tod Milligan who was to have
met her outside the umbrella shop there was no sign.

It was a nightmare scene with the shouting, the shooting,
the rushing feet. Blindly Pamela ran down the first alleyway
that offered, ran until the sounds of tumult faded behind her
and she could pause to catch her breath.

Gradually she took stock of her surroundings. They did
not impress. There were narrow streets, small, grimed
houses, a brooding emptiness. It was as if suddenly everyone
about had withdrawn suddenly from life. She felt like an
intruder in a ghost town.

Once more she began to hurry, pausing at each inter-
section to stare up and down for any familiar landmark. But
she could see nothing that brought back any chord of
memory. Not only was it as if she had left the familiar city
but had even moved into another time.

These mean streets were lit by gas, by ancient fixtures set
far apart which shed only a little yellow glow on the pavement
directly beneath. The violence at the city centre had been
frightening. This silence that came out of the past was even
terrifying.

Yet could she possibly be far from main roads? From
trams, from all the accoutrements of life as she knew it?

At last the silence was shattered by the sound of running
feet. Three men were racing towards her and at first she
thought that they too were fleeing the riots together.

Then appallingly, as they came closer, it was plain that
she was watching a chase. Two men were in pursuit of a
third. And because the quarry kept turning a panic-stricken
face on his pursuers he was losing ground. He was quite
young, Pamela saw, as he came under the nearest lamp. He
had fair hair and a big nose. His mouth gaped his fear and

she could hear the hoarse rasp of his breath above the sound of feet.

The pursuit ended only twenty paces from where Pamela had halted, pressed against the wall. The victim staggered as his foot caught the kerb. And before he could recover the other two were on him, dragging him down. Then for a moment there was hoarse breathing, the flailing of legs and arms and at last a low moan.

Three men had gone down. Only two rose. One of them stooped and seemed to wipe his hand on the other's back. But it was not his hand he wiped. Pamela saw the glint of steel in the lamplight, saw a knife slipped back into a pocket.

She knew that she had just seen murder done.

And then, as the two moved on, she realised they were bound to see her.

And to know what she had seen.

CHAPTER TWENTY-TWO

'Bogey, we had to bring her. She seen us kill O'Riordan and he was on the inform all right. You might have had the peelers here before us if we hadn't given it to him.''

"You could have cut her throat in the street."

Pamela Hendrick gazed at the grotesque form of the Bogeyman in mounting horror. The whole world had gone mad this night. To walk out for a simple date – and to mingle with riot and murder!

Her hair was still tangled for when they had seized her in the street they had up-ended her, stuffed her own skirt into her mouth and thrown her into the back of a car. She had no idea where she was now except that it had a taste of poverty about it; a mean house with shabby wallpaper, worn linoleum – and this fantastic dwarf on his trolley as the sole inhabitant.

Could it not possibly be a nightmare? And yet the facts remained so solidly plain in her memory. The Bogeyman gazed at her thoughtfully, rancorously, from his luminous eyes.

"Who are you? Name, address, a brief biographical digest. By which I mean – tell me all about yourself."

"I know what you mean," she answered peevishly. "I went to school."

"Ah. So you're English as well. I hope you're not going to ask for the British Consul. He's not available."

He smiled quite blandly but the smile was more frightening than another man's scowl.

Pamela began to tell her life story. The killers waited impatiently and when she had finished one of them broke in: "Never mind about her past, Bogey. What do we do with her now?"

"I thought I'd made it clear that I was the only person here who asked questions . . . Well, what would *you* do with her, Pontius?"

"Knock her on the head and dump her out in the country somewhere . . ."

"Which is exactly why I'm the one who asks the questions. You were lucky to get here with her. By now the streets will be packed with the Feet. If you got a hundred yards you'd be lucky. Go upstairs and wait till I call you."

They obeyed meekly and Pamela relaxed a little. Could this wheeled mommet in his book-lined room possibly be a serious threat? Yet had not the others' obedience proved his menace, his authority?

Now the Bogeyman gazed at her quizzically.

"Knocking on the head," he mused. "Those savages can think of nothing else. There are much better ways to silence a woman, very much better, ways devoid altogether of violence and in fact generally considered as affording mutual satisfaction. But before we go further, tell me more about your life in Belfast. I'd be interested for example in your reactions to the Reverend Mungo McMaster since your paths have crossed to some extent. What do you think of our good demagogue?"

Pamela, still eyeing him warily, told the man what he wanted to know; how she had come to the city, where she lived, her father's work and what she had seen and heard of McMaster. The Bogeyman listened in silence.

"From the little I've seen of him he hasn't much education. He has strong beliefs, sincere I'd say. He's a powerful speaker. I don't think he's after wealth or luxury or anything like that . . ."

"A simple, sincere fanatic? Would that describe him?"

"Perfectly."

"Dangerous?"

"I didn't think so at first – "

"Now you do?"

"I think he feels he's a man with a mission."

"And the nature of his mission?"

"I don't know how a man like him would think."

"But your father's a man with a mission, a trade union leader. How does he think of McMaster?"

"He loathes him." Then she had to explain the effect of McMaster's mission on her father's.

"I see. You've been very helpful, yes, very helpful. Just a little more on the same subject – what do you think of McMaster's personal life? Or putting it more bluntly, his sex life?"

"I shouldn't think it exists."

"Which would have been my own opinion. However, I have been informed that he makes a practice of seducing young girls. What do you say to that?"

"Whoever told you that must be out of his mind."

"Some of my informants are not very bright," the Bogeyman conceded. "But I don't think they'd lie. They've told me of seeing a young girl going at night to McMaster's tent. They have listened closely – and a tent is not soundproof, you know. The sounds they heard left no doubts in their mind. Now what do you say?"

"I think there must be another explanation," Pamela insisted. "Couldn't the girl have some spiritual trouble she's taken to him for advice?"

The Bogeyman laughed.

"I think you're shocked at the idea of a clergyman in bed with a woman. But it's not by any means unknown – even in my own church. If you've read Boccaccio and other slightly scatological authors you would realise that Holy Orders, far from subduing the sexual urges, tend to intensify them. Or perhaps it is that those who are attracted towards religion may also be those who have a considerable sexual drive. McMaster's admitted power of oratory, his domination over his mobs may well spring from that inner sexual drive. What do you say to that?"

Pamela's hands fluttered in a helpless gesture.

"I haven't read as much as you seem to have done. I don't know."

All alarm had left the girl now. In some way she had already grown to trust this strange, truncated man.

"Very few people have read as much as I have done. The nature of my body cut me off from the normal sporting activities of the young, from football, the other simpler games. In their place I read. Before I was twelve I was reputed to have read every book in Smithfield Market, though this is not true. There were many into which I did no more than dip, appalled by the vapidity of the minds that conceived them, and many more whose shoddy, tattered state – for they are second-hand for the most part, these books – offended me. But certainly I am one of the best-read persons in Belfast, in Ireland, perhaps in Europe.

"No one minded my looting their stalls for books. To the traders the books were only another commodity, worth a few pence to them. And I – I was 'Yon poor wee Bogeyman, rest his soul, ah, God love him, let him read what he wants.' There is in the Irish character a very strong vein of mawkish sentimentality, as you may have observed."

He wheeled his trolley suddenly to a sideboard among the bookcases and opened it.

"I think you would like a drink. It has been a disturbing evening for you."

"I'd sooner go home," Pamela said. "My father will be frantic, phoning the hospitals, the police – "

"I'm afraid he'll have to suffer. You'd have no chance of getting through the streets after a night like this. Besides it is still not quite certain that you'll ever be able to go home."

He poured two large glasses of Irish whisky and rolled towards her – like, she thought with an inner giggle – a dumb waiter. He had ways of projecting himself without the use of his hands by controlled flicks or jerks of his body.

"I told my thickheads now upstairs that they had no imagination. They have a curious belief in violence as a solution to all problems. Kill enough people and there will be no opposition. History indicates the fallacy of the proposition, for if it could succeed there would be no Irish problem today. England has often decided to battle or starve or murder the Irish out of existence. Lines of conflict can never be solved by conflict."

"What are you going to do with me?" Pamela said quietly, sipping the whisky, not completely believing that this was happening.

"When I was only thirteen or fourteen," the Bogeyman answered with apparent irrelevance, "I discovered that I had a peculiar advantage with women. I will tell you how it came about.

"Around here the girls had always looked on me as something of a baby, a living doll that they could play with, carry about, stow in their dolls' prams if they had one – it's a poor area and they had few enough toys of any kind.

"You might suppose that I excited some horror in them but horror is a quality of the unfamiliar. They had known me since I was literally an infant. They had seen me naked. They knew the circumstances of my birth – I suffer from what is known as phocism. A word which derives from the Latin for the common seal *phocus phocus.* Through some dietary deficiency no doubt on my mother's part I was born without legs. Instead of legs I have minute stumps with dwarfed toes and toenails which do in fact resemble the flippers of the common seal. Other victims are even less fortunate for phocism often extends to the arms also.

"This deformity was then familiar to the girls. It excited no horror. Rather I think – as I grew older – it produced another excitement. In any case since I was accustomed to be carried and cuddled and handled by girls, I grew very familiar with their own physiology.

"And as they had explored me in their earlier years so now it became my turn to explore them. I can remember quite well the first time I slipped my hand up under a girl's skirt, fumbled through the tatty tangles of her underwear and came at last to that organ which though lacking any aesthetic appeal remains still the principal magnet to the male.

"The girl's name I have long since forgotten but her reaction stays with me, the mute and eager acceptance, the parting of the thighs, the panting. Then it was as if I had not been there. She scarcely knew me, lost in the pleasures of her own body.

"Later, though, later she came to know me. They all knew me. Once I had made a beginning, tasted my first girl, there was no turning back. One brought another and they whispered and giggled as if I was not really a person. With me – and I am sure they were sincere in their belief – it did not count as if I had been a real person."

A shade of bitterness came to his face now. He had moved close to Pamela and his hand stroked her ankle and her calf as he talked on.

"I could pleasure the girls with sex but I was still not a man to them. The idea of marriage to me would have horrified any one of them – as indeed it would have horrified me. They were so foolish, so ignorant, so filled with all the mindless prejudices of this city, of this Ireland.

"They thought, because I was on my little trolley, a childling, that they had the power over me an adult has over a child. But soon they began to learn what power I had over them.

"I read many esoteric and erotic books, which were sold under the counter in certain of the stalls; dirty books you can get anywhere and I think more easily in religious countries than the others. I learned all the subtle ways of caressing, kissing, heightening desire. And I learned that I had in myself a unique quality of priapism. The same accident of birth which had deprived me of my legs had endowed me with organs of unusual size and capacity. If I wished to be, I could be insatiable. I think for many of those girls – and most of them are married now, mothers of families, even grandmothers – what I did for them was more than any man did afterwards."

By now his stroking hand had passed the girl's knee. Unhurriedly yet implacably it was creeping up her thigh. And in Pamela Hendrick there was no resistance to the encroachment. But it was a dream, she assured herself, it had to be a dream. And if it was a dream, was resistance of any use?

"I had power over women and when I was young I used it sometimes cruelly, revenged myself for their innate contempt, their emotional indifference. But cruelty began to die in me when I saw so much around me. This is still a land of horses for all the electric tramcars, the motor cars and cycles. I was revolted at the drivers of the carts and the way they used their animals. Then I grew revolted by the way they used each other.

"Now I knew that as well as power over women I needed power over men. This would not be for revenge but to bring about the changes I knew were needed. I set up an illegal organisation, not a political party like the Republicans or Nationalists, and not a violent group like the IRA, but an organisation whose first purpose would be the gathering of knowledge. That organisation still is in the building. It needs, for its growth, money; and tonight the riots were to be a chance to gather that money. No doubt we have done well but not I think well enough. My men have looted inns and warehouses and feel themselves great heroes. But . . ."

He fell silent and Pamela sensed her legs parting to the intrusion of his hand.

"You wonder why I tell you so much? Why am I not afraid you will betray me? You will know in a little. When you leave here in the morning your wish will be to return. I speak without vanity, knowing my power. You will be as incapable of betrayal as you are now of resistance."

He drew her to him, gently pulling her up from her seat. Her knees wobbled a little and her eyes would not meet his as he fumbled at the fastenings of her skirt.

It was true, she knew, as she heard the garment drop softly to the floor. It was all true. She could not resist him now. She would not betray him.

CHAPTER TWENTY-THREE

The meeting in the tent that was the Tabernacle had continued indecisively for some two hours. In the air was a sense of crisis, even of disaster. Mungo McMaster had felt it from the time he first took the chair where his pulpit stood normally.

The Tabernacle was packed now, perhaps two hundred men standing shoulder to shoulder there, muttering, angry, almost disillusioned. Speeches had been made which were fiery. Others had the dismal pessimism of convinced failure. McMaster himself had scarcely spoken, save to terminate an overlong address or to give the floor to a speaker. He had learned his tactics already, moving by instinct from the preacher whom none could silence to the shrewd politico.

The tent was full now, he was thinking. But for how many days would it stay so, how many weeks? How soon would it be before his congregation began to diminish? How soon before there were only the few women at his meetings and then at last not even the women?

He had started a movement and this he knew – a movement must move, must grow, must progress. Growth is life and life is growth. Even as a man begins to die when once he comes to maturity, so the movement which has ceased to spread is beginning to die back to its roots.

And this could be the time of decision. In minutes or moments he could take the actions and say the words which would determine whether McMaster's Movement, which was how it was already mostly known, would continue as an organic entity or begin imperceptibly to wither. This was known to him though it was not thought out in words and phrases. But he had the feeling, as he had had the feeling that he must accept the challenge of the prayer for the ship. His feelings he always trusted for surely God did not speak to man in words but rather in the pervading, irresistible sensation of compulsion. He must be inspired.

Now two speakers were ranting only half-heard and now suddenly McMaster himself rose from his chair, dark and brooding above them all, hands outspread for silence. He got it at once. A movement that was almost a shudder of relief passed through the tent.

"The Scots poet, Robert Burns once said: 'Facts are chiels that winna' ding.' Facts are what we face. We must not let ourselves be misled into the sideways and the by-ways. Facts. With the facts we can make decisions."

They looked puzzled. They did not know what came next. Nor did McMaster. But he would know when he came to it.

"One fact is that our movement, a free movement of free men, gathered in a free city under the Crown of His Majesty and in the very shadow of that monument to His Majesty's great and peace-loving ancestor to praise the Lord in the way to which we are used, was set upon viciously and wantonly and wickedly by a mob of hooligans. That is a fact.

"Many were grievously hurt in that vicious affray. Even now many still lie abed of their wounds. Brethren who should be gathered with us this night lie hurt and wounded close to death. That is a fact.

"And sorrowfully we know that there are brethren we shall not see again, who gave their lives in that terrible time when we were beset as were the children of Israel beset by their enemies about them, by the Moabites and the Amalekites and the Philistines with all their abominations. That is a fact."

In fact four men had died, one of them of a heart attack. Twelve others were in hospital.

"And where were the forces of law and order when we were beset? Were they driving back the hosts that assailed us or were even they seeking to destroy our meeting to nullify our Witness? Did they set their strong arm about us and respect our loyalty?"

"Did they bloody hell!" came a voice.

"That is a fact," McMaster intoned. "Also those same so-called forces of law and order now seek to prevent our peaceful gatherings, order us not to walk the streets and praise our God and our Sovereign with loyal tongue. That is a fact."

Notice had been served on McMaster that any future processions must be notified in advance, together with the routes they would take and the times. Police instructions had been reinforced by statements from various Cabinet Ministers deploring violence and, by implication, McMaster's Movement.

The Government was in a quandary. The Movement's members were certainly among its own supporters. And the very sentiments which McMaster was expressing had been voiced on their own platforms at election time. Nonetheless they wanted no widespread civil disturbance. Nor did they want to take repressive measures against either side at a time when tempers had only just begun to calm down after the Troubles, when there were some prospects of an end to the Depression – and when in England itself there was some recrudescence of Radical influence. The Cabinet at Stormont could never ignore the existence of a large and vocal body of opinion opposed to the very existence of Northern Ireland as an entity.

But mainly the Stormont Government's worry was domestic. They were themselves Ulster people, living in Ulster. Memories of civil war were still too close, too harrowing for anyone of responsibility to wish to see them re-lived. They were held in the horns of a dilemma that must persist for generations and perhaps all that they could do was to damp down the flames, let the fire smoulder harmlessly.

"Now, brethren, you do not need me to tell you that this is not a Movement of wealthy men. We labour with our hands in the vineyards of the Lord. And it is written truly that the labourer is worthy of his hire.

"Can it be that there are those in high places see us, see our humble, God-fearing Movement as a threat to their wealth? Is this the true reason why they ban us from the streets, seek to crush us down? Is it their own wide lands, their ownership of mills and foundries and shipyards they protect? Is this a fact?"

He thundered out these words and at the same time a new brightness came into his eyes and his face seemed to harden.

"So here are the facts. We seek to walk the streets, to bear witness to our beliefs in humility before God. There are those on either hand who would oppose us, deny us that freedom of speech which is our God-given right. From the hosts of Midian they oppose us, yea, with sticks and stones and the fire of their guns. And on the other hand stand they like unto the Pharisees who took up the laws in their hand and swear: 'They shall not speak.'

"But I say to you, brethren, we shall speak. We shall not be silenced. And if they who should guard us are as the shepherd dog who runs with the wolf or stand afar off and cry: 'I see not, nor do I hear' then it is very plain what we must do.

"We shall not be silenced. We shall not be denied. We shall take as our motto 'Man, mind thyself.' If none shall guard us we shall be as our own shield and buckler. Our enemies we shall not seek out nor shall we attack them. But let them take heed. Let them not attack us. For we shall find the means of defence. As our fathers found it in the olden times so shall we. And as in those short years ago men rallied to sign the Covenant and to take up their arms to guard Ulster for herself, so shall we also take up arms. As they smite, so shall we also smite. Brethren, I give you the watchword: 'Man, mind thyself.'"

Mungo McMaster had spoken. And again the Movement would move.

Mungo McMaster had become a subject of general conversation by now in the city. In the nearby rectory of St Cyril's the Reverend Roger Simms talked of him very often with his curate. Curiously, their positions were now almost completely inverted from the early days of McMaster's coming.

They sipped a delicate manzanilla sherry, brought back by Simm's brother from Spain itself.

"He seems to have a strong practical sense at least, your rabble-rouser," Simms remarked. "This bodyguard thing he's started, a practical idea, don't you agree?"

Richard St Leger's lean and ascetic face was hard.

"Our Lord found no need for bodyguards."

"Our Lord never preached in Belfast."

Simms was in a jovial mood, as usual. St Leger was very much not.

"It's not merely a bodyguard. It – it's a private army. Why the Government permits it I don't understand."

"Oh come, Richard! It's a stabilising factor. His meetings don't get attacked now that the . . . others know they'll get a bloody nose if they try it on."

"It's Fascism, Rector, exactly the same tactics as Mussolini has used in Italy – "

"Well, at least Mussolini has got the Italian trains to run on time, my brother says. And Rome's a good deal cleaner than it was. Maybe McMaster could get the Dublin trains to be punctual."

St Leger's fury burst out in a flood. "You haven't heard him, Rector! When he started he was an evangelist preaching the love of God. Now it's hatred that is on his lips – and hatred begets hatred."

St Leger's lips compressed suddenly into silence and he

stalked gauntly from the room without even finishing his sherry.

*

Even on the gracious lawns of the Royal Yacht Club in Bangor they found time to talk of Mungo McMaster and the Movement. There were of course much more important matters for discussion on the lawn.

In particular there was Sir Thomas Lipton's forthcoming challenge for the America's Cup. The challenge was being made through the Yacht Club and every new detail of the latest *Shamrock* was awaited avidly.

Despite his wealth there were members of the Club who despised Lipton for his earthy origins. The millionaire yachtsman who had expanded a fortune in trying to win a cup worth originally a hundred guineas had started his way to fortune as a cut-price grocer and to some of them this is what he was still; a cheap little grocer who happened to have a lot of money, even though he might hobnob with the King himself.

They were fond of the Kaiser's description of a Royal visit before the Great War. Asked if he had seen the King, Wilhelm answered bitterly: "No. He'd gone boating with his grocer."

While their own less impressive craft bobbed at their anchorage before the big red Victorian splendour of the clubhouse they demolished the hopes and pretensions of *Shamrock* and at the same time flayed the New York Yacht Club for its interpretations of the deed of gift under which the races were sailed and which, it was said, made it virtually impossible for a challenger to win.

The Earl of Dail was taking tea on the lawn with a cousin from Cowes and the managing director of a tobacco manufacturing firm which he owned. Their wives were with them and in fact the gentlemen were drinking brandy, not tea.

"Personally," said Dail, loudly enough to be heard at the

djacent table where Lipton was under some particularly scurrilous fire. "I've always rather liked Tommy Lipton. A charming little chap, full of virtues. If he's a self-made man, he's made a good job of it. He knows what he's at as my butler would say. He knows what he's at and he goes for it. A sound chap."

His voice dropped. "I can't stand these jumped-up Belfast bookies' runners. They'd kiss Lipton's backside if he let them but he's not that sort – not a toady man."

The ladies looked suitably shocked at the mention of backsides and Goulding, the tobacco man, felt his own face tighten. He was inclined to agree with the others about Lipton.

"Like this fellow McMaster," the Earl continued. "He knows what he wants, he goes for it. It's the only way."

This was too much for Goulding.

"I'll have to disagree with you on that, your lordship," he said, his adam's-apple wobbling in his turtle-like throat. "McMaster is a dangerous revolutionary, a mad dog. Why the Government don't arrest him I don't know. If his doctrines spread we might as well close Donague's. The workers are restive enough as it is. These damned unions – and now McMaster preaching social equality in the name of religion. It's not Christian."

The Earl would have laughed if his mouth had not been full of brandy. Instead he choked painfully and the other two men had to clap him on the back.

"Thank you for those words, Goulding," he gasped at last. "I will treasure them always."

The Bogeyman, he thought, would be as amused as himself. He must remember to tell the little grotesque when they talked again. Bogey relished verbal absurdities as much as he did every other social anachronism.

Milanda, the Countess of Dail, was talking to Goulding's wife. As ever, the Countess looked the picture of elegant aristocracy, slim, beautifully groomed, fine-drawn as an

Afghan hound. Mrs Goulding was plump and dumpy with big, horn-rimmed glasses on her pudding face. The contrast was painful.

Yet it was not so painful as the contrast that sprang unbidden into the Earl's mind each time he remembered the Bogeyman's words, the picture of that loathsome little beast making love to Milanda . . . and Milanda liking it.

Was it true indeed that Bogey had that strange power over women? Could he indeed seduce Milanda? Had he?

The thought came to torture Dail again and again and he wondered if it was true that, as the Bogeyman implied, he enjoyed the thought in some perverse way.

Dail wondered why he allowed himself to dwell so often on the thought. Was it, as Bogey had implied, that there was some perverse, masochistic element within him? Why indeed should the thought of whatever happened to Milanda worry him at all? He was full of a vast indifference for his wife, an indifference whose origin went back to a marriage which had been contracted for no pressing reason that he could now recall and that had seemed an error as soon as consummated.

Perhaps he had been thinking of an heir. For if he had no heir the estates would go to his cousin Hector, a London stockbroker whom he detested.

And if an heir had been the purpose he had failed miserably in it. Either Milanda was barren or he was sterile – and he felt almost certain that within himself the juices of virility were as fecund as ever.

It was a long time though since he had put them to the test with Milanda. The cold, unstirred and unstirring body beside him in the bed was as anaphrodisiac as sago pudding.

Looking at her now, every inch the countess, he formed a mental picture of the expressions on her face if he ever introduced her to Bogey. He began to picture Bogey in bed with her, thought of her slimness swelling in pregnancy, her elegance and poise brought down to an earthy level. It was what she needed, of course.

And the thought continued to vex him deliciously as the conversation wandered on, and out in Ballyholme Bay the yachts stood in towards the finish line beyond the club jetty.

CHAPTER TWENTY-FOUR

"Onward Christian soldiers," thought Mungo McMaster, "Marching as to war . . ."

And indeed but for the absence of uniforms the men on Gonagal's Bit had a very warlike aspect. They were drilling by platoons, marching and counter-marching across the muddy ground as war veterans of the Battle of the Somme and other Flanders hell-holes barked their orders.

Some in the ranks wore medal ribbons as proof that they too knew the meaning of war but more of them were too young to have seen action. They marched with a pleasure that an old sweat would have derided and there was a frightening enthusiasm in their eyes.

Some still wore their shipyard dungarees. Others were in the overalls of their shops or stores. More were simply in their ordinary clothes.

Apart from enthusiasm they had only one feature in common. About their necks each of them wore a red scarf, a feature that had gained them already the nickname of 'the Rednecks.' To wear uniform though not against the law would have been too expensive, but the red chokers were badge enough to hold a unit together, to enable men to recognise their mates.

Visibly they carried no arms for that would have been against the law – though it had not stopped the Ulster Volunteers of a generation earlier – but down each trouser leg there hung more than flesh and blood.

Mungo McMaster watched them train, watched with a

swelling pride and affection. They were his men, his army – or rather, they were the Lord's men. They were dedicated to the protection of righteousness, to guarding the witness of the Word.

Also watching, but without affection or pride, were two men whose plain clothes were so much alike as in themselves to be a uniform. They were plain clothes detectives of the Royal Ulster Constabulary. They knew they had long ago been identified and they made no real pretence at not being policemen. Probably, they thought sourly, it would have made little enough difference if they had. McMaster's Movement had its adherents in the Force also. At least one clerk in the Inspector General's own office in Waring Street had been rapidly transferred to a country district. There might be more.

They watched, bored, and knew that their report that night would be identical with their other reports.

"By the right, right wheel . . . Smartly there in the rear rank! Lengthen your stride . . ."

Sometimes Dulcie McMaster watched the men also, diffidently and from within the shadow of the Tabernacle. The marching men made her uneasy with their hint of implied conflict. Worse was the effect that they had on Mr McMaster. The Movement, the Rednecks, the Tabernacle even, everything seemed to be conspiring to take Mr McMaster from her. Who cooked his food now? Who comforted him in bed? Mr McMaster had unleashed forces that were driving an ever-deeper wedge between the pair. Or rather it was not so much that there was a wedge as that she was increasingly ceasing to exist.

The meetings, all the meetings, the public meetings and the private meetings in the Tabernacle – McMaster was hers only to serve his food and accept an occasional caress like some docile but useless dog.

But even all this would not have mattered, she thought, if Mr McMaster had been happy in himself. She wished nothing but that she could see him happy, contented. If this involved pain or discomfort for herself, then so be it. But now – was he happy? Was there content in him? There were times in the mornings when she saw him lying on his bed before he awoke, when she was sure she saw lines of strange anguish deepening on his face.

But that indeed might have been imagination. She admitted as much to herself. She had little sureness about anything or anyone now. Maybe this mounting power that gathered about her husband was what he wanted and needed. For this it might have been he was born. Certainly he displayed no doubts to her, no doubts at all about his mission.

Perhaps men like Mr McMaster could not doubt themselves ever, if their mission was to succeed. How could a man lead others if he could not totally convince himself?

A flat cart drawn by an elderly bay pony rolled slowly past Gonagal's Bit, its load of coal briquettes still smoking from the kiln where they had been moulded from coal slack and pitch into the little semi-cubes that were the city's cheapest fuel.

The driver did not pause as he drove for he was known in the district. He had hawked briquettes there for twenty years and his father had hawked them before him. His name was Kevin Dougherty and the name itself was almost a guarantee of his religion.

Tomorrow he would be delivering beyond Smithfield and tomorrow he would be telling the Bogeyman what he had seen today.

Yet another watcher of the men was Janey Anderson and she was less watching than gazing out of her window at Gonagal's Bit. Her blue eyes were not really focused on the scene. They were troubled. She had a strong suspicion that they had every reason to be troubled.

"Me Mam," she thought. "Me Mam will just kill me."

*

Wee Hughie Macatammany was troubled about the plan. His small, serious face puckered almost as if he was going to cry.

"Never! The McNulty Street Gang. You'd never bring them in, would you? Not the McNulty Street ones! The Minister would never have it. Not them ones. Didn't they try to bash him right at the start?"

He was in the headquarters of the Movement which was also the John Williams Cowan Memorial Hall. This was a meeting of the Executive Committee of the Movement. Present at the meeting were Harry Makins, Eric Webb, a butcher's helper, Thomas Gill, a moulder in the foundry, Tom Parfray, an unemployed plater, William McGoogan, a painter, and Alec Price, a carpenter and glazier.

Price was a small man with hands soft-skinned and clean through working so much putty through them. His voice had the smoothness of putty; a persuasive, oily quality.

"Hughie, it takes a painter to paint. It takes the man for the job. You have to fight fire with fire. The Scarves are fine for the body of the Movement but you have to have the experts for the big jobs. We won't be always on the defensive. If it's ever coming to fighting back we'll need the experts . . . We've had a word with Herbie Vignoles and he's willing enough to come along – "

"He's willing! Yez've had a word? Yez had this whole thing cooked up behind me back before ever the meeting took place!"

"It wasn't just like that. We happened to be talking and Vignoles happened to be there. We went ahead. Hughie, the work of the Movement has to go on. It has to go on."

"But the Minister!" Hughie cried. "What about the Minister? Sure he wouldn't have that irreligious crowd of street hooligans . . ."

"The Minister isn't to know," growled Makins. "D'ye hear me? He's not to know. And what he doesn't know 'll not hurt him."

Price was more persuasive.

"Hughie, this is for the Minister. We're out til protect him. The McNulty Street ones – they can keep a better eye on him than anyone."

"What about the Scarves, then? D'ye think we'd let anyone next nor hear the Minister?"

All of them there wore the red scarf about their necks.

"Oh aye, we can guard him. When we're there. But the way it is, we can't be sure we'll be there all the time. Herbie can have men on duty at all times, just keeping an eye. They'll be professionals, see, doing the job right. For ourselves – well, it's not really in our line now, is it?"

Gradually Wee Hughie Macatammany's resistance was eroded. Grudging consent came at last. But as he went home to his mother he felt a deep sense of unease. The Movement had come a long way from its origins. Had it come too far?

Hughie had more than the Movement on his mind. There was his mother. As he stopped at Macari's for chips for their joint supper he thought of his mother. She was a problem which grew with every day. Her deafness had reached a point at which she heard virtually nothing. Her whole personality was crumbling as well.

She had been as house-proud as any Belfast woman but now Hughie came home often to unmade beds, unwashed dishes, floors which had not felt the touch of brush or mop. Sometimes she was not even dressed properly. She would wander about in long, baggy knickers and unlaced corsets. Hughie suspected that in his absence she also drank, for he had found an empty bottle of cheap wine in the dustbin when he was emptying the ashes from the fire. Certainly he had found no bottles thereafter but that might only be because she had grown cunning.

Nowadays she complained a lot.

"It's no' fitting at my age, all this work. You should have more respect. All this big house to keep clean and none to help me. When your Da' was your age he was wed and had me to help his Mammy."

There had been a lot of talk of marriage recently. But who

would marry him? Hughie Macatammany had no illusions
about his own attractions. He had only to look in the mirror
to know that no girl could fancy him. If the mirror was not
proof enough he had his memories. Other fellows could get
off with girls but not him. He could remember church
socials and Sunday School outings and dances. He could
remember the disgust of a girl called Louella Cassidy when
she learned that she had to kiss Hughie as part of a game.
That screwed-up face came into his mind every time he
thought of marriage.

And yet there was no doubt that a wife would have been a
fine solution to the problem of the old woman. Some quiet,
decent girl who wouldn't mind Mam's haverings and would
cook a decent hot meal for him of a night when he came
home from the Yard. His aspirations rose no higher than
this, shied violently away from bed and what went on in bed.

Prudery was no feature of Yard life. There was as much
bawdery and bad language there as would be in any exclusively male gathering. Hughie shut his ears to it, to the
relished tales of what men had done to women and what
women had done to men. And when some peripheral image
from that talk came into his mind when he lay in bed he
banished it with a desperate fear.

"Think of the Minister," he would reprove himself. "What
would Mr McMaster say if he knew thoughts like these were
in your mind?"

And yet each night when the sour smell of the uncleaned,
frowsty house greeted him at the door and the longing for a
wife came to him it was not entirely as a domestic servant
that he visualised her.

*

"Really, you do please me greatly," the Bogeyman told
Pamela Hendrick from the depths of her thighs. "There is
some quality to your sex which is absent from any of the
local girls."

"Maybe I feel less guilty about it than they do," Pamela answered.

She lay on the floor before the fire, body rippling in a slow, sensuous rhythm in response to the Bogeyman's expert caresses.

"I could never understand why I shouldn't enjoy it. And I can't feel guilt. Everybody does it at some time and that's what it's for when all's said. Maybe if I'd had a mother – I mean if my mother hadn't died when I was so young – I think mothers have a lot to answer for. 'Don't you ever let anyone touch it or even see it. It's dirty . . .' All that sort of thing. The other girls used to talk about it in school, in the lav. What their Mums said and— Oh, that's nice. That's delicious."

"Guilt," said the Bogeyman after a little. "Yes, I suppose guilt has a lot to do with it. For men also. I was fortunate in my infirmity. Not being regarded as a normal person no one every thought to equip me with the normal inhibitions . . . I wonder if the depilation was such a good idea as we thought. The presence of public hair lends that faint air of mystery to an organ which in itself lacks much grace or beauty."

"Well, thank you very much!"

"I was generalising. A carter described it to me once. 'Bogey, all the time you're a boy you try to get a look at one but when you do at last what do you see, only half a pound of chopped liver. I tell ye, man, the whole thing's a great oul' cod.' "

Pamela's laughter gurgled helplessly.

"The male organ, on the other hand," said the Bogeyman severely. "Has its own objective beauty when in an erect state."

"Long live the State!" cried Pamela.

"I'm being serious. You have an object of such curves and lines as are the fundamentals of art. Look at it, consider it. Is it any wonder that the Hindus in their wisdom have from ancient time set up phallic symbols, lingams, about their villages?"

Pamela had not stopped laughing but she contrived to gurgle out: "Less fucking art and more artful fucking."

The very use of the forbidden word was a rich source of titillating pleasure.

CHAPTER TWENTY-FIVE

Afterwards Tod Milligan wondered to what extent he wa
to blame for the development of the Movement. It had beer
he who gave the first publicity to Mungo McMaster and i
had been he, above all, who had introduced Brek to th
preacher. But for Brek would matters have gone as they had

No one would ever forget Brek. He was a small, ebullien
man in a plus-four suit carved rather than tailored from ver
large and loud checked tweed. He wore highly decorated
brogues and he looked like a golf professional. He talked i
a parody of an American accent which was made the mor
appalling by the fact that he was American. As Sid Levin
commented later, 'Absent from his country for his country'
good.'

And yet at first meeting there was something rather fetch
ing about him; his sheer and apparently animal high spirit
which only after some acquaintance revealed their totall
mechanical source.

Tod met him first in the bar of the Grand Central Hote
where he had been reporting a Rotary meeting. Tod wa
sorting through the notes of some abysmal speeches wher
Brek bounced up.

"I'm Brek," he announced and offered a hand which wa
disproportionately large, swollen no doubt by a life of shak
ing. "Calvin Brek. I know you're a newshound, name o
Tod Milligan, so no call to introduce yourself. Well, Tod,
greatly like to meet newsmen. Boy, I like to meet everyone

ust everyone. Now what's it to be, Tod, boy? What d'ye
rink?"

Bemused, Tod Milligan blinked at a face like a walnut
with small simian eyes and vast drugstore teeth. He accepted
Scotch which was made a double and for the next ten
minutes listened to a lecture on the virtues and attainments
of Calvin Brek, who was about to give a new look to Ulster.

"For you're slow. Oh my, but you're slow! No hustle here,
no go, no zip, no zoom."

"No wham?" Tod ventured.

"That neither. Man, you're living in the last century!
You need a hustler. You need fire in your bellies – "

"The bit in our teeth?"

"You said it, man. You certainly said it. Now how do I
get to meet the top men around here?"

"Why not just call them on the phone?"

"Heck, that way you just get secretaries. Secretaries I can
always speak to. And 'in' is what I need. I want to meet the
big, big people. Say, they tell me your shipyard is the biggest
in the world. So who's the President? Who do I meet?"

Milligan gave him names and addresses and telephone
numbers with the enjoyable feeling that many a staid nest
was about to suffer something like an explosion.

How the name of Mungo McMaster cropped up he could
not afterwards remember. But Brek was positively interested.

"A hot gospeller! Him I've got to meet. I helped a whole
lot of them back home. You've heard of Aimee Semple
Macpherson? The Swami? Dr Lincoln? Brother, I helped
put them where they are today. You fix it for me to see this
McMaster."

And because he was in any case going to see McMaster
later – for by now the preacher was on the chain of those
asked for quotes on any issue of the day – Milligan did just
that. He left Brek with Mungo McMaster and it did not then
strike him that the two could possibly have anything to offer
each other. But that was then.

"They were really rather comical," he told Sidney Levine.

"Opposites in every possible way – height, speech, though I expect each would be a real curiosity to the other."

"It's hard to see what interest Brek could have i McMaster," Levine commented. "He doesn't sound exactl the religious type. How are things going with your lady lov Pamela Hendrick?"

"Oh, you know . . . Sometimes I see her, sometimes don't."

But the very mention of the girl's name started a feeling desire in Tod Milligan. He was seeing her later. And h knew how the meeting would develop.

To Milligan Pamela was more than just a girl. She was a education. Even to hear her name was to set up a ticklin erotic irritation in his loins. For to hear her name was t recall experience, to remember that fantasy could be tran lated into actuality.

Existing on the periphery of events for ever, reporter incline eventually to an acceptance that the events never exi save as they describe them; that beyond the pasteboard the stage there is no actuality. It is a self-protective mechan ism in a profession that piles disillusion on disillusion for th genuine romantic (which a reporter must be at heart).

Therefore the reporter assumes an ever denser skin of pre tended cynicism in which dreams can be nurtured tenderly Politicians could be dismissed in the knowledge that withi the reporter the knight waited on his white charger; gir could be bar-room jokes while somewhere a sweet, etherea princess waited to ennoble with a kiss.

In the midst of all the hurly-burly the reporter was th extended eye of his editor, uninvolved, a recording machin that passed on the messages while absorbing nothing of th events.

Tod Milligan had read as much pornography as the nex man. He had heard and told as many dirty jokes. He was a interested in sex. But his experience was so totally negligibl that the impact of Pamela Hendrick on him had been quit shattering.

Now everything he had read in the books, had hinted at and laughed at was actually happening. And yet something was lacking which as yet he did not understand though later he knew that the lack was emotional involvement.

He felt nothing for Pamela Hendrick other than for her body though he did from time to time delude himself that he was in love with her. He did not make the error of supposing she returned the passion. Sometimes he wondered if she even liked him. She laughed at him more than he cared for.

And with it all she had become indispensable to him. Or she had been. Already he was perhaps moving away from her. But not very far. He would have liked to tell Sid about the girl and later he would do this but not then. There still remained some inhibitions in him about Pamela Hendrick and he was not absolutely sure that he was not in love. And yet he would have liked to tell Sid the Yid about his last visit to the house at Ballyhackamore. Sid would have appreciated it.

The door was on the latch when he arrived on the step and she called him to enter, to shut the door behind him.

She had been having a bath and this required no exercise in deduction for the steam was still rising from her body. This also was evident for she was quite naked save that she held a towel in her hand with which she was drying her hair.

He stared and felt the colour gathering in his cheeks. Her laughter mocked him as she led the way into the living room where the gas fire was burning.

"Tod Milligan has never seen a naked woman before," she taunted. "He's embarrassed."

"Naked women are very rare in Ireland," he temporized.

"Then you should be pleased. Or is that the word? I can see you're something all right."

She crouched at the fire to dry off her hair and her body was rosy from the bath, almost glowing, intolerably tempting now with every curve and secret visible at last.

"Come on then," she said. "Don't just stand there. And I mean that in every sense. We've work to do. I've got a book

here about the Hindu art of Love. Khama Sutra or something, and they think of all sorts of things we haven't tried
yet. So off with those trousers before they strangle you."

*

Long after Milligan described the scene to Levine.

"It was weird when I think of it. There she was, naked in
front of the fire with that book in her hand and ready for
anything and everything."

"The Khama Sutra," Levine mused then. "Recondite
don't you think? Didn't you wonder where she got it?"

But Milligan had been then too absorbed with the results
of the book to wonder about its source, which was of course
the Bogeyman.

Pamela Hendrick, though, was thinking of the source of
the book, even while the pair wrestled in the convolutions it
inspired.

*

"McMaster," he had said suddenly. "They say McMaster
has a naughty predilection for the ladies."

"Naughty? I wouldn't have expected that word from
you," Pamela murmured from where his lap would have
been if he had had legs. "Not naughty."

"In his case the word is appropriate," The Bogeyman's
fine fingers ran through her hair. "A minister of religion.
Fie on you! At any rate, the rumour exists. Of its truth I
would like some confirmation."

"Aren't you a bit obsessed with that man?"

"Extremely interested. At any rate – I want the facts. I
want you to get them."

"Me? How?"

She sat up abruptly and stared at him.

"My dear young lady, the methods I leave to your own

genuity. But the broad lines of inquiry should be obvious enough."

"You mean . . . ?"

"I mean."

The first moment of outrage passed swiftly and Pamela felt a sudden swift excitement, an eagerness that surged through her body.

"Like . . . Samson and Delilah?" she breathed.

"Appropriately Biblical. Yes. Like Samson and Delilah."

PART THREE

CHAPTER TWENTY-SIX

Belfast was a city inured to processions – or so it had supposed. Each Twelfth of July the Orangemen walked, twenty or thirty thousand strong, through the city with their great banners flaunting their loyalty to King and Constitution. In every Protestant street bunting was strung across from house to house. Great plasterboard and wood arches crossed at the street ends displaying scenes from the past and legends of solidarity with Britain.

On March 17, St Patrick's Day, a similar display though on a slightly smaller scale was given by the Hibernian lodges, their loyalties being of a different hue but equally fervently announced. For both parades there were brass bands and pipe bands and accordion bands, and indeed many of the bands played, with a fine impartiality, for both parades, music not knowing any religion and one crowd's money being as good as the other's.

But there had never been a parade like Mungo McMaster's first Grand Display. There had been talk beforehand, whispers and rumours about the city that this one was going to be very, very different, that no one would ever have seen a parade like this.

Nor did the rumours lie.

The newspapers carried advance notice of this Grand display – for that was how it was described.

'A GRAND DISPLAY OF OUR FAITH IN OUR BELIEFS' said the half-page advertisements. 'LET ALL WHO HOLD FAST TO WHAT IS GOOD AND WHAT

IS TRUE RALLY IN SUPPORT.'

And because this Grand Display was to be held at night the lack of a public holiday did not at all hamper the crowds that thronged the streets. The hawkers were out in force with their barrows and trays, selling dulse and yellow-man and monkey nuts and fruit and whatever gewgaws might catch a penny.

Everyone was willing to be entertained. Most were ready to disapprove. McMaster's following was still localised, confined to Ballymacarret and the shipyard workers, to a minority from the rest of the city. An uneasy peace dwelt over the city, a peace that the majority wanted to maintain whatever their beliefs. Where they were physically neighbours there was little enough difference between Protestant and Catholic. It was in the separated parts, where enclaves of Protestants dwelled among Catholics or where Catholics themselves were segregated that rumour and hatred were able to build and seethe.

In Anne Street, a Catholic called Carroll from the Antrim Road remarked to his Protestant neighbour McClintock with whom he had come to watch: "Your man's really putting on a show tonight."

"Not my man, you needn't say it," McClintock bristled. "Sure he has no connection with any church at all. He's just a chancer. You could call him a Papish as easily as a Protestant."

"It's nothing to what the Papishes could call him . . . Is that them coming?"

*

Faint music could be heard now from across the river, the shrill of pipes, the thinner shrill of fife and flute, the rumble of drums. Especially there was the sharp thunder of the Lambeg drums, biggest of all, bigger than any bass drum played with two canes instead of a pair of drumsticks.

"You know, it's a stirring sound, the brattle of the drums,"

Tod Milligan told Pamela Hendrick as they watched the gathering of the men at Gonagal's Bit.

"What?" she shouted. "What did you say?"

"Stirring – it's a stirring . . . Skip it, dear lady, skip it."

There were four drums, in pairs, members of a local drumming club.

There was a fifer to each drum, the shrill notes of his tiny instrument virtually unheard save in the moments between the drum strokes. The fifer walked slowly backward before the drummers, who were themselves strained back against the monstrous weight and bulk of their own instruments. They waddled like women grotesquely pregnant.

As they waddled they played, the flexible canes raising strange, spine-chilling rhythms from the taut skins in what seemed a continuous thunder until the ear became at last attuned to the sound. Then there became apparent strange subtleties of counterpoint, of beats within beats as stick tip and belly struck at a different time.

Already one of the drummer's wrists was bleeding as it chafed the drum's rim and it was popularly held that this drawing of the blood was the sign of a good drummer, proving the suppleness of his wrist and the closeness of his hands to the drumskin.

The drumming club was an Ulster phenomenon, its origin locked in the past. Tod no more than the bulk of the populace knew anything about them other than that they made an uncommonly loud noise on occasions of Orange rejoicing. He had assumed that they had something to do with the Battle of the Boyne, like everything else in Ulster history. Sidney Levine had assured him once that they were survivals of the ancient Irish war drums, beaten to terrify opponents and hearten their own side.

Sidney had gone so far as to assert that within recent years there had even been Hibernian drumming clubs and the two would meet in friendly contest, or as friendly as any inter-denominational contest could be in Ireland. Sidney might have been right. There was a primitive power to these drums, an imperative harshness absent from the douce beating of the ordinary band bass drum.

With the sound echoing from the buildings around, beating in on every ear, there was no doubt that there was a mass hypnosis. It was a sound to put tempers towards the edge, to make the blood beat more hotly. Whatever their origins these drums were war drums now.

Abruptly the music ceased and across the waste ground shouting voices were caught in the vacuum before ears readjusted themselves.

"Is it a sort of endurance test?" Pamela demanded.

"Something like that. They claim there are different beats – but I'm damned if I can tell them."

"While they're quiet, how about introducing me to the Great Man?"

Tod looked down quizzically at the girl, wondering what fancy it was that had now interested her in Mungo McMaster. She had, so far as he knew, no religious interests beyond a vague affiliation to the Church of England. She had never seemed more than vaguely aware of McMaster before. Why should she now want to meet a man who had been available to her from his first arrival with the donkey?

It was curious, he thought, how attractive fame could make a person. A man's name had only to be in the papers a few times and everyone wanted to meet him. Fame was its own attraction.

He started to edge forward through the crowd of Rednecks towards the Tabernacle, noting that on this occasion there were no Orange banners in evidence, no collarettes worn. The Grand Lodge of Ireland had seen to that. At an emergency meeting it had forbidden the brethren to parade as Lodges save on occasions authorised by the Grand Lodge. The 'Grand Display' was no such occasion or any other function organised by the Reverend Mungo McMaster.

Several members of the Government were members also of the Grand Lodge and it was regarded as a moot point whether the Grand Lodge ran the Government or the

Government the Grand Lodge. But the Grand Lodge had yet to go so far as banning the brethren from belonging to or supporting The Movement. As ever, the Grand Lodge proceeded cautiously, for it might be eventually that it would receive McMaster to its bosom.

A tension hung over the crowd, which Milligan estimated at about four thousand. The tension did not come entirely from the throb of the drums but rather from an intense feeling of anticipation. Implicit on every face was the expectation that soon there would be something rich and rare, that this night great things would be done, that they were then in the presence of history.

There was not very much talking, rather there was a shuffling of feet, coughing, occasional mutters from one man to another, as men speak in church before the service starts.

Milligan tried to analyse the feeling but found it beyond him. These men had all taken part in parades before. There seemed no logical reason for them to expect that this one would be different. It was, he reflected, a measure of the spell Mungo McMaster had woven that when he held a parade it was expected without question that it would be stranger, richer, better than any other.

Nor were expectations to be disappointed this time.

Pipes skirled suddenly within the Tabernacle and Mungo McMaster came out of the tent, creating for himself a path through the crowd as effortlessly as Moses had created his across The Red Sea.

As ever, his appearance drew every eye to him. But for once he did not retain the crowd's attention. The piping grew shriller. The band was coming out to the tune of 'Cock of the North', which in view of its effect on a good many there was afterwards thought to be very appropriate.

For there had never been a band like this before – not in dour old Ulster. It was a pipe band all right. But the pipers were girls.

Ten girls were piping, ten were drumming – and leading the way were ten drum majorettes, twirling batons, stepping high – and looking at the start a shade uneasy about this public display of their bare knees.

The girls wore semi-military Highland uniform, red tunics with broad epaulettes and dangling gold braid. On their heads were black bearskins. Their kilts were of the men's style, in the green and red Cameron tartan. Chequered green and white stockings and shoes completed their outfits as their fingers flickered on the chanters and their red lips pursed round the mouthpieces of their instruments.

Afterwards, when Milligan described the girls to Sid Levine, the lawyer commented: "It sounds as if they were got up to assault every form of erotic sensibility, suggestions of fellatio, homosexuality, lesbianism and plain or normal screwing."

At that time Tod Milligan could only stare. He was not alone. Several thousand pairs of eyes stared. From several thousand throats came a murmur that was a compound of admiration and desire, a hungry murmur that was a tribute in itself. The musicians marched the smarter, the drum majorettes lifted their knees still higher and twirled their batons with still greater verve. It was evident from this moment that the Grand Display was about to be a success. Mungo McMaster had done it again.

Or was it Mungo McMaster's doing? A chord of familiarity throbbed in Milligan's mind when he saw the drum majorettes strut onwards. Somewhere he had seen something like this before.

"It's like one of those American college films," said Pamela. "Tod, d'you think the girls are like Scotsmen? Have they anything under their kilts?"

"There's plenty of men just dying to find out," Milligan quipped. But in his mind another word was blazing.

"Calvin Brek," he thought. This must be Brek's doing. The little American had somehow talked McMaster and the Committee of the Movement into this altogether un-Ulster activity.

There had been talk before, Milligan remembered, of a

190

girls' pipe band. But the idea had quietly died, loaded down by all the prejudices of tradition. Brek must have found the girls somehow, dressed them, persuaded them to take part.

How did those sober, sour men of the Executive Committee square this display of pulchritude with their consciences?

And Mungo McMaster? What did he think of it? Where did it fit into his own cheerless brand of puritanism? Milligan could get no clue from the preacher's craggy features. The deep-set eyes blazed as brightly as ever and McMaster marched like a general leading his army.

*

And yet in those first minutes as the procession moved towards the Queen's Bridge, named for Queen Victoria naturally, the Grand Display which was to have such momentous effects, dissolved almost into farce.

Ahead of the advancing band a group of urchins stood. Milligan saw a man speak to them, saw some coins change hands.

And as the girls neared, two of the boys ran out into the road. Their intent was plain. The matter of what went beneath the kilts was to be put to the test – publicly.

A grubby hand reached for the flirting pleats of a piper's short kilt. But it never reached it. Behind the piper a tenor drummer, with a marvellous sense of timing, swung a stick at the boy's bending backside.

Moments later files of Rednecks were moving up to flank the band on either side. The Movement would look after its own.

The long column wound its way slowly into the heart of the city and turned eastward towards the Ormeau Road. McMaster planned to end his rally on the green grass of the Ormeau Park and make his speech there. The route had been approved, reluctantly, by the police and detachments of police led the procession and followed it. Constables marched on either flank and riot cars were at readiness in the barracks.

But the real protection of the long, slowly marching column was in its own numbers, in its silent, introspective discipline, in the implicit threat of the bulge down every trouser leg.

This was one protection. Another moved through the streets parallel with the main road, not with the procession, not apparently even connected with it.

But the McNulty Street Gang was there too, skirmishing along the flanks, ready for whatever dark plans their own leader might have. They wore no scarves about their necks, had nothing to identify them as a corporate body. Yet there was about them all the same grim, indefinable ferocity, like a wolf pack that for the moment was protecting the sheep.

Down the Ormeau Road the band led the long column of McMasterites, the kilts flirting saucily, the pipes droning the girls' brief repertoire of the 'Cock of the North,' 'Hielan' Laddie' and 'The Forty-Second.' They played the three marches through, paused, then played them through again.

They were at the Holy Land when the lights went out.

*

They called this small area the Holy Land because of the street names – Jerusalem Street, Palestine Street, Damascus Street and the rest, the legacy of some speculative builder, perhaps, with a taste for the Bible.

The lights went out all together, the street lights, house lights, shop lights. Abruptly a quarter of Belfast was plunged into total darkness of an overcast northern night. Ironically they had just passed the gasworks whose product had only recently been supplanted by the power station.

Afterwards there was an inquiry at the power station. A fuse had burned that should not have burned; a stand-by relay had failed to function. There was evidence of sabotage – but sabotage by whom? The Movement members? Their opponents? Afterwards The Movement was held guilty by many – for The Movement was prepared for the darkness.

*

The pipes wailed mournfully into silence in a moment or two after the lights went out, the bags gasping out their last puff of air as the girls halted. There were a few last indecisive taps on the drums. The shuffling sound of those thousands of feet edged into stillness and for a few long seconds there was silence in East Belfast, silence in the ranks of the Movement, silence on the crowded pavements.

The silence had fear in it, for all men fear the dark and there were women there, and children also.

The coming of the darkness had been like a visitation of divine wrath, like a black hand stretched down in disapproval across the earth. Thus might the end of the world come. Thus does death come to each, with the darkness.

Here and there a child began to whimper. Women's feet shuffled uneasily on the pavements, turning this way and that, not knowing which way lay safety – if there was safety, if there would ever be safety again.

The policemen who had them began to fumble for their torches but torches were not standard equipment. A constable supplied his own torch and he had it with him normally only when he was going on a night patrol. He did not expect to need it in a well-lit city on crowd control.

Among the watchers and among The Movement also panic was only a few breaths away. And it was then that Mungo McMaster's voice rang out very clearly above all the petty noises of the street.

"Light!" he cried in a great voice. "Light! Let there be light."

Now he was even more than Moses leading out the Israelites. Now he had become God Himself.

"Light. Let there be light."

It was inconceivable that that vast voice should not be

obeyed, that it should fail to create out of the primordial darkness the light that it had ordained.

Let there be light, McMaster had ordered.

And in the lightless street, down its length, lo there was light.

This, if ever, was Mungo McMaster's finest hour.

CHAPTER TWENTY-SEVEN

"Torches," Tod Milligan marvelled. "They must have been going to have a torchlight procession. The clever old rascal!"

As the lights went out he had drawn Pamela Hendrick with him into the shelter of a shop doorway, not sure what was happening, finding the shelter by luck rather than judgment.

Free from the press of the crowd he was able to watch the golden glow spread up and down the Ormeau Road as the men of The Movement lit one from another the oil-soaked torches they had been carrying secretly. The glow was considerable, brighter probably than the street lamps' light. It threw every building into a flickering relief. Men's faces were distorted as the swaying torches cast shadows this way and that.

In some minds there was the thought that this light had more in common with Hell than Heaven.

"Now we know they did have more down their trousers than legs – "

The procession had been halted for perhaps a couple of minutes. Now, in answer to McMaster's orders, the band began to play again. The pipers led the long, glowing worm of people across the Lagan River for the second time and in through the gates of the Ormeau Park.

Within the park everything was in readiness. A platform had been set up on the grass and sconces placed in which torches were already flaring as the band piped McMaster forward.

It was immensely impressive, immensely theatrical. Calvin Brek, thought Milligan, really knew his stuff.

The pool of light in the midst of the darkness, the branches of the trees catching the upper glint of the radiance, the square focal point that was the platform – and on it that great, gaunt, gesticulating figure in black. No one who saw Mungo McMaster that night would ever forget the scene.

And yet somehow no one afterwards could remember the words which had been said. Certainly not Tod Milligan.

"Look," he told his news editor. "No one can take a short-hand note in the dark."

"What about those torches you make so much of?"

"No more use than candles."

"When I was a cub reporter there were lots of courts and council meetings which met by candle or lamplight."

Milligan was inclined to inquire if shorthand had been invented in those antediluvian days. But the chief did not appreciate sarcasm, other than his own.

In any case, that was later. The fact was that while McMaster was speaking Milligan did not even attempt to take a note of the words. Pamela Hendrick was clinging tightly to his arm and that in itself was a distraction. Also, the sheer emotional atmosphere of the gathering, more intense than anything he had experienced, the long, rolling phrases from the platform, the occasional hysterical outburst from the crowd all prevented clear thinking.

These intermittent cries of 'Hallelujah' and 'Strike them Lord, strike them!' were a new feature in the Movement, a self-generated desire to participate even more than by hymn singing.

McMaster's voice rose over everything, a supreme instrument that had its own wonderful power to strike a sympathetic vibration in every ear.

And the message? Listening, everything was clear. All the problems of the world were solved in that full, rousing rumble that rose and fell with the innate subtlety of a violin played by a Paganini. But afterwards? What had the words been? What had McMaster actually said?

To some the message was clear enough, to those like wee Hughie Macatammany, of faith and perhaps simplicity. To The Movement's true believers there was no need to ponder the semantics of the speech. To them it was all so plain and no words were needed. Perhaps indeed they did not hear the words but only the echo of their own past, their own existing beliefs and prejudices and hopes.

We are right, was the message confirmed in their hearts by the figure. Our ways are the right ways, the true ways. Our faith is the only faith and all else is idolatry and paganism. Our people are the Lord's people and all else are of the Devil. And because we are the true people the land is ours and all in it. This is God's wish. Man lives by work and it is God's will that man shall earn his bread in the sweat of his brow. Therefore those who would hinder us in our demand for work are enemies of God, whether they be of the Popish faith or not.

We are right. All others are wrong.

God loves us. He hates all others.

We are God's people and what we do is God's work.

Among the throng the great ecstasy mounted.

*

Dulcie McMaster stood beneath the trees on the outskirts of the crowd. She felt no resentment at being there, ignored, unacknowledged. To her it was very right and proper that Mr McMaster should stand high on the platform and be the cynosure of all eyes. It was for this that God had called to him in the Goat's Bit, for this he had been born. And in any case, Mr McMaster could do nothing that was wrong in her eyes.

And yet the platform with the lights glowing about it seemed to emphasise the gap that was growing between herself and her husband. He was up there and she was down here. And so it would always be.

There were tears trickling down from her blue eyes across

her wasted cheeks and she seemed in that faint light to have grown very old.

*

The Bogeyman sat in a new invalid chair under the trees with a blanket draped where his legs would have been. Pontius Pilette had wheeled him there and stood restively in attendance behind the chair.

"Look, Bogey, you don't want to hear any more of this," he complained from time to time. "Suppose some of them guess who we are?"

"Be quiet," the Bogeyman answered implacably. "You've got for once the opportunity of listening to a very remarkable man. So listen."

And listen he did himself, intently, his massive head cocked a little to one side, an odd smile on his lips. From time to time he made brief notes in a book on his lap.

"I just don't understand you," Pilette complained. "This fellow wants us all destroyed as far as I can make out. He doesn't want a Catholic left in the country. And you listen!"

"I listen. A man learns more by listening than by talking."

And yet the Bogeyman was not so much listening as absorbing, taking in with all his senses the strange, rich flavour of this torch-lit scene in the park. He tried to divine what lay within the tall figure of the preacher, what forces compelled him into his ranting denunciations, what inner fire and inner disappointments motivated him. There was something more here than a simple ranter, more than an Orangeman with a loud voice.

More than anyone else there, the Bogeyman appreciated the true nature of the message that McMaster preached, the underlying Socialism, the substratum of pure Christianity that existed despite those tirades against Roman Catholicism.

Perhaps, he thought, he knew better what McMaster was trying to say than the man himself did.

Pilette remained uneasy, continually eyeing the others

around, almost visibly wondering what would happen if they knew that in their midst there was one of the opposition. Like a lion in a den of Christians, thought the Bogeyman.

"Look," Pilette whispered. "You're not thinking of turning or something, are you?"

The Bogeyman lifted his head slowly and gave him a long, icy stare.

"You have to know your enemy before you can destroy him. You have to know him and love him. Only then can you destroy him."

Pontius Pilette sniffed his disdain.

*

At first Pamela Hendrick had been quiescent in Tod Milligan's arm, his caresses hidden in the shadows and their closeness unremarked in a crowd whose gaze was concentrated on one point. But after a while she grew restive and her muscles hardened against the exploratory fingers. At last she pulled his hand away, face averted from him.

"What's wrong?" he murmured in her ear.

There was no answer but she rejected each new contact as he made it. She even moved away a pace or so in an unmistakeable gesture. Milligan's eyebrows rose. What had happened? What had he done?

Then he caught a glimpse of her face in profile. He had never seen her look like this before, never seen such a naked exposure of feeling on her face.

With a sort of wonder he realised that to Pamela Hendrick at least Mungo McMaster's message had struck home.

*

"And they went up on the breadth of the earth and compassed the camp of the saints about and the beloved city . . . And fire came down from God out of Heaven and devoured them."

Afterwards there were plenty to say that it was as Mungo McMaster pronounced these words that the first tongues of fire were seen about the Roman Catholic Church of St Malachy. There were always those to say that the fire was a direct response to McMaster's words.

Police evidence and that of the Fire Brigade, on the other hand, spoke of the discovery of 'combustible materials' in the burned-out shell of the building. There were witnesses to speak of the furtive manner of men seen in the area. At an identity parade various members of the McNulty Street gang were dubiously stated to have 'been very like' the skulkers.

But to the Movement gathered there, the fire was very plainly God's answer to McMaster's words.

Nor did it seem in any way illogical that when he saw the flames soaring in the darkness McMaster should pause in his peroration and, in a changed tone, declare: "The fires consume. Yea, as it shall be at the Latter Day. And yet it may be that there are human souls in the ultimate peril. Yea, though their souls shall be already lost to the Dark One, yet we must aid them. To the fire, men, to the fire!"

The Bogeyman laughed in pure delight.

*

The irruption of the men of The Movement into the narrow streets about St Malachy's could have only one interpretation as far as the inhabitants were concerned – and it was not rescue.

This was invasion. This was war.

A barrage of stones met McMaster and his people as they swarmed about those streets. As swiftly as the errand of mercy had begun it ended and became a punitive expedition.

This was a bizarre war, a strange battle fought in the darkness between unseen armies. The police moved in with batons swinging indiscriminately. And when the firemen tried to link their hoses to the hydrants they found them cut and cut again.

Over all the blazing church towered and flared, sparks rocketing and the grotto in the minute front yard being rocked by the stones that fell from the walls.

There were men still who plunged into the flames and McMaster was one of these. In the vestry he came on one of his people locked it seemed in a life and death struggle with a naked man.

"Brother, we are here to help, not to fight," McMaster shouted.

"Craven images, Preacher, graven images. Shall they not be cast down and destroyed utterly?"

And it was a figure of Christ wrenched from the wall that was being pounded against the ground.

In the street outside there were men on the rooftops throwing down slates on the milling throng beneath. Glass was shattering and women screamed as doors were kicked in and the tensions that McMaster had generated in his people by his words were dispelled by them in their own actions.

Darkness was a cover then, a mask in which no man knew his neighbours or remembered their deeds.

In darkness as in drink men may do things that daylight or sobriety would totally inhibit.

*

Wee Hughie Macatammany found himself in a house, borne into it by a press of men. There was the crunch of smashing furniture and the tinkle of breaking glass and a woman's voice wailing: "Ah, Sacred Heart, it's the end of the world! Mother of God, pray for us."

A man was shouting hoarsely: "Never mind your prayers. Get them drawers off."

Hughie was forced towards the stairs and part way up them. There was someone above him. He could hear the heavy breathing and he lashed out blindly and instinctively.

"Ah, Mister! Ah now, Mister!" a voice whispered. "Ah

now please, Mister, sure you've no call for that."

It sounded like a girl's voice and when his hand stretched upward he felt the softness of a woman's leg and the folds of a skirt.

"Mister, could you ever keep the others off? Come up the stairs, Mister, come up the stairs."

There was no light in the bedroom but he knew it was a bedroom because he was dragged almost at once onto the bed.

"Mister, you'll keep us safe? You'll not let them hurt us?"

And as the voice spoke, hands were fumbling at his own body, stirring up sensations that had lain dormant for so long.

The body beside him on the bed had drawn up its skirt, pressed itself closer to him. Warm, smooth female skin was close to him and his hands clawed by reaction rather than intent for every part of the body, touching, exploring in a sudden frenzy that afterwards he would seek to dismiss from his memory.

Half-remembered jokes came into his mind now, the coarse bawdry of the shipyard. He had no experience but he was not entirely ignorant.

And in his mind also there phrased themselves little words of self-justification. For was this not war and were the women of the enemy not by tradition the spoils of the conqueror?

Though indeed there was little enough of the conqueror about Wee Hughie Macatammany then as he was dragged over on top of the woman's body and felt her adjust herself to him, felt the first delicious onset of the rhythms of congress seize him in their pleasure.

There were long seconds when he was lost to all knowledge of the present and to anything but the urgency of his own body responding to the woman's. To him it did not seem strange that she of the enemy should be so eager for him, should devour him with her body. Nothing was strange to him in those moments when his body at last received its long-denied fulfilment.

And then it was over and he was weak and breathless

above the woman with guilt starting to take the place already of the more imperative urges.

There were screams here and there in the street as other women found themselves less willing victims.

Then suddenly the street lights and the house lights were shining again in the city as the repairs at the power station were completed.

Hughie Macatammany found himself looking into a wrinkled, aged face. Grey-white hair was spread across the pillow and an almost toothless mouth grinned slyly up at him.

"Come on, Mister, do it again. Ah, come on. Yon was awful nice."

The horror that remained afterwards in the back of Hughie's mind came not only from this woman's age but even more from the tawdry figure of the Madonna on a little shelf above the bed.

"Idolator!" he cried as he ran from the room. "Idolator!"

The wheezy laughter followed him down the stairs.

CHAPTER TWENTY-EIGHT

The Earl of Dail gazed round the Bogeyman's room with considerable interest.

"So this is your place, eh?" he commented at last.

"Well, it's not always so neat. In honour of your lordship's coming we put the pigs in the bathroom – or we would have done if we had such a chamber."

The Bogeyman was annoyed to find himself in a defensive mood, nervous almost. He regretted now having invited the Earl. And he was angry with himself for this admission. He had nothing to be ashamed of, he thought.

"Not so grand as Castle Dail," he said. "But then Castle Dail wouldn't be so grand if your forefathers hadn't robbed mine."

"Ha!" chuckled the Earl. "But your forefathers wouldn't have had anything to be robbed of if they hadn't come to Ireland and robbed the Firbolgs of the country."

He paced over to the fireplace and examined with interest the gaudy picture of the Sacred Heart which hung there.

"Somehow I wouldn't have expected this of you."

"And would ye deprive the poor of the consolations of religion, yer lordship? I have only Irish whisky. If that's not good enough for you, you may go thirsty."

"Never apologise," beamed the Earl. "That was what I was taught in the army. Never explain, never apologise, never something else. . . . When dealing with your inferiors that is. And you do regard me as an inferior, don't you? Where's this drink, then? Let's see some of this ancient Irish hospitality."

The Bogeyman rolled over to his little sideboard and poured two large drinks.

"And what about your McMaster now?" he demanded. "If it had been one of us who started that riot how many would have been in jail? But it's one of your crowd and – "

"Steady on, old chap! Not by the remotest effort of the imagination can I think of Mungo McMaster as one of my crowd."

"He sure as hell isn't one of ours."

The Bogeyman gazed thoughtfully at the tall, bucolic figure in the baggy tweeds. He was thankful that his mother was out. He could guess the sort of kow-towing humility the Earl's presence would have reduced her to. The old peasant still lived in them all. A lord in the house would be better than the Lord in the house.

"What about McMaster?" he insisted.

"For what it's worth," said Dail, "I gather that the Government are even more worried about him than your lot. He certainly seems to have a remarkable influence."

"He has all of that," the Bogeyman agreed sourly. "He's just about the greatest rabble-rouser I ever heard. Talk about your Edward Carson and your Craigavon! They wouldn't be in the same league with him."

"Come now, Bogey. You can't put these distinguished statesmen on the same level as a back street preacher."

It annoyed the Bogeyman greatly that he was never entirely sure when the Earl was joking or not. That large, red-cheeked countryman's face could assume a mask of solemnity while the most outrageous statements issued from its lips.

"Did you speak to the Prime Minister about him?"

"Not in exactly that form. Craig is not the kind you question. He has his own moods too. But put another way, I did have a word or two with him during which the name of McMaster came up. Craig is worried, very worried. McMaster has a great deal of support and unfortunately it is support in the same area from which he derives his own power. You can't expect him to make widespread arrests of Orangemen for being Orangemen."

"Long live democracy!" jeered the Bogeyman.

"Shit on democracy," answered the Earl. "It's only a word – and one without much application to Ireland."

"Democracy is the curse of the ruling classes," agreed the Bogeyman.

"I suspect you're really a Bolshevik," murmured the Earl. "And come to that, there's something of the Bolshie – or something of the new crowd, the Nazzis – in McMaster. I think that's what really worries Craig."

"I'll bet it does. Never mind what the McMasterites do to the poor Papishes – what about the established classes? If he goes on the way he's going you'll have some real worries on your hands. Suppose McMaster became Prime Minister, for instance? Just suppose – National Socialism wouldn't be in it. He'd have all your lot – and I mean the rich – out scrubbing the streets. Just like what Hitler wants to do with the Jews in Germany. He'd have Castle Dail set up as an orphanage. Hitler! Ulster would be ages ahead of Hitler!"

Dail plucked at his lower lip and nodded his agreement.

"That's what's really worrying Craig," he nodded. "Belfast is ripe for some kind of revolution, just like the Clyde."

"So what's he going to do?"

"That I don't know. I really don't know. Whatever he does will be something quiet and shrewd. You won't hear him making speeches about it. I think it'll be a matter of pressures from a lot of directions, indirect pressures."

"Pressures!" The Bogeyman laughed harshly. "How do you squeeze a stone? McMaster's a rock, hard as that Rock of Ages that the Proddies are always singing about. There's nothing you can take from him, for he hasn't got anything. If you put him in the Crumlin Road Jail you make a hero and a martyr of him. Even if you have him killed he's still a martyr. I thought of that myself."

"You did?" The Earl's eyes had a new interest as he gazed at the truncated shape of the Bogeyman. "You're a ruthless little swine too, aren't you? I should have told Craig about you when I was at it."

"I expect he knows all about me. He's got a pretty good network of spies and informers. So have I. Oh, I expect Craig reckons that if the need comes he can lay a hand on me all right. After all, I'm not equipped for running . . . By the way, what do you think of my new wheel-chair? But it wouldn't do, either. Arrest me and then I'm a martyr. And I'd be as creditable a martyr as McMaster – a poor legless cripple, incarcerated by the brutal totalitarian Ulster Government."

He laughed joyously.

"Sometimes I feel quite sorry for the people in power. A man hasn't got his troubles to seek when he governs a country."

" 'Uneasy lies the head that wears a crown' – really, Bogey, you're extraordinarily serious today. I'd rather expected we were going to have one of those orgies you tell me about, lots of naked girls and so on."

Again the Bogeyman laughed.

"You must admit it is funny. There you are, a peer of the realm, a belted earl – rich, too, and yet when you want a girl you come to a little monster like me. Oh, you should think shocking shame of yourself! And not only girls, Papish girls. Suppose they have horns?"

"I think I can do all that's needful in that direction."

"Ah, a witty, aristocratic pun. I'll send for the girls now. What kind do you fancy? Blondes, brunettes, redheads?"

"You really are an extraordinary man, Bogey, quite extraordinary."

"My own belief entirely. Wait while I find a boy and I'll send for some girls – unless of course you'd sooner keep the boy?"

"Not me," said the Earl hastily.

*

Dulcie McMaster was quite sure she knew what was wrong with Janey Anderson. The girl had come to her in the Tabernacle a few times, ill at ease, something plainly on her mind. She had not, however, said anything. Yet Dulcie knew, divined intuitively or through long experience on the farm when the different mood of an impregnated cow or sow was always plain to the accustomed observer.

Dulcie knew and knew also that she could say nothing. To admit even to acknowledge was to criticise in some degree Mr McMaster. That was impossible.

And yet something must be done. As something had had to be done for her husband, so now something must be done for the girl. Dulcie thought hard and, for her, deviously. She must contrive and she must contrive without seeming to do so. In her mind it was quite clear what had to be done.

*

Wee Hughie Macatammany spent a good deal of time in the Tabernacle. He was a fair enough carpenter and there were any amount of small jobs to be done within the tent to add to its comfort; a set of shelves to hold cooking utensils, a bedside table, a sideboard – and his magnum opus, a proper lectern that would hold the Minister's Bible firmly and at the right height for his eyes.

He had grown used to Mrs McMaster bringing him cups of tea and had taken her increasingly into his confidence. She knew about his mother, how he lived. And what little she did not know she divined, for he was so very like herself – meek, a sufferer of all the buffets the world could bruise him with, not a man to turn and fight.

"I often wondered," she remarked, "That you never married, Hughie."

He blushed deeply.

"Och, Mrs McMaster, who'd want the like of me? Forby, there's me Ma. She's a bit astray in the head, don't you know. What girl would have the like about her house and under er feet?"

"Well now, you're very foolish to think so little of yourself. And there's many a girl would be lucky to get a good steady young fellow like yourself. There's some I know . . . But there, I mustn't be saying too much. You could have your mind set on being a bachelor maybe."

"Me! I tell you, Mrs. McMaster, if I thought a woman would have me, I'd . . . I'd . . ."

He turned away and hammered fiercely. But the seed had been sewn. A night or two later it was Janey Anderson who brought him his tea as he worked on the lectern.

"Mrs McMaster has a wee bit of a headache." She smiled shyly. "I hope ye don't mind, Mr Macatammany?"

"Mind! What way would I mind?"

He blushed suddenly and attacked a piece of oak viciously. From a corner of his eye he could still see the girl. He picked up a chisel and returned to the attack, hoping Janey would go and yet afraid that she would. The chisel slipped and nicked a piece from his thumb.

Blood welled and spilled, glittering drops as he stared and then clapped the thumb to his mouth.

"You've cut yourself. Let me see . . ."

And as he held out his hand obediently there was the first delicious contact between them. In that instant his future was determined if it had not been before.

*

The power of Mungo McMaster was still ascending. Councillor McCullough chose a bad time for his first challenge.

McCullough had never forgiven McMaster for his brusque refusal of support at his election. Now, as convener of the Parks Committee, the chance came for him to retaliate.

The minutes of the Committee read: "That the Corporation acquire that area of land known as Gonagal's Bit for the creation of a children's playground.'

And Dulcie McMaster came out from the Tabernacle one morning to see lorries from the Works department grinding their way onto the waste ground. Men began to unload tools.

She hurried to tell McMaster, who came to the door of the tent and stared out bleakly at the intruders. But he did not go over to question them.

"It would be best, my dear," he said shrewdly, "that we should have no direct knowledge of what is doing."

In any case information came quickly enough. Mrs Anderson was the first to bustle into the big tent.

"Oh, Mr McMaster, oh, what'll we do? What'll we do! The Corporation's going til level off the whole Bit and make a children's playground of it."

"A children's playground? Well now, Mrs Anderson, that's an amenity that is greatly needed in this area. For you know yourself that there's nowhere for the children to play but the streets."

"And what's wrong with the streets? Didn't I play in the streets and my father and mother before? What ails the people they have to have playgrounds to play next?"

"Nonetheless, the days are coming when there will be more and still more cars and lorries on the streets and there will be no place then for the children. Did not our Lord himself say: 'Suffer the little children . . .'?"

"But yourself, Mr McMaster! Don't ye see? If they build the playground here – what will you do? Where will you go?"

"The Lord will provide," McMaster said calmly.

And he gave the same answer to all the others who came to him with their indignation and their worries.

Perhaps he knew or perhaps he did not know that there would in any case be no need for him to take any part in the campaign that sprang into swift life.

This was a woman's campaign. From start to finish the men took little part in it. Some of them, it is true, went to the City Hall where they were met with bland regrets from Councillor McCullough.

"I'm surprised that you would wish to deprive your own children of an amenity such as this playground," he told them. "When the Corporation is trying to do something to help you it really does surprise me that you should take this attitude."

"But that's Mr McMaster's place," one protested.

"Well now, according to the law that piece of ground belongs to a Miss Margaret Jameson and the Corporation is acquiring it from her. I'm afraid your Mr McMaster has no title to it whatever. Thank you, gentlemen, and don't hesitate to call on me at any time. You know I always have the interests of my Ward at heart."

The men could be fobbed off, over-impressed by the City Hall surroundings. Not so the women. A tide of indignation swept up and down the little streets about Gonagal's Bit.

"Whoever asked them for their oul' playground? The Minister's far too good; he should talk them down from the pulpit. Suppose he was to go away . . . Who was it prayed for the ship and got it? Supposing he goes . . . suppose he goes . . ."

And this was the principal consideration. Suppose McMaster did go? They could not define what their actual loss would be but in their hearts they knew it would be grevious, intolerable. In his few months there Mungo McMaster had woven himself into the fabric of their lives. To the women, more even than to the men, Mungo McMaster was a figure on whom all hopes were pinned. Without McMaster, what comfort could there be?

It was the women who acted.

"Missus," a labourer complained, "You're in my way."

"And I'm staying so," growled Mrs Anderson, seated firmly on the muddy ground at the start of the trench that was being dug.

All across the Bit it was the same. Men tried to dig, to swing their picks, cart earth in their barrows. And at every turn a woman barred their way.

The ganger shouted at his men to work. But to swing pick or push shovel meant hitting a woman.

And there were other women carting off the men's tools, stacking them in the road. The sacks of cement which had been stored under a canvas sheet were ripped open. Wheelbarrows were tipped up as they were filled.

For the men it was a torment. Unable to hit back, unable to work, they drifted at last from the Bit to gather in a muttering, smoking group despite the ganger's angry oaths.

At last the ganger turned on the women.

"I'm warning yez. Quit this now or I'm for getting the peelers."

"Get them then."

Arms folded implacably across their bosoms the women stood their ground. The ganger made good his threat. The young constable he brought gazed unhappily at the gathered females.

"Now you can't do this, you know," he told the women mildly. "You've no right to stop these men working."

"What do you know about it?" snorted Mrs Anderson. "Away and get your nappy changed."

The policeman flushed and tried to take a firm line.

"I wouldn't advise you to adopt that attitude. Now, I'll just take your names and addresses and then you can all go home." He produced his notebook and pencil. "You first, madam – "

"Away and kiss your granny's backside."

The constable flushed a deeper shade of red and looked round helplessly for aid. There was none in sight. Then, turning, his elbow caught Janey Anderson in the chest. She doubled up immediately and collapsed.

"Did yez see that? Did ye see? He hit her! He *hit* her!"

The constable vanished instantly under a surge of furious bodies.

"Goad!" breathed a workman. "See that? I'm for out of this afore they start on us."

It was Mungo McMaster who came to the policeman's rescue, striding swiftly across the muddy ground and bursting into the throng of women with a violence which took little heed of their sex.

"Ladies!" he cried. "Ladies!"

But he did not treat them like ladies. He grabbed at whatever part of their anatomy that offered, hair or neck or arm or leg and he scattered them like some giant forward in the midst of a Rugby scrum of midgets. Women flew out from the conflict in every direction and if it had not been McMaster who mishandled them he would have joined the policeman on the ground.

As it was, the policeman's breath had been almost battered from his body. His trousers had been removed in their entirety and one sleeve of his tunic was also gone.

"Up with you, lad – "

McMaster hustled him to the Tabernacle amid the women's jeers.

"Bare-bum!" they called. "Hey, bare-bum!"

The policeman was even then aware that he had in all probability acquired a nickname for life.

CHAPTER TWENTY-NINE

"Who's running this city anyway?" demanded Councillor McCullough belligerently. "Us or this jumped-up street corner preacher?"

For once he found himself supported from the Nationalist benches. But on the Unionist side of the chamber it was different. Everyone on that side of the house was very much aware of the danger of the position. They were dealing now with those who could be called their own supporters. And they were dealing with women. They had no confidence. It was very touchy, very difficult.

McCullough demanded more police intervention, a firmer line from the Corporation, prosecutions. From the opposition came whole-hearted agreement.

"Well now," said the Lord Mayor judiciously. "It seems to me we could very well adjourn debate and action on this matter until such time as the ground becomes vacant. After all, there appears to be no demand from the local residents for this facility and since they are the parties principally concerned in the matter . . . Yes, I think we would be well advised to leave it alone."

Which was the feeling of the majority of the councillors and aldermen there assembled. This was a very hot potato and no one wished to burn their fingers.

And yet McCullough was not without support. Afterwards a dozen men gathered in the Committee Room, angry men for the most part, worried men.

"This McMaster'll have to be got rid of one way or the

other," said McCullough. "Yon oul' woman in the chair is scared out of his breeks. The police are scared – "

"They don't want to lose any more trousers," a man guffawed.

"It's a tricky job for them," McCullough cautioned. "It's one thing running in a lot of tarts off the street. But public opinion would be behind the women. If one of them got injured, there'd be heads rolling at Waring Street."

And certainly the Inspector General's department was moving with a great deal of circumspection in the whole McMaster affair. They were on a hiding to nothing whatever they did.

"Now I've got a good friend round there, in Waring Street," said McCullough with a wink. "And he says they're fair sick of Mungo McMaster and his cantrips. They wouldn't be one bit sorry if something was to happen to him – suppose maybe some fellows was to go round one night and pull down the tent and clear him out, lock, stock and barrel. They wouldn't be in too much of a hurry to come running either, supposing they knew who was doing it. I mean, they wouldn't have the Papishes at it, but if it was our own that'd be a different job – "

"It'd be a great thing to see him gone, there's no doubt," agreed the owner of a small machine shop. "I tell you, since he started all this Bolshy talk you can't get a decent day's work out a man . . . Who'd do the work, anyway?"

"I know a few hard men," McCullough winked. "They're not the best pleased with McMaster as it is. A pound or two a skull and they'd be in amongst him like a shot."

"A bit of peace, eh? We'd have a bit of peace. Man, that would be grand!"

The little group of businessmen made their plans. Nor did it occur to them that they would be subject to the perpetual flaw in any Irish plot – that amongst them there could be a traitor.

*

The attack on the Tabernacle started at eleven-thirty, a time when Belfast was long tucked up and in bed. Twenty men bore down on the tent, five from each side. The plan was simple enough. The tent was to be pulled down. It and all its contents were to be burned. McMaster and his wife were to be thrown off Gonagal's Bit. And if they were bruised a little in the process there would be no complaints.

McCullough waited in his new Morris Cowley car at the corner of the Bit, not close enough to be associated with the action but within sight of it. This was something he did not wish to miss. The stiff-necked preacher would bite the dust and eat some of it, too, if his men did their bidding.

As for that old woman of a Lord Mayor . . . Well, there would be vacant possession of the ground in the morning. The playground would be built. And even McMaster would hardly dare to return with another tent.

McCullough relished the thought of McMaster's perplexity when once he was cast out. Much of his charisma – though this was not a word known to Councillor McCullough – came from his living in the tent, from his patent personal poverty which more than anything else was an affront to respectability. If man of God could flaunt their poverty then wealth was given an actual stigma. It was as well that the general run of clergymen had no such foolish fancies.

The shadowy shapes of the men were at the tent. In the moonlight McCullough could see them outlined against the canvas. His tongue licked his lips with almost physical enjoyment. This was the time.

That was the end of Councillor McCullough's enjoyment for the night.

From within the tent there burst a sudden flood of men and even from that distance McCullough could make out the red scarves round their necks.

There were about forty of them and it was obvious that they had waited in a deliberate ambush, that they had known of the plot. Some of them carried sticks but most of them used boots and fists with good enough effect.

The battle was so brief that it could hardly be called a battle. McCullough saw his men thrown down, saw them rise, fight for a few brief moments – and then run. He felt an all-consuming fury and for Mungo McMaster an unquenchable hatred.

Then he switched on his engine and started to drive away. The car jolted violently. While he waited someone had crept up to let the air out of his tyres. But by then he was beyond further exacerbation.

*

"Sid," Tod Milligan shouted above the roar of the engines. "Tell me something about the law on marriage."

"Oh, no! Blows the wind in that airt? A sly devil this Milligan, deuced sly."

There had been a period film showing in Belfast. It's curious pseudo-period dialogue had excited Levine's admiring derision.

Now, as the two of them watched the Ulster Tourist Trophy on the Ards circuit, the bogus historic phrases rolled from the young lawyer's lips.

"Don't be wet," said Milligan. "It's not for myself."

"'Tis what they all aver, my lord. 'Pray, good scribe, advise on a friend's behalf . . .' And the friend no doubt is the lush and – oh, so willing – Pamela."

"Oh, balls. Anyhow, I haven't seen her for weeks. Well, a fortnight . . . Oh, here's Prince Bira – and Nuvolari."

In silent admiration they watched the car screech past, wheels pounding on a surface meant for normal road traffic and not racing cars and vanish in an aura of benzine and burned castor oil with an over-flavour of scorching rubber.

There was a cheer from the stand and a local car, driven by Jackie Chambers, seemed to be in hot pursuit of the champions. Actually he had been lapped.

"It's McMaster," Milligan explained when a little silence followed.

"I understood he was already married."

"He is. What I mean is that he's planning to marry two of his crowd. You remember the girl, the miracle girl, the one he prayed over and she got well? Well, she's marrying tha funny little man with the glasses and the coat down to hi ankles – Macatammany. McMaster is going to perform the marriage ceremony."

"They'll have him if he does," said Levine firmly. "This'll be their chance to pop him in the Crumlin Jail. Preaching he can get away with, but purporting to perform a marriage ceremony, not being a duly licensed minister of religion – Oh, I should say that this is very much the one they've been waiting for. I think they could give him six months."

"I thought it would be something like that."

A Bentley roared past, driven by a sporting peer who waved gaily to the crowd and then almost charged them as the big car slid sideways. In Nuvolari's pit they were already popping the champagne in expectation of the usual victory.

"You'd better warn him that he'll really be for the high jump. Tell him – "

"I did. I wasn't quite sure but I did warn him he was on pretty dicey ground. He's going on with it."

"Then verily he deserves all he gets. I expect that will be plenty. When's the ceremony?"

"Today. In the Tabernacle."

*

The wheezy harmonium droned out the notes of the Wedding March under Dulcie McMaster's fingers. In her eyes was a light of triumph, subdued but recognisable. As she had planned so had she done.

In the eyes of Wee Hughie Macatammany, it was difficult to read an expression. The little man looked dazed, as if even now he did not believe that this had happened to him. He clutched Janey's hand as if fate might even now drag her from him, not knowing that a stronger power than fate would be needed now to separate him from Janey Anderson. 'What God hath joined let no man put asunder' he echoed in his mind with a wonderful gratitude.

Mrs Anderson was weeping softly and perhaps gratefully for she had herself wondered about the girl. Wee Hughie's mother was present in the flesh but almost totally absent in the mind.

Janey looked at her as she passed and wondered how soon it would take her to persuade Hughie that his mother would be happier in a Home. She felt relief and happiness and no guilt at all. She would be a good wife, she thought, quite good. Hughie would make a fine, obedient husband. And she owed it all to the Minister. Throughout the service she had gazed up at him with grateful, adoring eyes, wondering how much he knew, how much he suspected.

Whatever the facts might be it seemed to her that she owed all her happiness to Mungo McMaster.

And in McMaster's mind also there was a great content at this joining of two of his flock in matrimony. These were the first. But there would be more, many more.

"Go forth, be fruitful, multiply," he had told them.

And the land would fill with their seed, the Word would fill the land.

The congregation was small for that wedding because so many even of the Movement had been drawn to the TT races. It was not so often that Ulster stood in the middle of the world stage. The TT was not an event to be missed.

No doubt if more had been working they would not have gone to the race but the Movement had still to reach its zenith. Many, far too many, of its most faithful adherents were still unemployed. They were free to walk or beg lifts to the circuit and watch cars burning fuel that would have kept their families in food for weeks. But then it was sport, and they did not grudge any waste on sport.

There were strangers in the congregation and McMaster had expected to see them. They waited until the last of the wedding guests had followed the bride and groom to the

Anderson house where there would be cold chicken and ham for the wedding breakfast.

"Mr McMaster, we're police officers . . ."

*

If the District Inspector had not been almost totally bald he would have been tearing at his hair.

"Sergeant, you're a bloody fool."

The sergeant gazed unhappily into the middle distance.

"You could have found all this out beforehand."

"Yes, sir. But when I saw a wedding service and – "

The D.I. sighed. "I know. I suppose you're not really to be blamed. And yet it would have been so simple to check."

"Yes, sir. But I wasn't to know – "

The telephone rang and the D.I. braced himself visibly before he lifted the receiver.

"Good afternoon, Minister," he acknowledged the greeting and question. "Yes, sir, we brought him in. But we had to release him."

A faint smile twitched the sergeant's lips as he heard the words 'bloody fool' applied again.

"The fact is, sir, that no case lay. It appears that the couple had already gone through a Registry Office wedding. Therefore they were already man and wife before McMaster's ceremony. Therefore it did not purport to be a wedding ceremony. The Attorney General is quite positive that no case lies. Yes, sir. Sorry, sir."

He glared at the sergeant who took this, correctly, as a dismissal.

CHAPTER THIRTY

n its way this victory over the police had a greater effect
han anything else that Mungo McMaster had done. The
tory spread across the city with lightning speed and men
elished the idea of how neatly the preacher had baffled
authority. They liked the thought of the police being led on
nto a false arrest, they laughed over what the D.I. must have
aid – and shrewdly they assessed the improbability of the
police ever arresting McMaster again without very good
cause.

In higher places there was a certain sour appreciation of
the preacher's skilled tactics.

"Jimmy Craig has had a splendid laugh over it," the Earl
of Dail told the Bogeyman. "He's not altogether sold on his
police force. He has a liking for the sharper sort of trick."

They were now aboard the Earl's yacht, a fifty-ton
schooner called *The Gilaroo*, one of the Ulster names for the
big lake trout that had begun to draw anglers from England
and Scotland. Though the Earl fished his own river occasionally he was not an enthusiastic angler (indeed he was no
enthusiast in any respect). But the word had a flavour that
pleased him, a rolling euphony, an almost piratical smack.
It went well with the long, sleek black hull designed by Fife.

The Countess was not aboard. The Countess was never
aboard the schooner. To board a ship of any kind was for her
to succumb instantly to sea-sickness, terrifying, complete,
and disabling prostration for which the Earl had little if any
sympathy. 'Imagination', he called it with a lack of imagina-

tion on his own part.

But then, almost anything to do with the Countess evoked nothing more than apathy from him. She was a bishop's daughter and with her remote, almost ethereal beauty, she had undoubtedly attracted him strongly until the moment of consummation of the marriage, when it appeared that behind the beauty there lay nothing but a chill vacuum.

Nothing he could do would rouse her from her passivity. As a good wife she had to submit – but she did not have to like it.

Nor did she have to like Ulster. In fact, she hated it. It was nothing like England. Its attitudes were wrong. More than anything she disliked the curious familiarity of the lower orders. In the bishop's palace servants had been automatons who did as they were told and did not venture views of their own or presume on their superiors. Here they seemed to regard themselves as part of the family, free to offer advice or join in the conversation at any time.

"It's the semi-feudal outlook," the Earl had tried to explain. "The old clan system. You get the same thing in Scotland. After all, think of Queen Victoria and that fellow Brown. To an extent a servant *is* part of the family here, part of the unit, part of the tail."

"They should know their place," insisted Milanda with middleclass logic. "They presume altogether too much."

She had never told Dail about the incident at the river. She would have found it hard to describe for one thing, to put into words what the man had actually done. And she feared that his reply might be merely ribald laughter.

Milanda might well have left Dail long before, though duty might bid her stay, but for the Irish Sea crossing. The stretch of water prisoned her as surely as a wall.

Now, as the schooner glided along the coast of County Down with a land breeze driving her and scarcely raising a wave, the Earl of Dail was talking of his wife to the Bogeyman.

"Virtue," he sighed. "It's a fearsome thing to have a virtuous wife."

He lolled in a deck chair in the sun. In an ice bucket a bottle of champagne sat between himself and the Bogeyman, who found it more convenient to sit on the deck than trust himself to unsteady canvas. A few yards away the yacht's skipper was at the wheel. Some of the crew were below and some lay on the deck forward, enjoying – as Dail had pointed out – all the pleasures of yachting without any of the expense.

"Socrates said something about virtuous wives," the Bogeyman answered. "The reference escapes me now. Is that the Mull of Galloway over there or the Isle of Man?"

"The Island . . . Want to go over? It would take about four hours."

"No, no. I have a meeting tonight."

"At which no doubt you'll plot our destruction."

"What else indeed . . . As to wives, the unvirtuous kind are supposed to be even more trouble."

"Yes, but you can beat them – or divorce them. What can you do about a woman who is too good? I did try to beat her once but it wasn't a success."

"She wasn't too strong for you?"

"No. It was that look of patient, indignant resignation on her face . . . And I suppose I really didn't have a proper excuse, a reason to beat her except that she was there. I didn't give her a single cut after all."

The Bogeyman gazed reflectively at the cottonwool clouds.

"I told you the answer once. Let me at her – I'd bring her to life or . . . Wait, Tony, don't start coming the offended aristocrat! – or if I didn't waken her I'd give her a sense of guilt. She'd be so worried about being in the wrong it would quite change her nature."

He glanced slyly at the Earl.

"Bogey, I've told you this before – there are limits. How would you like to be pitched over the side?"

Dail was not altogether joking.

"You can't drown a man born to be hanged. I wonder what length of rope they'll give me; pretty long to make up for the weight I haven't got in my legs. Can you hang a man with a wooden leg? No, you have to use a rope . . . Proceeding. You've got a wonderful lot of illogicalities in your attitude, you know. You've a wife who can't stand you and you don't even like. But when I suggest screwing her in order to make her more likeable you got up in the air. Toothbrushes."

"Toothbrushes?"

"You wouldn't let anyone else use your toothbrush either and that's about the size of it. You'd give a toothbrush away but you wouldn't lend it. Yes, that's your attitude. Exactly."

He poured himself a careful glass of wine and as he sipped it he began suddenly to giggle.

"Now what filthy thought has rippled the cesspool of your mind?"

"Just a thought. Where it came from I don't know. But suddenly I had a vision of Lady Dail in bed with your preacher."

"My preacher? You mean McMaster? I've told you – he isn't mine."

"But how does the thought strike you? That great gaunt man brimming over with virtue and virility. Lady Milanda . . . Don't you think it has its risible possibilities?"

Dail scowled but from a faint quirk at the corner of his lips he was not unamused. But he changed the subject.

"McMaster. Why the hell do we always have to be talking about McMaster! A man doesn't seem able to get away from him these days."

"And maybe less so in the future," the Bogeyman assured him. "If I don't have him shot he will quite probably be Prime Minister."

"Now you're being absurd. A man like that? Without education – or breeding?"

"How much breeding did Stalin have? Or this chap Hitler? The present Shah of Persia was a sergeant in the army a few years ago . . . If the drive's there a man will get there. McMaster's got the drive."

The Earl of Dail showed distinct alarm on his rubicund features.

"You're not joking? But McMaster's never said anything about politics."

"My God! It's no wonder you people are dying out. What the hell do you think he's been talking about but politics? The Movement is as near as a curse to a Socialist crusade . . . Socialism started with Christ, you know. Don't you ever read his speeches? The papers give them fully enough."

"Good Lord," was Dail's comment. "I wonder if Jimmy Craig's thought of that. He wouldn't like to lose the job."

"You can bet your bottom dollar that your pocket Prime Minister knows all about it. He might laugh – but he'll be shivering just a little in his shoes, too. Mungo McMaster could sweep the lot of you from power, you out of your big house and your yacht, Craig and his pals out of Stormont. Or I'll modify that a little. He could have if he hadn't made one small mistake."

"And what was that?"

"He didn't get me on his side."

Dail laughed, a little uneasily perhaps.

"You really have the most ineffable vanity, Bogey."

The Bogeyman's eyes glittered. "Vanity, yes. A proper man has a deal of vanity. Which is another name for pride. And pride comes from self-knowledge. Maybe I am a physical dwarf, a grotesque little monster. But inside I'm a giant. Inside I've got legs."

He held out the wineglass in his hand and then slowly closed his fingers about the bowl, crushing the glass and letting the splinters fall to the scrubbed teak deck. The man at the wheel half-turned and then looked ahead again. Breaking glasses were no concern of his.

"You've cut yourself," said the Earl.

"I did something that you could not do. I've got strength. Great strength. Brains and strength. I could rule. I could rule over you all, Papish and Prod, rich and poor, aristocrat and peasant. I could rule if I wished. I could. I'm a better man than you, Tony Dail. Stronger, cleverer, better. I tell you . . ."

A little foam flecked the Bogeyman's lips and veins were standing out on his forehead. His head jerked uncontrollably from side to side and then his tongue stuck rigidly from a gaping mouth and his breathing rasped hoarsely from his lungs.

Dail stared, fascinated and frightened by this sudden attack. He started to rise, to go to the Bogeyman's aid, but as he did so the other's rigid muscles relaxed suddenly and the congested colour faded from his face.

"That scared you," he grinned perkily. "Maybe I'll scare you more before I've finished with you – if McMaster doesn't scare you all to death first."

*

Shane Hendrick was talking but he was not hearing himself. Neither, he suspected, was anyone else in the hall. He was talking because it was his job, because he was paid to talk, to deliver lectures and create organisation. The lectures he could give without thinking about them but so far as creating an organisation here, he knew he had failed. He had failed, was failing, and would continue to fail. He felt a dreadful, grey lassitude about him and he did not even care that he was failing. Worse still, he did not even care that he did not care.

The source of his failure was McMaster he told himself, and he knew that even that was not true. He had been failing before McMaster came and the preacher's coming, his attraction away of the union members had only highlighted Hendrick's own failure.

The fact was, he thought, as his voice droned on, he had no fire in his heart. Inside himself he was a little dead. Something was missing in his make-up. And yet it had not always been missing. Had that something died with Tansy? And yet long after his wife had been buried he had still held his own strong beliefs in the essential unity of labour, in the vital need for the work he was doing.

In London, in Union H.Q., he had had a fair reputation as a fire-eater. H.Q.! He felt a sudden and violent nostalgia for the desk and the graphs and the returns, for the telegrams to this branch and that and the hasty meetings with committees and secretaries. Above all, he longed for the wonderful days of the General Strike, for the swift march of events and the close comradeship of the office.

"The initiation of joint negotiation," he droned on. "Must be primarily the responsibility of . . ."

Belfast had seemed like a wonderful challenge when he knew the job was open. He had even intrigued a little to get it, emphasised his own Belfast accent, dropped hints. Now, if they recalled him in the morning, it would not be too soon.

And yet without McMaster, without that gaunt dramatic man's hypnotic fascination for his people could he not have succeeded? Without McMaster . . .

How could there by any solidarity among the workers when McMaster was deliberately separating them, making of them two classes? The Catholics were as entitled to Union membership as the Protestants, as entitled to the jobs. And if they combined then there could be justice for all, work for all, higher wages for all.

The dark magic of the preacher had even reached into his own home. What attraction could Pamela find in the man's mouthings? Pamela had never in the past shown the slightest interest in religion and yet now she could scarcely be kept from McMaster's meetings. Where did this uncouth countryman get his power over men – and women?

Glumly he gazed at the bored men on the benches before him. For Pamela's sake as well as his own he must get a transfer. Tonight, perhaps, he would write to London.

*

"I'm sorry, Bogey," said Pamela Hendrick. "I can't help you any more."

She was in the Bogeyman's house again. She was naked and relaxed.

"Can't?" he said. "Or won't?"

"Whichever way you like."

"So the McMaster spell reaches out even to you. How? Has he an even greater priapismic power than myself? But that would be impossible. Has he had you, Pamela? Has he?"

"I've told you, I'm not helping you any more."

The Bogeyman's hand stretched out slowly and caressed the girl's breast. Then suddenly his pale fingers tightened and she gave a gasp of pain.

"Sadism is not one of my particular pleasures," he said, softly. "However, I am prepared to suffer a little myself."

There was no expression at all on his fine features as his fingers continued to tighten and the girl's face distorted with pain.

"Stop it! Stop it!"

Abruptly he released her and she slumped to the floor, rubbing a breast that bore the imprint of the man's fingers red on the pale skin.

"Why?" he demanded now. "Tell me why. And tell me truly. Or I shall hurt you very much. I could call the others and have them hurt you but they would do it less skilfully. Now tell me why you are betraying me."

"There's no betrayal. But I can't go on with it. I . . . Well, if you like he's cast his spell over me. Listening to him, I don't want him to be harmed. I . . . You wouldn't understand but he comforts a woman. Just to listen to him. Just to listen."

"And that's all? Only listening? No sneaking into the tent by night, no sweaty groanings with that big, tall man? No houghmagandy, which is an expressive Scots expression for the processes of generation? No sex at all?"

"None. Nothing. I've hardly spoken to him. I've just – listened."

"Are you saved then, little Londoner? Is your soul safely

228

gathered in? If so, what are you doing here consorting with the man's principal opponent? If you're saved, why fornicate? You make belief hard."

"This . . . I like it. It's good for me. And in any case McMaster has never dealt with it. The only fornication he's concerned with is Rome."

"Ah. But I'm Rome too. Or are you going to save my soul as well as gratifying my body? Is this some new and delicious perversion?"

Slowly Pamela began to pull on her clothes.

"You'll never understand him, not in a million years. All you can think of is to pull him down. You're no different from the others, the Unionist and the Orangemen and all the greedy bosses round the city."

"But that's where you're wrong! Listen. I admire this man. I admire him greatly. He is a tremendous force. But I admire a gale at sea also. That doesn't mean I want it to last for ever."

Pamela could not doubt the Bogeyman's sincerity.

"I still have to destroy him," he went on. "Someone will destroy him. And better me, I think, than others."

"Why? Why do you want to destroy him? Because he has long legs and you have none?"

The Bogeyman's face stiffened. For once the girl had driven a thrust home.

"I want to destroy him because otherwise he will destroy us all. He will destroy the country, his friends, everything. Don't you see it? Those parades. . . . His tremendous influence over his followers – and above all, the people behind him. That horrible little pseudo-American, (He's a Czech, actually) Brek. They'll corrupt whatever is good in his crusade. Our two peoples will be set even more at each other's throats. There can be nothing for this part of Ireland but increasing tension, bloodshed and ruin as long as McMaster lives.

"And above all – I think he must be destroyed because that is what he wishes in his heart. He sees himself, I think, as a re-born Messiah. The very way he came to the city – the donkey, his wife in that absurd blue cloak, his refusal to take money . . . Don't you understand? He sees himself as a new Messiah.

"And there can be only one end for a Messiah. If I do not destroy him, at last they will crucify him. Because of what he is I must destroy him – and if it could be done with your aid, by word of mouth, by attacking his reputation and his purity it would be gentler than by physical action.

"Seduce him, Pamela, make it evident. Make those strait-laced followers of his see him in another, earthy light. His mission will be dead, but he will live."

CHAPTER THIRTY-ONE

"These kidneys are uncommonly fine, my dear Dulcie. Rich fare for a poor preacher. But then, you are always good to me."

"Thank you, Mr McMaster," said Dulcie almost inaudibly. It was a pleasure and a relief to her that now the other women no longer sent food to the Tabernacle. Gradually and with a great deal of diplomatic skill she had discouraged them and indeed for many of them the novelty of feeding the Minister had lost its first edge.

She had no money to do her shopping, but money was not needed. The Executive Committee had seen to that.

"Since he will take no money we have spoken to the trades-people and they will be very proud to supply all your wants."

This Dulcie doubted. She had no high opinion of shopkeepers. They were always anxious to get their money. In her view the shops had either been bullied into supplying the Tabernacle, with the knowledge that almost all their customers were supporters of the Movement, or else the Committee was paying for the goods. The Committee had money now, plenty of money. Collections were taken at every meeting and the funds were probably considerable.

Mr McMaster did not know, she thought, about these collections. Certainly he never mentioned them. In the past Dulcie might perhaps have raised this matter but not now. It was sufficient for her that the food was there, that butcher, grocer, bread-server and milkman came each day. Mr

McMaster was well fed; he was well. That was what mattered.

"I see the Government has had another ding at me," chuckled McMaster over his kidneys. "They're a touchy lot up there in that House of Parliament. Maybe it's time I had a real ding at them. I wonder now how it would do if I marched on Stormont."

Dulcie looked at him aghast.

"You'd never, Mr McMaster. March on Parliament! Oh, you'd never!"

"I might just indeed. They're not a bit complimentary, this government of ours. They make little of the Movement."

McMaster's tone had been bantering at first but a purpose began to grow in his eyes even as he spoke. Dulcie quailed as she looked at him, for she had learned recently how swiftly an idea could be turned into a determined intention.

"Maybe the time is nigh for a trial of strength," he said. "Let us see whether the Lord stands on my right hand or his."

"They'll arrest you – put you in prison."

"I think not, Dulcie. I think not at all. I think perhaps there could be another day of glory for The Movement. I think I can outface this Laodicean Prime Minister that thinks to hunt with the hounds and yet run with the hare. I think when my men march fornenst him he will have two thoughts about whether he is the great man or I. Aye, I think the time of trial is very nigh."

*

"March on Stormont! They'd never let us."

That was the unanimous opinion of the Executive Committee save for Brek, who was not an actual member but attended.

"Do you think they could stop us? D'you think they'd dare turn guns on us? On loyal Ulstermen seeking only to put their grievances before the Government?"

"I reckon Mr McMaster's right," Brek said. "I guess if you march up there as if you'd every right to they won't even try to stop you."

"And if they do, we'll smash them!" breathed a voice.

McMaster frowned.

"We're peaceful men. Our cause is just. We'll have no need to fight. We're Christians, so let us not even talk of fighting," McMaster put in then. "But also we are prudent men so if there be fighting it would be well to win the fight. How many men can we muster?"

Though the Yard was open again only a tithe of the unemployed had been taken on so far. In the first stages of a ship most of the work was specialised. Nor for a month perhaps would the gates open to the real flood of men, the platers, the riveters, the caulkers who would clothe the skeleton with its skin of steel.

As well there was still short time working in most of the linen mills and in the city's other engineering works.

"We'll have five thousand men marching," McMaster was promised.

"And women too," Brek put in then. "Say, don't forget the women. If you've got women in your column the Government will sure as hell not be inclined to any shooting. March behind the girls' band, have women in the column – you can't go wrong."

"Mr Brek's right," McMaster nodded. "And there is a place for women this time. Our fight is for them as much as for our men."

The old familiar enthusiasm was glowing in his eyes.

"We will march. The Scribes and Pharisees who have set themselves in judgment shall be toppled from their high places, yea, those that worship the graven images shall be cast down. For I tell you that inasmuch as we have heard the truth and know it, therefore will we bear this truth before us as a shield and a banner."

*

233

In fact, there were a great many banners waving above the long column that wound its way out the Newtownards Road towards the new Houses of Parliament in their open parkland that had once belonged to Stormont Castle and was now in the public domain.

The girls' pipe band led the way, their high-stepping drum majorettes at the forefront, drawing out the occupants from every house along the route and indeed most of the inhabitants of Belfast who were not at work to watch this greatest of all McMaster's displays.

Tod Milligan was there and Sid Levine had abandoned his clients for the day in the expectation that they too would be out to see the fun.

"Isn't that your girl?" Sid asked. "The Pamela one?"

"That's her – but not mine any more, I'm afraid."

"A quarrel?"

"No. Just – I don't know . . ."

This was the truth. Tod Milligan did not know the cause of the rift between himself and Pamela Hendrick. It was there and that was all he knew. Since the torchlight procession Pamela had grown increasingly indifferent to him and it was a fortnight now since he had talked to her.

"She looks a real Movement girl now," Levine commented. "All for it."

He chuckled slyly. "Not one of McMaster's bits, is she? I hear he has quite a way with the girls. All those high-stepping fillies in the short skirts – "

"Listen long enough and you'll hear a lot!" Milligan snapped.

"My, we take umbrage, do we? I didn't think you cared as they say on the cinema screen. Do you? Are we somewhat heart-broken at the loss of our English lass?"

"Don't niggle me, Sid."

Levine was in a mood that came upon him sometimes, a mood of cruelty.

"Do you think he doesn't fancy the girls then, the long fellow? From what I hear he's been through half the distaff

234

side of the Movement. They even say that girl he married off
– remember when they arrested him? – was in the club and
had to get married."

"Look, just drop it will you?" Milligan pleaded.

*

In the column was Hughie Macatammany marched
proudly. He had a new coat, one that fitted him, for he was
at work now. Janey had insisted on the new coat.

His heart swelled when he thought of Janey – and how she
herself was swelling with the promise of their first-born.

Hughie had heard the rumours too. In the Island there
were always men to make sure of such matters.

"Hey, Hughie, is it right your big fellah had a nibble at
your icing before the wedding? Whose cake is it in the oven
anyway?"

The following fight had been very brief for Hughie was
not equipped by physique or temperament for battle. He
had been pinioned against a gantry upright while his
opponent, a heavy-shoulder caulker, sought clumsily to
soothe the little storm he had roused. Nor was it only because
Hughie had friends and influence through the Movement.
The big man now regretted a jibe which had been taken
more seriously than he expected.

"Look, look, I was only joking, Hughie. Don't take on
that way. Sure, no one would mean the like of that. It was
only a wee bit of fun. Sure, I'm sorry, Hughie. I take it back."

Honour was satisfied. Hughie shook his ruffled feathers
back into place.

"Well, all right!" he snapped. "But mind what you say
next time."

Then, unexpectedly, he added: "And if it was true – d'ye
think I'd care? A man should be proud to do anything he
could for the Minister – aye, and a woman too. I tell you,
there's plenty of fathers and husbands too would be walking
six foot tall did the Minister fancy their women. God, man,

when ye think what he's done for us, what he's doing . . ."

He clambered up the gantry to his station. The rivet boy tossed up the next glowing rivet from the brazier in a glowing arc to be caught by the riveter in his steel cup and in the same movement thrust it through the hole to be held on the inside by Hughie while the riveter rounded off his end with a swift rattle of blows like a machine gun.

Hughie's shoulders straightened as he remembered that brief exchange, transmuted in his mind to an all-out defence of Janey's and the Minister's honour. He thought too of the boy who would surely be born. He would call him Mungo.

*

Anne Foss presided decorously behind the bar where the Members gathered without, for once, the urge of the party whips. She watched them sip and stroll and stare from the window down the long mile to the entrance gates on the Upper Newtownards Road.

This Members' Bar was well placed above the pediment surmounting the pillared entrance to Stormont. The long slopes on this sunlit day were speckled with picnickers and sightseers come to view the confrontation of McMaster and the Government.

There was not much conversation in the bar. The tension was too great and no one really wished to speak about what might or might not happen when Mungo McMaster came marching up that broad processional way. There was perhaps an unvoiced hope that the march would not take place, that somehow the Prime Minister himself would stop it, would call in the troops or the police or the 'B' men or maybe even an Act of God.

As well, in the politicians' way, each was wondering how best to utilise the incident for the future, how so to posture himself as to have seemed, retrospectively, correct. With something like suspicion men eyed each other and sipped at their drinks and waited.

The Prime Minister himself came into the bar and passed through the balcony above the portico. There was nothing in his solid, expressionless face to indicate that he thought or what he intended. Annie Foss, unbidden, sent him a double whisky but he did not touch it as he stood on the balcony and stared down the long avenue through eyes that seemed always narrowed since the tissue round them was puffy. His down-turned nose, broad and heavy like his chin, seemed to sniff hungrily at the wind.

In the distance the first shrill of the bagpipes could be heard.

From the balcony there was a splendid view down the whole length of the mile-long driveway, surfaced in a reddish kind of chip, from the front gates.

Beneath the building, a little way down the drive, was the statue of Edward Lord Carson, the Cork man who more than anyone else had been the creator of Northern Ireland as a separate entity.

Hand aloft in his familiar declamatory stance, Carson's statue seemed not to be shouting its defiance at the column advancing from the city.

On the balcony now were most of the members of the House of Commons and a scattering of Senators. The Prime Minister himself stood a little apart; a tall, monolithic, in-scrutable figure with a big blunt nose and eyes lost in puffy lids. About himself he created a small pool of silence amid the uneasiness and the subdued excitement. Of all those there he was the only one who could possibly know what was going to happen or at any rate what was likely to happen. As usual he kept his own counsel.

The little knot of Nationalists were enjoying the situation, apart as usual from the others, delighting quietly in seeing the body politic of their opponents apparently about to tear itself apart.

For the others it was a traumatic time.

"He should have closed the gates – "

"He should have the troops here – "

"Where are the police?"

"They'll wreck the place – "

The sound of the pipes came thinly up the broad sweep of the grounds, the rhythm of the drums almost lost in the distance, become no more than unapprehended vibration.

James, first Viscount Craigavon, rested his big farmer's hands on the Mourne granite of the parapet and stared at the distant colour of the banners, listened to the mounting skirl of the pipes and remained as determinedly impassive as ever.

CHAPTER THIRTY-TWO

For Mungo McMaster walking alone behind the girl pipers it was a disappointment that the gates, those twelve feet tall gates of gilded wrought iron, had not been closed against him and his people.

There would, first, have been a moral in that. It would have shown The Movement that without doubt the Government was turning against the people, that it regarded itself as too high-and-mighty to hold converse with the commonalty.

And there would also have been the opportunity to put into action the plan he had devised to meet this contingency.

In the column behind, carried by the inner files, were a dozen twelve-foot ladders. McMaster had planned that when they came to the closed gate they would set up their ladders and scale it and the flanking fences and surge forward like an invading army. If there were troops there, or the police should resist them, so much the better. They would be overwhelmed. Nothing could resist the power of The Movement.

But the gate was open. There was no resistance, only a lone park-keeper in his uniform who saluted with ex-service smartness as the column wheeled through the gateway and began to ascend the slope towards the buildings.

On either side lay the green slopes of the park and the band itself had begun to play 'The Green Grassy Slopes of the Boyne.'

Ahead lay the Houses of Parliament with Stormont Castle

and Mr Speaker's House to one side, dwarfed by the modern classicism of the big building, half-hidden by trees.

It might have been on the Gates of Heaven that McMaster was marching. Parliament buildings had, in the bright sunlight, an insubstantial quality, brighter than the sky behind, windows glancing back the sun's rays.

The heart of Mungo McMaster was swollen within him as his long, black-clad legs scissored their way up the slope.

For this was surely the time of decision. Now was he surely at the zenith of his career. The false glitter of that great house of sin ahead might deceive others but this day he would purge it of its evil. As the money-lenders had been scourged from the Temple, so would the false leaders be driven from their high places, the unrighteous would be cast down and a new sweetness and purity would occupy the land.

There were curious bystanders all the way up the long drive-way and others seated more prudently on the grass a little out of danger's way. They watched the high-stepping drum-majorettes and the flirting kilts of the girl pipers and the long, red-scarfed procession with the women in a solid phalanx at the rear.

Most of all, though, they watched Mungo McMaster.

Separated from the band, separated from the leading files of the column, walking in a little open space of his own on which none encroached, McMaster was bound to be the cynosure of all eyes.

"He walks big," a man said. "He walks proud."

And yet to Dulcie McMaster, far back in the throng of women, Mungo McMaster looked very small, very fragile as he led the way up the hill.

*

"If he gets away with this," Milligan told Sid Levine, "There's no limit to what he can do. Bearding the Government in its den – "

"You could be right," said Levine noncommittally. "It's

240

ot over yet . . . Did you say you were covering this for the *Express?*"

Milligan grinned broadly. "Both their local men are in ospital. They got boozed up and crashed a car. I'm standing n – with a good chance of a permanency."

"Ill wind department," Levine nodded. "We move up in he world then?"

"Well, at least the *Express* doesn't think five pounds a week s the height of generosity like the Belfast papers. If it goes ight I could be making a thousand a year in no time – more, naybe."

"You'll be wanting some investment advice then. They've topped. What now?"

*

There was a sort of terrace in the long slope and the road divided here, passing to right and left of the Parliament building. The band halted on this plateau and McMaster came up to them and from his gesture dismissed them.

Above him a broad flight of stone steps led to the final broad plateau on which stood the building itself. McMaster mounted a little way up these steps and with hands held high beckoned to his people to come close, to gather at his feet for his message.

The great throng surged silently closer, slipping on the slopes, falling on the grass, but very orderly for all that. The men crowded the closest with the women packed in behind them, looking up, all of them, to the dominating, dramatic figure that hovered over them; scarcely linked to the ground, almost hovering in the air. At that time it would not have surprised anyone if McMaster had in fact floated gently from the ground, poised himself in the air. Perhaps even McMaster would not have been surprised.

Dulcie, looking upward, could almost trace the thoughts in his head, the exaltation, the passion – and the unknown self-glory. Of them all, only Dulcie McMaster really knew the changes which had taken place in the man she loved.

To the others it might seem that Mungo McMaster trul
spoke for God. But Dulcie knew that in his own mind, un
acknowledged, was the belief that perhaps he was God.

And this day was his proof. For surely man alone could no
challenge unscathed all the temporal powers that the bi
long building behind represented. If there was no othe
power behind him and within him, then surely the Govern
ment would have struck.

But perhaps they were waiting. Perhaps behind the cove
of the Parliament building the soldiers waited with thei
armoured cars, ready to rush out and drive the people fron
the grass. Perhaps the police were massed in squads witl
batons at the ready, night helmets on their heads, preparec
for the moment when the order would be given to clear th
rabble from the slopes. And somewhere in her heart Dulci
McMaster hoped this would be so; that in a sudden swif
violence McMaster's pretensions would be shattered, th
Movement scattered to the winds, sanity restored to th
world . . . and Mr McMaster. If she prayed then it was fo
this she prayed.

A little way to one side of her, Pamela Hendrick stood witl
her eyes fixed on the gaunt black figure, the words he wa
saying rolling over her unheard but with a strangely physica
effect, as if they were caresses. Muscles within her flexed and
tightened to the words and her eyes were blank and un
focused.

Wee Hughie Macatammany was in the forefront of th
men, holding one of the cords of a banner as it bellied in th
breeze. Unashamedly, he was crying, gulping every fev
moments and drawing his wrist across his eyes.

Nor was he alone. The mass emotion which Mung
McMaster could evoke at will had the whole Movement i
its accustomed sway, phrase after rich, vibrant phrase strikin
home to the respondent chords in his hearers' hearts.

"Work . . . Money . . . God. . . . Usurpers of the people'
birthright, desecration of the Lord's appointed places . .

Woe to the land where such things be . . . Betrayed by corrupt leaders . . . led into the Valley of the Shadows by false shepherds . . ."

*

Brek had not marched in the procession. This was not, he thought, his function. He was strictly a behind-the-scenes man, an organiser, an ideas adviser. But he could admire.

Well on the outskirts of the crowd, in a position from which he could easily disassociate himself from the whole project, Brek listened and admired.

He had never heard McMaster in such voice. He had never seen the response so complete.

"The hollow of his hand," he marvelled. "He's got them right in the hollow of his hand."

Looking ahead, he thought what money was to be made from this man when he had been divorced from his parochial surroundings. In the States McMaster would be worth millions.

He had the message and he had the delivery.

Brek allowed himself a small smile. For McMaster's message had subtleties that were not apparent to his followers or even probably to McMaster himself.

McMaster had given his people both an aim and an enemy and these were vital to any campaign. Most important was perhaps the enemy. Hate and love were the two great emotions and hate was ever the easier to rouse. McMaster had provided a broad spectrum of people to hate: the Roman Catholic Church and by association its members; the Government and by implication the wealthy members of the community who were that Government. Equally intelligible to men with empty bellies were the aims of the Movement. Work, prosperity, comfort. These were aims that anyone could understand.

And anyone could understand that the Government and the Catholics were linked in an unacknowledged alliance to keep the aims from being achieved.

Almost as important as what McMaster condemned were those things he did not condemn. He had never raised his voice against drink. Nor had there been any suggestion that sex was sinful. Rather there had been always the implication that The Movement should go forth and be fruitful and multiply.

McMaster did not, in short, condemn the simple pleasures. Only the metaphorical whoring after Rome was denounced. Only drinking the waters of iniquity, which was to say supporting the Government was sinful.

What a lot of money was to be made from him! What a lot.

*

"The Sermon on the Mount, would you say?" Tod Milligan murmured. "Or has he more a touch of Moses heading for the Promised Land?"

In a pause in McMaster's words the clanking of a tramcar sounded very far away and the buses passing at the foot of the long driveway were like toys in the distance.

This was another world here on the slopes of Stormont, a world that was McMaster, a world which had no existence beyond that terrible, yearning voice dragging the souls behind it in a long comet trail.

Milligan had been watching the Parliament building, able to make out the heads and shoulders on the balcony, recognising the Prime Minister himself, seeing the others. He would have given a lot to be up on that balcony now, to hear what was being said. What would the big man do? How was the Prime Minister going to react?

As McMaster thundered to a conclusion, the same thought must have been in every mind on that grassy slope. There was no sound at all when McMaster finished. And yet the silence seemed also to exclude other sound – the city sounds that should have been heard. Minds were immersed in their own pools of thought and emotion and nothing could touch them but the mesmeric voice and gestures of Mungo McMaster.

And what Mungo McMaster did then was to turn his back on his people.

Slowly, deliberately, he mounted the steps towards the front gates of Parliament and every footfall could be heard distinctly by the people, the faint clink of the nails in his boots, the rasp of leather.

Though he was receding he seemed actually to gain in stature as he walked towards the building, to rise bleak and black and irresistible, like some moving machine that would come to the building and walk through it, bring it down and in the same instant irrevocably destroy the fabric of all their lives.

No doubt people breathed but for them all it was as if they held their breath collectively for the long seconds as McMaster's unhurried pace took him to a point beneath the balcony.

There he halted and though he turned his head up and his hand raised high in a gesture of command, it was almost as if his head was already on the balcony's level.

"Come down, James Craig!" he called in a great and terrible voice. "Come down!"

Nor did a single person there doubt at that moment that James, Viscount Craigavon, Prime Minister of Northern Ireland, would indeed come down.

Afterwards it seemed incredible but then it seemed utterly inevitable, that the Prime Minister could no more refuse to come down than the sun could to set.

Tod Milligan was one of the few, probably, to feel any incredulity as the Premier's massive body appeared at the door and walked slowly out into the sunlight – a big, impassive man who was yet dwarfed by the conquering scarecrow in the black suit.

*

Beneath these two men and above them also no one could hear what was said, neither the members of the Government on the balcony above nor the members of the Movement on the grassy slopes beneath.

They stood immovable in a long survey of each other, a survey which could have been silent or in which words could have been said.

Above and below were the watchers, silent, enthralled by this strange confrontation, the words forming in their own minds for the speeches which should be said, each according to his own view.

And these imagined speeches were perhaps the only speeches made for the very fact of confrontation removed the need for words. Words had no longer any relevance. What was relevant was the fact.

The fact was that Mungo McMaster had come to the crest of his wave. In the sight of his people, in the sight of the world, he stood talking as an equal or perhaps as more than an equal with the Prime Minister. Nothing else mattered beside that astounding, irrefutable fact.

And when at last the man parted, when Craigavon stepped to the Parliament House and McMaster moved down among his people it was McMaster who seemed to be rising.

Could there be any limit to his rise was the question in each mind. How much farther might Mungo McMaster go and in going take them with him?

PART FOUR

CHAPTER THIRTY-THREE

Wee Hughie Macatammany had never been drunk before. But he had never become a father before, either. To be in employment, to have a son, to have his mother now safely in a home – these were reasons in plenty for getting drunk in Googan's Bar just around the corner from Gonagal's Bit.

There were plenty to join him in his celebration for at last the good times had come. There was work again, work at the shipyard, work in the linen mills, work in the foundries and machine shops.

"And all Mr McMaster's doing," Hughie declared. "Who took us all til Stormont? Who faced out Craigavon himself? Who made the ships come and the mill orders and everything? I tell ye, if it wasn't for Mr McMaster – "

No one argued, though in a corner of the bar someone murmured: "Aye, and if it wasn't for McMaster maybe there wouldn't be the wean, either." This, though, Wee Hughie did not hear. He was absorbed in contentment, face blurred, legs unsteady, voice tapering gradually into incomprehensibility as the pints and the whisky went down.

The others watched him with a genial contempt as he swayed at the bar and tried to buy more drinks and more.

It was not so long since anyone buying a drink would have been surrounded in that pub with a host of eager takers. Now everybody had money in their pockets and the talk was of football or 'the grus', for greyhound racing was gathering momentum again now that there was money in the city, or of what this one and that one was doing at the weekend.

Especially there was talk of the 'big one', the new ship whose order had set the seal on the new prosperity. A forty-thousand tonner, a passenger liner, work for joiners, upholsterers and all the other ancillary trades which the first ship had not brought since it was only a cargo tramp.

The newspapers had shown an artist's impression of how 'the big one' – unnamed yet – would look; sleek, gracious, transport which would be forever beyond the means of the men who made her.

But this was nothing new for the Yard men. Of them all only a tiny handful had ever travelled in the creation of their hands. All the great ships that moved down the ways into the grey water of the Lagan were not meant for them to use. Nor indeed did they resent this, any more than a Rolls Royce mechanic would resent not being a Rolls Royce owner or a goldsmith his lack of a crown. The important thing was that 'the big one' had brought them work, would bring more work, was the source of the new blood beginning to pulse through the veins and arteries of the whole community.

The 'big one' was prosperity and if Mungo McMaster had been the instrument of its coming, then good luck to Mungo McMaster.

But there were plenty of people who ignored Mungo McMaster's part completely. The Unionist papers praised the Prime Minister and Minister of Finance for their far-seeing wisdom in making it possible for the Yard to undercut rivals for the contract for the 'big one.' The Yard's Board was similarly praised for their foresight and business acumen. The city and province as a whole was allowed to congratulate itself on its perspicacity. The workers were praised for their famed craftsmanship which had drawn the order. Shoulders generally were bowed beneath the weight of patting. Euphoria was general.

*

For Mungo McMaster this time was one of ultimate triumph. He walked like a king about Gonagal's Bit. Women came to their doors as he passed by. Men touched their caps or even crossed the street to shake his hand.

Gonagal's Bit itself was scarcely large enough for the crowds who came to his evening meetings, though the daytime gatherings were already beginning to shrink now, reduced to women for the most part and a few men who were either too old for work or not capable of it.

But the evening meetings, that vast crowd spilling over into the streets about the Bit, they were something never to be forgotten, intent faces listening, lifting up their own voices when the hymns came, moving in a great unison.

At this time McMaster's favourite relaxation was to walk slowly from the Bit across the Queen's Bridge and down the Donegall Quay to a point where he could watch across the river the work beginning at the Yard, see the ribs of the new ship rise like some organic growth amid the gantries, hear and almost taste the flavour of the work.

Going down the quays he would be saluted by dockies and stevedores whose numbers also had grown with the new work at the Yard. Sometimes a passing tug would blow a blast on its siren and a skipper wave a greeting at the tall gaunt figure.

McMaster could sit there on a bollard and if the sun shone he could be content for an hour at a stretch; not so much thinking consciously as lost in a gentle meditation, in a pervasive gratitude for the swift answer to his prayers. Or so he told himself.

*

"Monarch of all he surveys," said the Earl of Dail. "Wouldn't you say that's his pose, Bogey?"

"I'd like to see inside his mind," answered the Bogeyman.

He was seated with the Earl in the rear seat of Dail's Rolls. They were on their way to the schooner, then lying in a basin near the quays where some maintenance work was being done on her. The little cocktail cabinet built into the dividing seat was open and each had a glass of brandy. Through the voice pipe Dail called on his driver to halt.

Drinking, the pair gazed at Mungo McMaster and speculated on his thoughts.

"Everything's gone right for him," Dail remarked. "He's made good every promise he ever gave to his followers. They've got work. He's shown himself almost above the Government. I should think he's feeling pretty God-like by now, wouldn't you?"

"I'm not sure. I think I would be a worried man if I was Mungo McMaster. He's achieved a lot, I'll admit. But he's gone so far so quickly – where has he got left to go? What new aims can he set himself? What fresh promises can he give his people?"

"Interesting." Dail smiled and then laughed. "That's almost what Jimmy Craig told me. It's curious that you and he should think alike."

"Curious? I would have thought that it only went to prove that the Right Hon and noble gentleman has more intelligence than he's credited with."

"Meaning?"

"There are more ways of killing a cat than stuffing it with cream – but not necessarily better ways."

"That's profound. Does it mean anything?"

"I'll tell you on the yacht."

McMaster was still brooding as the Rolls glided on its way.

*

From the schooner there arose already sounds of a party in full swing.

"They've arrived, it rather seems," Dail observed. "And found the keys also."

He had invited a few friends to meet the Bogeyman, or perhaps for the Bogeyman to inspect, to study and, later, to comment on.

There was no crew aboard and in fact the guests had not

found the keys of the main companion. They had simply smashed in the door. In the main cabin they had found the drink cupboard and opening it had been even less of a problem.

The long cabin seemed full of people, though in fact there were only about half a dozen. They were moderately drunk and getting drunker. They greeted Dail and the Bogeyman with hoots and jeers in the hybrid accents of the Irish upper class.

There seemed to be three girls and three men, though since the men were long-haired and the girls shingled the difference was not immediately apparent. Dail did not try to introduce the Bogeyman.

"Well, cut off my legs and call me Shorty," tittered a long-haired, florid-faced baronet, seeing the Bogeyman for the first time. The joke seemed so apposite that he repeated it – several times.

The Bogeyman gave a thin, dangerous smile and trundled to a seat at the long, fixed table.

"Tony does have some odd friends," a girl told him, a plump, eager-eyed little blonde.

"So I've noticed," agreed the Bogeyman.

She stared and her eyes narrowed momentarily.

"I meant you," she said.

"I meant you," the Bogeyman answered equably.

Unsure whether or not to take offence the girl laughed uneasily and drifted away. The Bogeyman took stock. To watch this little group of the aristocracy at play confirmed what he had long suspected – that there was even less difference in the natures of people in upper and lower classes than seemed reasonable.

*

"Mr Hendrick, just how far can a shop steward take a dispute with management?"

"Well, it depends on the nature of the dispute. The first

stage is, of course, up to him. Let's take the case of a man dismissed for falling behind on output rate. It may be that the shop steward could have the actual rate examined in case it had been over-set in the first place. In any case of doubt the shop steward would be well advised to consult his branch secretary . . ."

The questions coming from the floor of the hall indicated how little attention had been paid to Hendrick's earlier lectures. But they did not disturb Hendrick. Rather they delighted him. They indicated that at last there was some interest in the work he was doing. Now there could be some progress.

The reason was not far to seek. Before everything had been very largely academic. Men without work had no real interest in union procedures. Now, however, it had real point. Men at work wanted the best conditions, the highest wages. They had wakened from their long slumber.

Glancing through the window Hendricks could see McMaster making ready for his evening service. The platform and pulpit had been set up outside the Tabernacle. A crowd was beginning to gather.

Hendrick had long conquered his resentment of the preacher. Whether or not it was true that Mungo McMaster was responsible for the new prosperity in the city, for the first steps towards the boom years that must surely come, there was no doubt that the men believed in him.

And between himself and the preacher an arrangement had been reached that McMaster would not hold his service until the trade unionist had finished his lecture. Thus the trainees would not miss the talk and the preacher's congregation would not be diminished.

Yet, while he talked and answered questions, Hendrick wondered if the latter supposition was true. For it seemed to him that the crowd was smaller than in former days. Gonagal's Bit was packed, it was true, most evenings, but they did not shoulder each other quite so closely. The crowd did not overspill into the side streets as before.

But perhaps this was only to be expected. Men worked overtime and shift work now. They simply did not have the chance of attending.

Pamela was still there, though, he noticed, well to the front. What did she get out of it? What drew her to McMaster? She puzzled him. At home she was silent, brooding on her inner thoughts. And she would not share them . . . But then, she never had. Perhaps after all he should have married again. The girl needed a mother, or at least a companion in the house.

But trade union organising was no metier for matrimony. The women in it were all too dedicated to the cause and were rarely enough attractive anyhow. A wife from outside the Movement was almost impossible. He hardly ever met a woman outside the Movement.

Shane Hendrick closed his notebook.

"Tomorrow evening I'll be dealing with the Workmen's Compensation Acts in greater detail. You'll want to take notes . . ."

*

To Wee Hughie Macatammany the proposal was next to treason.

"We've never yet put off a march," he said. "And McMaster won't stand for it. Sure, even the peelers couldn't stop us marching nor the Government nor nobody."

"You'll have to look at it this way, Hughie. The Blues hasn't played Celtic since the work started again at the Yard. Half the men hasn't had a make in their pocket to get til a match these long months. Was we to march the morroah we'd get a lot missing. I'd say it'd be better we didn't take the chance."

"I guess the man's right," Brek agreed. "I guess our people need a bit of fun in their lives. If they have to choose between the march and the match it'll rile them up inside."

And indeed the meetings of Belfast Celtic and Linfield

Football Clubs were always clashes of the giants that no one wished to miss. Linfield, The Blues, represented the Protestant faction and Celtic were of course Catholic – though their team often included Protestants. But Protestants playing for Celtic became for the period of the match at least honorary Catholics, part of the enemy.

"You'll have to ask the Minister," Wee Hughie insisted doggedly. "He'll hardly be for it at all. What's an oul' match anyway . . ."

It was not even put to the vote. Only Hughie of the Executive Committee of The Movement was in favour of a march that Saturday.

And to his surprise when he told McMaster of the Committee's views, the preacher was not greatly disturbed.

"Indeed, I might very well go to the match myself," he declared. "It is a long, long time since I watched a game of football."

"But you'd hardly want to go til Celtic Park!"

"Why not?"

"Sure, the crowd will be full of Papishes. There's bound to be plenty there will know you. Losh, Mr McMaster, there'd be riots there that'd frighten the French!"

McMaster smiled. "Maybe so," he agreed.

Wee Hughie stared and then comprehension lit his face. A smile spread across his compressed features.

"Losh, Mr McMaster, but it's the quare head you have on you right enough. Man dear, but it'll be the match to remember."

A great gush of warm pride filled his heart as he pictured Mungo McMaster in the midst of the green square of the football ground, bringing sinners to repentance, vast voice moving the hosts of the Catholics to repentence. This would be indeed the apotheosis of the Movement.

"It'll be great, just great," he said fervently.

*

And indeed that match could have been the ultimate peak of McMaster's career had he ever gone to it. With the crowds both of the Movement and other uninvolved Protestants gathered there and an almost equal number of Catholics, the result could have been either a scene of mass conversion or the bloodiest sectarian battle that Belfast had ever seen.

But McMaster was not there. McMaster lay in his bed, that long, gaunt body racked with unaccustomed pain, helpless to stir.

And those with a fancy for signs and portents might have seen in this some augury of events to come.

McMaster had walked out the evening before to take his accustomed place at the evening service.

And abruptly his legs had shot out and he splayed clumsily and heavily to the ground

Women cried out as the tall body fell and, strangely, no one came forward to help; no one but Dulcie McMaster who ran out from the Tabernacle almost as McMaster hit the ground.

It did not look a bad fall but McMaster did not rise. He lay there with his face twisted, seeming helpless to move. And with Dulcie crouched over him it seemed a scene that was crystallised in time, the woman crouched by the fallen hero in the old, ordained way.

Then, long seconds after someone shouted: "Jeez, McMaster's fell . . . He's down!"

There was an apocalyptic ring to the words.

CHAPTER THIRTY-FOUR

"Dog shite," said the Bogeyman long after. "A little bit of dog shite and that was the end of McMaster when you boil it down . . . And no doubt it was a Papish dog, God rest him."

But that was long afterwards. Then it was a matter that McMaster had slipped and fallen and there would be no service that evening.

The tall figure was carried into the tent, groaning a little, and a doctor was sent for.

A strained muscle in the back was the diagnosis, rest the remedy. McMaster had never rested before. It irked him immensely to be lying in his bed while the world went about its business. He did not like to admit that the world could go about its business without him.

On the afternoon of the match he waited for Wee Hughie to return and report.

*

Tod Milligan was not normally a sports reporter but the *Express* had asked him to cover the big match and he packed into the Press box with the rest.

Sport reporting is different from any other kind. Few men can be enthusiastic about the proceedings of a Borough Council Meeting or even a Parliamentary debate. But it is hard to watch any game with complete detachment. Inevitably some form of identification grows in the mind. The reporters were almost as partisan as the surging crowd filling the big stand, divided clearly by their favours into two sectors, the green and the blue.

Party songs were hurled across the grass and even before the game began a few bottles, toilet rolls and other missiles were in the air too; not seriously thrown as yet, not with the venom that must accompany decision one way or the other, lightheartedly thrown as an augury of what was to come. In any case, ammunition must be conserved.

"I hear McMaster's not coming after all," said an *Irish News* man with a sidelong glance at Milligan. "You got anything on that, Tod?"

Milligan did his best to look omniscient.

"Which particular angle do you mean?"

"He was all set to make a big speech here, right in the middle of the match. But he's sick, they say."

"He had a fall," Milligan corrected. "He's twisted his back."

This he knew from Brek, who kept him informed on all probable future actions of the Movement and anything else that was likely to get a line or two in the Press. But Brek had said nothing of any plans for this match. In fact, Brek had said that the Movement's Executive Committee had played down a march for the day just so that they could all get to the match.

"A pity," said the *Irish News* man. "No hurt to the fellow, but if he'd started his preaching here he'd have got murdered and that wouldn't have done him any harm."

"Those are hard words from a man who's bought himself a car writing about McMaster for the Dublin papers," a Northern Whig man taunted, and the Press box's dignity degenerated for a little into an adolescent scrummage with a good deal of pushing and shoving but not much rancour.

The welcoming cheer of the Celtic supporters for their team running out onto the pitch restored order.

Down near the touchline, Wee Hughie Macatammany felt a tightness in his chest, a swelling lump in his throat. The crowd about pressed heavily on him but he hardly felt the

press ires. Inner pressures sustained him, the knowledge o
what he planned and what he would do.

McMaster might be absent, but that did not mean hi
message must go unheard.

The Linfield team trotted onto the field to the cheers o
their own supporters, and the match began.

In the Press box they were betting on the result. It was on
of Celtic's big years and three to one was the best offer or
Linfield.

"Not that it's fair, mind," said a *Newsletter* man. "Celti
has the pick of every Catholic in the Province whereas th
Prods are split up over a dozen teams."

"Your Granny's backside," snorted the *Dublin Iris
Independent's* Belfast man. "We've got the GAA to contenc
with. If it wasn't for them we'd have a real team."

The opening exchanges of the match were dull enough.
The reporters could argue on the effect of the Gaelic Athleti
Association, formed to further the cause of games Gaelic and,
by inference, the cause of nationalism generally. Specifically
the GAA banned its members from taking part in what i
called foreign games, particularly Association football
Even to watch a Soccer game meant expulsion from the
GAA. Thus Soccer-playing Nationalists could represent only
a minority.

The game came alive suddenly when Celtic probed the
Linfield left wing, brought the ball into the centre and only
just failed to score when the Blues keeper put the ball over
the bar.

Wee Hughie's sigh of relief was as great as anyone's. And
when the Blues took the ball away from the resultant corner
kick and launched an attack of their own in turn, he almost
forgot his own design in the mounting excitement.

"Ah God, he's missed!" roared a man behind him. "Oh,
the cag-footed eejit, he's missed an open goal!"

The game settled again, and Hughie could think once more
about what he would do. In his mind he could see it clearly,
himself leaping out onto the field, holding up his arms in a

great, commanding gesture, the words that would flow out from his mouth, McMaster's words, filling the ground with their sonorous echo, bringing tears and repentance to the sinners, bringing the idolators to a knowledge of the true faith.

This day he would make himself worthy of Mr McMaster. This day he would show the Minister that his lessons had not fallen on stony ground.

Truly the Papishes might revile him, stone him, kill him. But they would not silence the accusing words that would flow so freely from his tongue, that would bring the tears to their eyes and melting repentance to their hearts. The master might be laid aside for a little but his message would be heard.

Let them try to silence him, thought Wee Hughie Macatammany. Let them just try.

Celtic scored suddenly and subtly, a move improvised with a casual brilliance that took the Green supporters as much by surprise as the opposing team.

There was no real heart in the Linfield supporters' cries that the referee should buy himself new glasses, should carry out various involved and impossible physical contortions. The fact was that it was a good goal and they knew it.

"Five to one on the Greens now," said a gloomy evening paper man. "I can't see the Blues coming from behind."

In fact, Linfield equalised four minutes later from a penalty which drew howls from the Celtic crowd and whose cause, a borderline tackle, even had the Press arguing its justice.

A section of the Linfield crowd began to sing 'Derry's Walls' and their voices were answered by counter-singing from the Celtic supporters of 'Johnson's Motor Car.'

Everything was as usual and the police scattered round the ground relaxed a little, a singing crowd was hardly ever a fighting crowd, no matter how bloodthirsty the songs.

Only Wee Hughie, hardly seeing the game, did not accept it for what it was. For the game was surely only the prelude.

This day would not be remembered for the figures in the scorebook but for the Message.

Celtic scored again, a lucky goal from long range that flighted in just below the crossbar and brought renewed songs.

In the middle of the ground, Wee Hughie thought. He would be out there in the middle of the ground and they would all be listening to him.

They would all be listening to McMaster's words as they came from the mouth of Hugh Macatammany and some of the glory of the master must surely glow about the head of the disciple.

He could picture himself back at the Tabernacle, telling the tall man how it had been.

"Just your own words, that's all I ever said. Your own words . . . I gave them the message – and they listened."

He could see the smile on the gaunt face, the hand outstretched in approval.

"Well done, thou good and faithful servant . . ."

Then it was half-time and Wee Hughie wondered if now was the moment. But a band was playing and it would drown his words. Also, half the crowd was in movement, the devout fans heading for the areas behind the goalposts where they could watch their own side score, barrack the opposing keeper. With so much movement and men drinking or munching sandwiches there would not be enough attention to the words. The message would never be heard.

Through the second half was the best time, about halfway through. All eyes would be on the field. He would go out then. He would speak.

*

In the Press box someone had brought up McMaster's name.

"Physician, heal thyself," someone forecast. "That's what they'll be saying. Didn't McMaster really make his name as a faith healer? And isn't he lying now on the broad of his back? Oh, there'll be plenty of digs at him for sure."

Somebody passed round a half-bottle of Scotch, taking good care not to release his own grasp on it, for hospitality is one thing, folly is another.

"I heard they were going to build him a church. Is that right, Tod? You're well in with him."

"It's possible." Milligan was annoyed. The church story was an exclusive little piece he had thought was his alone.

"They've got a right bit collected, too. That's what I hear. So he's just like the others, after all."

"How do you mean?" Milligan demanded.

"Ach, wouldn't you know?" said the *Independent* man with feeling. "Money, money, money. That's all any church is for. Prod or Papish, they have their hand out all the time. If they're not building a new church they're repairing an old one or buying the priest new vestments or paying someone through Maynooth . . ."

"I don't think McMaster knows about it," Milligan defended the preacher. "The collection's in secret and they plan a big surprise for the long fellow – taking him up to his new church and giving him the key and saying 'It's yours' . . ."

Someone blew a raspberry.

"In a pig's arsa he doesn't know! Who the hell would start it only him? Priest or minister, the first they want is a roof over their heads . . ."

The teams trotted out on the field again. Milligan did not argue the issue. But he did not think McMaster knew about the building fund. Brek, at any rate, had assured him it was a complete secret.

More than two thousand pounds had been collected already, Brek said. A site had been picked. Building would soon start.

The game began to absorb him. It was even better than the first half, Celtic's ascendancy growing clearly and their artistry sufficient to make their next goal draw reluctant clapping from the Linfield supporters.

"A man who can kick like that," growled a burly docker behind Wee Hughie, "he can't be all bad. Even if he is a Papish."

Wee Hughie heard nothing of the comment. He was listening to the words in his own mind, to the message that was now his whole existence.

His body was trembling a little with excitement. If there was another score, he thought, that would be the time. He would jump the barrier – Just as soon as there was another score. Over the barrier and out onto the field while the ball was being centred.

His face was flushed and his mouth hung a little open. He had to take off his glasses and wipe them several times.

Linfield were fighting doggedly but unavailingly. Not even the most bigoted partisan could deny the justice of the beating they were getting.

The next goal came quickly.

Wee Hughie heard the roaring in his ears as the referee pointed to the centre spot and he forced himself past the one man between him and the barrier. Clumsily he pulled himself over.

Still the roaring was loud in his ears as he ran forward with stumbling steps on the close-clipped grass. The referee had whistled for the re-start.

And in Hughie's ears the roaring was louder still, a tumultuous roaring that drowned everything. He turned to face a stand that was swaying as he looked; a pink-and-white sea of faces that seemed now above him and now far below.

"Brethren!" thundered his voice. "Let us put aside sinful things. Let us live according to the Word of God. Follow the teachings of McMaster . . . Cast aside the heathen idols. Honour they father and mother . . . Remember the Sabbath that thou keep it holy . . ."

Like thunder his voice sounded in his own head. But around the ground they heard nothing and few even saw the small, pathetic figure with the waving arms that swayed for a moment near the touchline before it fell in an untidy heap.

"Drunk," said some of those that did see.

"Eejit," said others.

And returned their gaze to more important matters.

The ambulance man who stooped over Hughie had seen this sort of case before.

"Wouldn't you think a man with a bad heart would have more sense than come to a football match? Come on . . . He'll maybe live yet."

Celtic were scoring again as Wee Hughie was carried from the ground.

CHAPTER THIRTY-FIVE

"You helped me," said Janey Anderson. "You'll can help Hughie. You've got to help him. The doctors can't."

Watching the girl and her husband, Dulcie McMaster felt a deep foreboding. Mungo McMaster was still a little stooped, a little slow on his feet. In her view he should have been in bed still. But nothing would keep him there as soon as he could walk at all.

Without him there had been a few abortive attempts to hold meetings. Hymns had been sung and prayers read. But without the magic of his presence there had been a distinct lack of fervour in the gatherings.

In his bed McMaster had heard the flatness and had sensed the reduced numbers who had come – though Dulcie had tried to assure him that the crowd was as big as ever.

Despite her protests he had risen. Now Janey's anxious and yet defiant face confronted him with a new problem.

"No, no," he said now. "It was not I who helped you. Mine were the prayers but the work was God's."

"Then you'll do nothing? You'll not come? – and Hughie the one who followed you from the very first."

"Of course I'll come. I'm saying only, child, that you must put your faith in God's mercy and not in me."

This was not his first outing but it was his longest. He could feel the eyes watching from behind the lace curtains and he wondered why no one came to a door to greet him. But as he crossed Gonagal's Bit one door and then another opened and the women smiled shyly at him, waved or murmured greetings.

Yet there had been less enthusiasm in the greetings than he had expected and he wondered if this was because of his companion. Was there an element of jealousy that he had Janey Anderson at his side?

Wee Hughie was sitting up in a chair in the kitchen, strangely shrunken, face diminished to eyes and mouth. He started to rise as McMaster entered, but the preacher motioned him to sit back.

"No need to get up, no need at all."

The two men stared at each other for long moments, a tacit shock in each face at the appearance of the other. Janey broke the silence.

"Would the Minister like a cup of tea?"

"No, no. Nothing . . ."

From the other room the baby began to cry and Janey left the two men together.

"Won't you take a seat, Mr McMaster? I'd rise to get one but – "

"I'll manage fine. Just fine."

There was another uneasy silence which Hughie broke: "You're better yourself, then? And the Movement?"

"It's been quiet . . . quiet. It's been very quiet."

McMaster spoke almost to himself. The sound of the baby's crying faded.

"Well now," said the preacher with an almost visible effort, "Let's see what the good Lord has to say about your affliction. He'll hardly want you to be lying there when there's that much work to be done."

He knelt at the side of Wee Hughie's chair.

"Let us pray. Merciful God, look down now on thy servant, Hugh Macatammany . . ."

*

The plans for the church were before the Executive Committee and very fine they looked on paper.

"I still reckon there should be a house attached," said Brek. "Where's he going to live if there's no house? Why spoil it all for lack of another few hundred?"

"He's always been terrible set against living in a house. Didn't he live here from the start in his wee bit tent . . ."

The Committee argued pleasurably with the knowledge of the two thousand pounds they had already in the bank warming their hearts. There was no doubt in their minds that a built church of brick and plaster would alter things. It would demonstrate that the Movement had really arrived. Bricks and mortar confessed the ultimate respectability.

"Just the same, how are we to get the building done without himself knowing? A church isn't like a tent. It can't be thrown up overnight."

"Leave that to me," Brek insisted. "Just you leave that to me. I have a little plan to deal with that."

The conference went on. There were pleasant little details to be decided as to where the pulpit would be and what sort of lighting, and how many seats. The Committee was enjoying itself. And when the time came it would enjoy paying out the money.

*

"No," said the Bogeyman softly. "Positively and definitely no."

There were sour looks on the faces of the men about him in his own room.

"Look, Bogey, how long are you going to let him go on?" demanded Pontius Pilette. "Sure, the place is open now. They don't have guards on the tent any more. I think they've even taken off the peelers. This last week we haven't any spotted any around at all. We could go in there and deal with him and be clear before a soul knew we were at it."

"You could," agreed the Bogeyman. "You could do that all right. And put the city in flames the next day. Not that it

268

would be any the worse of a burning – but that's not how we do it."

"Since you've got so pally with his lordship," Pilette said savagely, "you've gone very quiet, Bogey. Has he bought you over? You won't be the first."

The Bogeyman did not answer verbally. Instead he shot forward in his wheel chair at frightening speed and one of his hands gripped Pilette's right wrist while the other shot up inside his raincoat.

"Pontius, you're getting above yourself," he growled. "You're thinking altogether too largely."

From the other there came a croaking cry as the Bogeyman's hand squeezed tightly.

"They say you were thinking of getting married," breathed the Bogeyman. "Maybe there won't be much point in the ceremony."

He squeezed again and, as Pilette cried aloud in grey-faced pain, the Bogeyman threw him backwards. He collapsed on the floor, groaning, his hands tucked between his legs.

The Bogeyman rolled back to where he had been before the interruption.

"Two cocks don't ever crow on the same dunghill . . . McMaster we don't touch because there is no need to touch him."

"You're joking!"

"McMaster," said the Bogeyman implacably, "is finished. It doesn't show yet but he's finished. He's like a tree standing with its inside rotted away. The first gale that comes along will bring him down. But if it's action you want, I've a little operation that might please you all."

*

"McMaster?" mused the news editor. "No. I don't think so. I've had enough of McMaster recently. And anyhow he's not making news any more, is he? If you ask me, that accident he had has taken some of the stuffing out of him."

269

Tod Milligan shrugged as he stood before a littered desk in a drab room that seemed never to have been cleaned because fresh accumulations of paper piled up more quickly than they could be dumped in the wastepaper baskets.

"I still think he's worth a piece," he insisted. "This march he's planning – "

"I doubt if there'll be a march," said the news editor. "From what I hear, support's been falling off from Mungo McMaster like dandruff from a reporter's hair."

"Well, most of his people are working now," Tod pointed out. "On the big one. You can't expect them to give up the chance of overtime after all the hard years. If they're working they can't be at meetings, can they?"

"Or march either," growled his superior. "If the march comes off it'll be a flop. I don't think he'll even start it. Anyway, I'd sooner have some new material on the big one. Go down to the Yard and see if you can dig anything new out of the hats there. Maybe something on the furnishing or perhaps they've got some revolutionary new equipment. Forget McMaster."

Tod Milligan had bought a car with the money he had made from the *Express*. It was a little Morris, battered but serviceable. He was in a strict minority in the city at the time. Press wages did not run to cars. This one even made him a profit, for he could charge taxi fares on his expenses account on occasion.

The looming shape of the Big One was brooding over the Yard, over all Ballymacarett, a great, red-leaded giant which had sprung into a skyline feature with amazing speed. Already some of the finishing trades were at work within the hull – painters, panellers, woodworkers.

Like scurrying ants men hurried up and down and along the stagings that surrounded the hull now at every level. Girders and drillers and milling machines shrieked in a hundred tones.

Milligan knew a foreman shipwright called McCusker and he sought him out.

"I doubt there's nothing for you here, Mr Milligan," said McCusker. "Barring maybe you're looking for tips for the grus."

He was himself a greyhound man, a breeder and a shrewd backer also. He gave the reporter a tip for a certainty the next night. But so far as a story went he was barren.

However, Milligan's time was not completely wasted. He recognised some of a gang working with timber near a staging.

"I've seen those lads before," he said. "Playing hurley."

McCusker looked troubled, knowing the implication of Milligan's words. Hardly any Protestants played Gaelic games like hurley.

"Look, Mr Milligan, the way things is, there's work for all now. I'm not asking a man if he comes from the Falls or the Shankill. Nor no-one else. If they'll work they're in."

Did McMaster know this? Milligan wondered as he drove from the Yard. How had he reacted? On the other hand, would it be responsible journalism to go now and ask him his opinion? Would it not count as inflaming the situation?

But then, if it was a fact he would be failing his duty not to learn about it. And, worse, he might be losing money he thought sourly as he drove to Gonagal's Bit.

Nothing seemed to have changed here since his last visit. The Tabernacle still stood. The houses about the Bit were as silently uncommunicative as ever, pipeclayed steps, washed windows – and no one visibly looking out.

It was round the Tabernacle that it seemed to Milligan he noticed the first indications of a sort of decay. Weeds were growing in the paving which had been set with such loving care around the big tent. The plants in the little flower beds had died or were dying. There was a feeling of neglect, of an inner uncertainty now given outer expression.

Yet McMaster himself did not seem greatly changed. He walked a little stiffly, for his back still hurt. He greeted the newspaperman warmly and there seemed no diminution of the harsh strength of his features.

Milligan had decided not to put his question directly after all. He fenced a little, asked some general questions.

"Well now, Mr Milligan, you ask how my campaign goes." McMaster brooded at the door. "I must tell you that in these days it goes less well than before. There are times when I feel I have unleashed a demon to devour me."

He gestured towards the Yard, towards the soaring stem of the Big One rearing above the rooftops.

"The ship," he said. "The ship. I hear dark tales of this ship. My ears tell me that with their hammers and their drills and paint-brushes and saws they are desecrating the Sabbath. Six days shalt thou labour, Mr Milligan. But they are labouring the seventh day also and surely God must withhold his blessing from the work."

"But don't they have a contract date they must meet?" Milligan asked. "Even with overtime during the week they'll never be ready for the launching day if they don't work on Sundays."

McMaster's powerful jaws clamped tight and the muscles stood out in ridges.

"For sinning there is always an excuse," he spat. "But here we have no ignorant men. They know the wrong they do. They work on the day when they should worship . . ."

Or, put another way, Milligan thought cynically, they did not attend McMaster's meetings. They did not contribute to the collections. Poor attendances would put back the date for the building of the church.

Milligan did not ask about the church. He knew it was intended to be a surprise, though he had a suspicion that McMaster must already know about it.

"But it is little wonder that my people are corrupted," McMaster growled, "When they are yoked unequally with the unbelievers, how shall they not be tainted? Woe to the shepherds that set the black sheep amid the white, that bring into the folds the very wolf that destroys, that poisons the sweet water of their innocence by communion with dark practices . . . There are children of Rome on that ship, Mr

Milligan. Dupes of the priests and that great whore of Rome. They spread their poison amid my flock. They corrupt. And if they are not weeded out then surely all shall be destroyed."

His eyes glowed sombrely in their deep sockets. Milligan's question was answered.

McMaster knew all right. And it remained only to learn how he would act.

CHAPTER THIRTY-SIX

"Well now, Bogey," said the Earl of Dail petulantly rather than angrily. "This is rather much. It is really very much rather much. In fact, I'd say it's a bit off."

Dail Castle had the appearance of having been struck by a hurricane. The furniture in the long and gracious drawing-room was shattered. Carpets had been ripped up. The portraits of the Earl's ancestors on the walls had been decorated with moustaches where inappropriate or more simply slashed across.

Paint had been splattered elsewhere and great slogans scrawled on the walls, also in paint:

"Up Ireland! . . . Hang the Queen . . . Erin abu . . . The Hell with Carson . . . Craigavon is a big fat bastard . . ."

Cupboards had been smashed open and a sideboard of drink had been opened and rifled – perhaps as a start to the festivities. And this was only one room. The rest of the house was in a similar disorder. Dail's butler was in hospital, having, he claimed, put up a desperate struggle. A gardener was nursing his bruises and a housemaid was still having hysterics.

The Countess of Dail was in a nursing home, suffering from shock.

"A broken window or two is one thing," bemoaned the Earl. "But this . . . How could you do it?"

"I had to give my people something to stir them up," the Bogeyman answered equably. "They've been growing restless. They think I've been getting too friendly with you – I

274

was merely restoring confidence. And no one's been really hurt, you know. It might have been a good deal worse. I stopped them smashing anything valuable. You can see that."

"But it's such a bloody mess!" Dail protested. "Some of them have shit all over the place too. Really, it's disgusting. I think I should have you arrested."

"Proof would be hard to come by. My alibi is quite cast-iron. My only connection with the raid is that I told you I was connected. That wouldn't stand up in law."

"Why did you tell me? I don't think I'd have guessed. I mean, we are friends, aren't we? – in an odd sort of way."

Dail's ruddy, farmer's face showed perplexity even more than anger.

"A very odd sort of way. I interest and disgust you. You interest and infuriate me. I told you because I wanted to see what you'd say. I thought you'd have been even more furious. I suppose you would have been if you'd been here yourself, experienced the affair."

"Someone would have been killed quite probably. I learned my shooting on pheasants. I'd try peasants too."

"Quite. In fact, you'd have enjoyed it. I'd have lost some men. I might even have been identified."

The Bogeyman licked his lips reflectively as he gazed around the room and remembered.

*

The organisation of the castle was known to the Bogeyman, as also the fact that the Earl would be absent that night. Most of the staff would be at a local dance. Quite simply his men had driven to the castle's front door, knocked politely and, when the butler answered, had swarmed in.

The butler's resistance had been very brief and the housemaid who was the only other member of the staff at the castle that night had been silenced very quickly by having her dress pulled above her head and tied in a knot.

The Bogeyman himself had supervised the destruction, enjoying in particular the desecration of the portraits which Pilette handed down to him and then returned to the walls. Deliberately the Bogeyman had allowed his men a thoroughly adolescent expression of destruction.

He wanted nothing at all that would point to a superior mind at work. Not that he expected anyone to think of him as the instigator, not even Tony. He wanted to be sure.

Just the same, the gardener's interruption was a surprise he had not expected. The gardeners – there were two – had cottages at the foot of the long driveway. This one, perhaps, was courting the housemaid. If so, he had plenty of opportunity to further his suit.

When the men took him he was thrust into the same deep linen press as the half-naked girl. The Bogeyman trusted that he appreciated the gesture.

Despite their violence the attackers had been quite silent except for an occasional tinkle of breaking glass or a laugh. There was nothing to alarm the Countess, sleeping in the castle's principal bedroom on the floor above. That she took sleeping pills the Bogeyman knew from Dail – not a lot, two a night, Nembutal, very regularly.

This was, the Bogeyman had always thought, the most revealing thing the Earl had ever said about his menage. What sort of a man would leave a beautiful wife to a drugged sleep every night? And what sort of a wife would seek it.

Now the Bogeyman made his way up the broad, heavily carpeted staircase, lifting himself from tread to tread like some stunted anthropoid ape, balding head gleaming in the light from the landing. In the drawing-room his men were drinking the Earl's brandy and, he trusted, keeping a good look-out. He would cut their hearts out if they failed him now. Not that anyone else was likely to come. But he liked to feel sure.

The bedroom was a surprise. He had expected something Victorian like the drawing-room; massive, carved furniture, rich hangings, lush carpets. Instead this room was delicately

276

designed in a style that was subtly French, old French, that is, not modern. He had seen pictures of a room like this in a book and he tried to place the period in his mind. Louis Quinze?

He paused in the doorway taking it in; the double bed with a half canopy and gauzy drapes pulled back to the bed-head. Beside it there was a small, fragile table. A slight dressing-table that yet contrived to bear a looking-glass that seemed far too heavy held a sparse array of neatly laid-out beauty preparations. There was a small wardrobe. There was a smoky grey carpet, insubstantial in colour and texture.

The light beside the bed was on and he could see clearly as he paused at the door, his gaze led artfully, inevitably, to the bed and to the figure on it.

There was something here of the Fairy Princess, he thought. Sleeping beauty waiting to be kissed into wakefulness. Yet there was an almost self-conscious awareness about the pale slim figure on the bed, as if it knew there would be a watcher, as if it had prepared itself for the moment, made itself ready for the scene.

He rolled forward silently in his chair and halted at the bedside. Whatever Tony might say or think, he decided, she was beautiful, this Countess of Dail. With her face relaxed in sleep and whatever asperity Tony found in eyes or lips lost altogether in slumber, she had an ethereal beauty that touched him.

There was no trace of facecream or night aids to beauty on her skin. Her hair spread across an embroidered pillow like spun gold.

And the fact of that single pillow in this double bed with its careful silk damask overlay told the Bogeyman almost more than he needed to know.

The woman breathed slowly and evenly, lying on her back, not stirring under his scrutiny. The Bogeyman thought of the Earl of Dail and the smile that slowly curled his lips had much of compassion in it.

He touched a hand that lay on top of the coverings and

there was no reaction. She was soundly asleep, drugged or not.

Slowly and carefully he pulled back the coverings.

The Countess lay naked.

This was strange. In his experience those who slept naked were either those who could not afford night clothes or those with a well developed erotic sense. Nudity in bed was a silent invitation to sex.

Or was there here an element of narcissium? He had expected, indeed he had been certain, that he would find the Countess wearing a neck-high, long-sleeved nightdress. And yet she was naked. Did Tony know that his lady slept naked? Had she slept that way while they still slept together? There was an interesting basic contradiction here, thought the Bogeyman, as he gazed avidly and with an almost artistic appreciation at the pale, smooth, slender body he had exposed.

The shoulders were narrow and sloping and yet the breasts were full and hard, with small, pointed pink nipples, youthful and innocent, touching almost. Though the waist was as slender as any he had seen, the hips spread fairly. The hair beneath had a red-gold glint above the long thighs and in all the body he saw only one faint blemish. On one knee the skin was rather red and puckered.

He wondered if the Countess did a lot of gardening. Kneeling could bring puckering like that . . . But then, people knelt in prayer as well as at work. Daughter of a bishop – did that explain anything?

The Bogeyman's powerful, well-tended fingers fell across the body, stroked a breast softly, teased at a nipple and then moved slowly down the belly.

Nor did his gaze leave the delicate oval of the face this while. His luminous eyes were alert for the first return to wakefulness of the Countess of Dail.

It would not matter perhaps if she did scream. But if she was going to scream he wanted to know first.

He was puzzled a little. For now the body was itself answer-

278

ing the touch of his hand. It was responding. And yet a sleeping body, a drugged body, should know no responses. Had his caress become incorporated into the fabric of a dream? Was she, in fact, less asleep than she seemed?

The thrusting, imperative, searching caresses went on – probing, exciting, insistent. And a body controlled by no mind at all responded yet more fervently.

On the finely-moulded lips, fuller than the Bogeyman had expected, a little smile had grown. The woman's breathing had changed. Sometimes there were almost imperceptible murmurs in her throat.

The Bogeyman heaved himself upward and the bed began its age-old, rhythmic creak.

*

"A good turn!" Dail's voice hardly forced itself from his lips as he looked at the photographs. "You were doing me a good turn!"

"Tony – "

"Don't call me that!"

"Your lordship, then . . . You want an heir; you want a divorce. My good turn has provided you with both, I imagine. The heir must be a virtual certainty. And the divorce – Well, would the countess dare to let these pictures be shown in court?"

"But it was rape! It must have been. She would never have – "

"Does it look like rape? Look, she's smiling . . . She's actually taking the initiative in this one . . ."

The Earl of Dail was almost literally stunned as he looked at the photographs the Bogeyman had taken. The bedroom was unmistakable. So was the Countess. In each picture she showed up very clearly, either her face or a distinctive birth-mark in the small of her back.

Less easily identifiable were her companions – for there was certainly more than one. They were bodies only, with scarcely an identifiable facial feature to be seen. The Bogey-man had been most careful.

"You took these pictures? She let you?"

"She was otherwise occupied – as you can see."

"I can't believe it! She's a . . . a lady."

The Bogeyman laughed uncontrollably. The Earl's statement had so many different risible aspects that it was some time before he stopped laughing.

"You can't deny I meant well," he said at last. "Though frankly, we didn't find her frigid."

A host of emotions had crossed Dail's broad red face. Anger had been the most frequent. Anger remained.

"I think I'll kill you, you little bastard," he decided.

"You can't kill us all. You don't even know us all. There's bound to be someone left. Or you'll think there is. And, of course, there are the negatives of the pictures."

Dail frowned ominously. "Blackmail, is it?"

"How could you suspect me of that? I've told you – I wanted to do you a good turn, in my own warped way."

Dail's face became impassive. "I think I begin to understand. The pictures are fakes. You've got someone to do a sort of graft, put my wife's face onto these . . . things. Yes. They have to be fakes. A joke. Not in the best of taste, but a joke. Well, I can take a joke I suppose. Yes, I can laugh with the next man. A clever, malicious joke in the very worst of taste, but a joke just the same. Well – we'll have a drink on this joke of yours."

The Bogeyman marvelled a little as he watched Dail in the actual process of deceiving himself. He had not supposed it could be done so quickly, and he was fairly certain that the processes of time would make the Earl believe that it had, in fact, been an elaborate joke.

He noticed, however, that Dail pocketed the prints and made no effort to return them.

PART FIVE

CHAPTER THIRTY-SEVEN

The ship mocked Mungo McMaster when he crossed the
Lagan to gaze at it from his accustomed bollard. It reared
up to the low grey clouds that hang so often over Belfast,
propped by its gantries, surrounded by its cocoon of scaffolding and staging, served by its myriad swarm of workers.

It was like an evil temple, McMaster thought. The workmen were its servitors, drawn from the true faith to a worship
of Mammon or Moloch. As they streamed in and out of the
sally ports the workers were the children that the great
monster was spawning. Once it had been the symbol of
McMaster's success, the ultimate achievement of The Movement. But where was The Movement now?

He glowered across the busy river at the steel and iron
incubus that now tormented him. He hated it. Whole-
heartedly, furiously, he hated it. Like Frankenstein he had
created a monster and now the monster was destroying him.

Of the destruction he had no doubt. He could feel it
within him.

The evidence of the destruction was in his meetings. Once
there had been thousands gathered on Gonagal's Bit. His
prayers had been echoed tumultuously. The sound of the
psalms had thundered across the city.

Now the crowds had dwindled. So swiftly they had
dwindled. It seemed to him that in the few days he had lain
in his bed with his back plastered his congregation had been
stolen from him. An outsider would not have seen it so. An
outsider would have seen that there were still hundreds

gathered there to worship and to listen. But an outsider would have been less aware that the gathering was now almost entirely women. There were a few men still, the old, the ailing, the ones who could not get work.

But the men who were the heart of The Movement were no longer there, the young, the fit, the men with drive and fervour. Those men were working on the Big One, part and parcel of that great monstrous ship that was destroying him.

They were working and could not attend the meetings. Or they had just finished work and were too tired to come, or had not washed . . . or worse still, had some pagan pleasure in their minds – a football match or the cinema or a dance, or else they were papering the house or going on a trip to the country or down to the sea at Bangor or Donaghadee.

The excuses were legion. The men had money in their pockets now and the pleasures of years to make up. They had no more time for The Movement which had brought them the money.

"What's the call for marching now?" even the Executive Committee members had asked McMaster. "Sure we have what we wanted. Didn't our marching get us the ship? Didn't we do what we set out to do?"

Only months before there would have been no 'we' about it. It would have been 'what you set out to do'. But now the past had begun already to blur in their minds. McMaster was no longer the lone prophet, the leader. Somehow it had become a co-operative enterprise in which each was elevated to equality with the preacher.

Success had destroyed McMaster and his cause. Success which was represented by that growing, flaunting hull across the river. Every blast of the Yard whistles was a taunt to him.

*

Mungo McMaster went almost unacknowledged as he stalked back up the quay, across the Queen's Bridge and homeward. There were a few still to greet him obsequiously but these were almost all women. And most of them were older women at that.

Was it to come back to this after all; as he had started so to end – the pastor of a few idle, ageing housewives?

For even the girls' band was disbanding now. The girls too had their work in the mills, making upholstery for the Big One, embroidering bedclothes for the ship, swallowed too by the monster. There were hardly any girls now at the practices, neither pipers nor drummers nor drum majorettes. Everything was going, everything collapsing. And the ship was to blame, the monster, the Big One.

Dulcie McMaster saw the mood of dejection on her man as he stalked across Gonagal's Bit and her heart was twisted. His gloom was her gloom, his suffering was her suffering. And yet, it was in her mind, all that was happening now was working to return her husband to her.

"The dinner's ready," she greeted him submissively. "It's but sausages. Will I serve them?"

"Aye," he grunted. "Aye. Do that."

As she followed him into the tent she had an impulse to throw her arms about him, clutch him close. She wanted to shield him – and at the same time she wanted him exposed to the arrows that were still to wound him, still to bring him back to her.

*

"He's no better," Janey Macatammany accused McMaster. "He's no better at all. You couldn't have tried."

Almost reluctantly she opened the door and let the preacher into the house. The baby was crying and there was a smell of potatoes burned in the pan.

Wee Hughie made less effort to rise this time than he had the last. But he forced a hopeful smile to his shrunken face.

"The doctor was saying rest," he said. "He said if I'd plenty of rest of the heart would take up."

He slumped deeper into the chair.

"They were in – some of them," he said apathetically. "They said it was sort of quiet with The Movement now."

"Sheep stray," growled McMaster. "Yes, the flocks stray and heed not the words of the shepherd nor his calls. And yet when the wolf howls by night they gather closer."

"No marches nor nothing," sighed Wee Hughie. "It's drastic right enough. Oh, it's drastic. I just wish I could get up and out and give them all a bit word, I'd tell them a thing or two . . . Deserting you after all you've done for them. They had nothing when you came here. You've given them work, self-respect, everything. And now they've got it all they turn their backs on you. I'd tell them all right. I'd tell them."

A faint flush of colour came to his cheeks and Janey came forward.

"You're getting excited. The doctor said you weren't to." She glared at McMaster with almost open animosity.

"Maybe you'd better leave him now. You'll not do him any good making him excited. He's not fit for it."

"You'll not speak til the Minister like that!" Wee Hughie said sharply. "Mind your manners, girl . . . Mr McMaster will bide as long as ever he wants. Sit you down again, Minister. Sit you down. Janey'll bring you a cup of tea."

"No, no, Hughie, I mustn't stay. I mustn't stay. I have many more still to see. I have my rounds to do. I can't wait too long. I'll just say a wee prayer with you for the good Lord to cast his eye on your affliction and to call to his mind you were always a trusty servant. Then I'll go along."

"Aye," said Janey. "Do that."

And it was not clear whether she referred to the prayer or the going along.

*

"Loss of confidence," said Levine didactically, "is loss of all. Surely you remember Quincy, the stand-off half? He had the best pair of hands in Ireland, never known to drop a pass or a catch. Then he had a bad match against England, as anyone could do. One of your chaps wrote it up on the lines that Quincy had lost his confidence. Quincy read the article – and believed it. He started dropping passes, missing tackles. Psychologically he went to pieces. He had lost confidence. He didn't think he could do it any more. He was even about to be dropped by his club side . . . Oh. Would you look at that bastard? He's offside a mile. The bloody referee's blind – "

Levine and Milligan were in the stand at the Ravenhill Rugby football ground, watching the match between Ireland and England. The white jerseys of England were very much in the ascendancy. The referee was less blind than Levine had suggested. He saw the offside, awarded a penalty and Ireland scored.

"I always think it very odd," Milligan remarked, "that you can get stout Orangemen to put on a green shirt and become as Irish as anyone for this game – and yet go off to a Lodge meeting after the game and thump the Nationalists."

"It's a British game after all," Levine countered.

"But more than half the team comes from the South."

"West Britons, Southern Protestants, remnants of the Pale, old Ascendancy men, or would-be's . . . Anyway, I was saying about Quincy. He got a knock on the head, concussion, played on – played a blinder, a real blinder, didn't drop a catch or anything. In fact, he scored twice. He didn't remember anything about it afterwards. When he was unconscious he didn't know he'd lost his confidence so he still had confidence, played as well as ever."

"He was cured then, was he?"

"Only for that game. Next time out he remembered about losing his confidence and no one had the decency to kick him in the head. He quit. That's what McMaster should do."

"McMaster?"

"McMaster. That's who we were talking about, wasn't it? Oh, very neat! Oh, lovely play! Did you see that side-step? Damn it, if only he was playing for Ireland!"

The cheering rose for an English score, English cheering

with a solid round of Irish clapping, appreciation – if reluctant, for a skilful enemy. Milligan and Levine clapped dutifully.

"McMaster's lost his confidence and his people have lost confidence in McMaster. Did you know that wee fellow in the long coat who used to be at all the meetings? He's ill. McMaster tried the faith healing on him and it failed. Word of a thing like that goes around. The Movement, I'd say, is as near finished as makes no matter. Unless McMaster can find some way of regaining his confidence. That's what I told Pamela – "

"Pamela? Pamela Hendrick?"

"Who else? – Oh, I didn't tell you I'd seen her. I had a few drinks one night . . . Tod, don't look at me like that! Sure, you haven't bothered with her in months."

"I didn't know I was looking at you in any particular way. I was just surprised. I mean, it is a little while since I saw her. I didn't think she was . . . well, your type."

There was an evident cold jealousy in Milligan's eyes, a jealousy whose irrationality he admitted to himself. He had no proprietory rights over Pamela Hendrick and strictly speaking had no interest in her. They had drifted apart and that was that. Yet he still felt jealous. Did a man never get a woman entirely out of his system?

"We were talking about McMaster, anyhow, not Pamela. It's been very interesting, you know. I think I could write something quite good about him. His rise and fall have been a microcosm in their way of Ulster life. If it wouldn't be too wordy I might even try a full-length epic. Blank verse . . . a little high-pitched, a little exaggerated. I think I'd give him a fancier wife . . . Give him a lot of women. If he didn't have them, that is. What do you think?"

"About the epic or the women?"

"Well, there's always been a strong rumour that he's a horny old devil when he gets the chance. He did attract women. There's no doubt about that."

"You're talking about him as if he were already dead."

"As a force, I think he is. Who was it described the Front Bench at Westminster as a lot of extinct volcanos? Oh, what a kick! They're going to score. Oh, damn – Oh, what a bloody fool of a man!"

An Irish attack had developed fierily and then petered out on the English line.

"You should have asked Pamela about McMaster," Milligan said carefully. "She might have told you what women feel about him. I often thought . . ."

"She did," Levine answered. "She did."

The game descended into interesting turbulence and McMaster was forgotten again.

CHAPTER THIRTY-EIGHT

Pamela Hendrick was annoyed with herself now that she had come to the Tabernacle. She had forgotten just how meanly extempore it all was, the mud that feet carried in from the ground outside, the sweating, soot-stained canvas that was beginning to fray in places, the lack of privacy since the tent walls were no barrier to sound.

What had been the magic here before? Where had it gone? What power had evaporated from Mungo McMaster? Now, seated, he looked merely a shabby, ageing, scarecrow of a man. His wife looked even more of a tramp.

"It was good of you to come, Miss Hendrick," The voice still had its sonorous timbre and yet some quality was missing.

"I thought . . . Well, we've been neighbours in a way. At least, my father was, when he was giving his lectures."

"I heard that his course had ended." McMaster showed no elation at news which should have meant that more of his congregation would be freed. "I had supposed he would stay in Belfast."

"The Union's sending him to Liverpool. I suppose in a week or two – we don't know yet."

Dulcie McMaster sat as always in a corner that was less physical than mental. Her faded blue eyes surveyed the girl and wondered. Young, so young still, strong, eager yet for life. Covertly she glanced at Mr McMaster. There was a hint of renewed life about him, as if the presence of the girl was stirring some deep source.

"Your father's ways are not my Father's ways," McMaster boomed. "Yet I wish him well. Will we see you again before you go?"

"The young lady's not going yet," Dulcie flustered as she rose. "She'll want a cup of tea . . ."

She clattered in her little cupboard, put on a kettle to boil.

"No, no. Really. I've got so much to do – "

Dulcie followed the girl to the door of the outer tent, sad, shrunken more than ever.

Her eyes were trying to convey some silent message that her lips could not utter. *You can help him. You – young, lovely, eager, loins, a body. You can help him. Help him.*

Pamela read the message and knew that once she would have answered it. She knew, too, that now such help was beyond her; that the gaunt figure within the tent had no more power to rouse or even interest her.

Her high heels squelched in the mud as she hurried away across Gonagal's Bit.

Dulcie McMaster's gaze turned from the back of the retreating girl to the looming shape of the Big One over the rooftops. Mr. McMaster had brought it to life and now it was taking the life from Mr. McMaster. And yet perhaps it was giving Mr McMaster back to herself. She did not know whether to hate the ship or love it.

*

"As to our brother in God," said the Reverend Roger Simms, "I fear, Richard, that he is falling on increasingly evil times. The salt hath lost its savour and the virtue hath gone out of the man."

With satisfaction he sipped a sherry which had not lost its savour.

"The Movement is one with Nineveh and Tyre," he added. "Do you agree, Richard?"

Richard St Leger shrugged. Local affairs were drifting from his interest. He had applied for a teaching post in an

English public school and he had been told that his prospects were excellent.

"This march on Saturday," he answered. "It should tell the tale, one way or the other."

"I thought the Council had already told the tale. I suspected that McCullough, like the Bourbons, would neither forgive nor forget. He has certainly gauged his time well. Hardly a hand was lifted to stop his men when they came again to start on the playground. I understand that next week they propose to demolish the – er – Tabernacle."

"It will depend on what happens on Saturday," the curate suggested. "If McMaster can recover some of his earlier fire he might even now get his Movement going again."

"I doubt it. Much though one decries at times the sheer, monolithic immobility of one's church organisation there is no doubt that the very fact of its existence tends towards a permanence that a more *ad hoc* system can never reach. The Movement was altogether too much dependent on the spirit and personality of one man. When McMaster became diminished so the Movement lost momentum. It is too much for one man to bear."

"I rather thought our own organisation was based on one man," said the curate drily, and received a frown for his impertinence. "I feel rather sorry for him – McMaster, I mean."

"I also. I indeed also. It must be humiliating to have the council workmen preparing to demolish one's church . . ."

A little smugly he glanced around his own snug room, reflecting on the impossibility of such a thing happening to any Anglican clergyman.

"He was a man of the moment," St Leger said. "He started something. He put life – and hope – into the place."

"He was the man of the moment, but the moment has passed. Now there will be children's swings and roundabouts where he used to preach. I would say that must be almost crushing."

"He won't think 'Suffer little children . . .?' "

292

His curate's levity brought a fiercer frown from Simms.

St Leger added: "Anyway, I understand that The Movement has already collected enough money to build a church for McMaster. The loss of that waste ground can't be so important."

"Oh, I hadn't heard that . . . Even so, to McMaster it must be a matter of chagrin at the least that his faithful followers did not turn up in their hosts to protect him from the workmen, to guard their Tabernacle."

"Perhaps he told them not to."

Simms put the sherry decanter away without offering the second glass which had been in his mind. Outside, a coal lorry rumbled past, hauled by a dark, massive Clydesdale.

"I feel a sense of doom about the McMaster situation – a dramatic, inexorable march of events. I feel a curious sorrow for him – and yet I can't say I ever liked him or his doctrines. Oh well. The accounts, I think, the accounts."

The routine of the parish proceeded on its way.

*

In his bed Mungo McMaster wrestled with terrible thoughts. The iron bedstead creaked to his movements, his brief flings from side to side, the involuntary kicking of his heels.

"Deserted!" he accused the silent tent top. "My God, why has Thou deserted me?"

There was anger in him, an accusing, comprehensive rage that began with God and ran down the scale to almost everyone he knew, everyone who had betrayed and deserted him.

He thought of the men and women of The Movement who had been so keen to march beneath his banner but who had left it when their petty material objects were attained.

"Do they not know how much is yet to do?" he charged, speaking the words sometimes and sometimes only thinking them. "So much to do – and they have to fall aside. So much to do."

His gaunt face tightened and relaxed and tightened again in a waking nightmare fantasy.

The moon was full that night and it lay beyond the river, throwing its pale light across the shipyard and casting the shadow of the Big One onto the very roof of the Tabernacle in a narrow, truncated triangle like perhaps a great black phallic symbol or again like some soaring pulpit against the sky; the tallest pulpit that ever was.

The preacher's rage fell most of all on the ship that mocked him and even now showed its power as it reared over him in shadow form.

Silent and still at his side Dulcie McMaster could not follow his half-voiced ravings, the grunts, the cries. She knew only that McMaster suffered, that Mr McMaster needed comfort.

For hours it seemed to her she lay and waited and suffered with this tall man. That surging, bursting energy had never been stronger, never more in need of an outlet. If only that English girl had helped, she thought, or any girl. Something, someone was needed to absorb that furious, thrusting strength, some safety valve was surely needed or within the man some terrible explosion would take place.

Her hand stole across his chest, caressed gently, tried to soothe. He flung from her silently as if her hand had been red-hot.

She tried again, more stealthily, tried to bring her body to his, to achieve some sort of diffident union. She felt the muscles tighten on the long, hard body. Then his spade-like hands thrust her away angrily, rejected her proffered comfort, spurned her . . . and all in silence.

This was worse of all, that she should be spurned in silence and if she had been able any more to shed tears Dulcie McMaster would surely have wept then.

But there was no place for tears in this broken yet indomitable woman, not while McMaster needed her, even though he did not know his own needs.

Again she touched him, feeling his skin hot and harsh under her hand as if fever raged in him.

"Mr McMaster," she begged timidly. "Oh, Mr McMaster . . . will you not listen?"

He said nothing, and she took heart from this.

"You are a man," she said. "And though this is not spoken of, a man has his needs and his rights and they should not be denied him."

Still he did not reject the caress and the exploration of the worn hand.

"A man must have a woman even as David had his women and Solomon and Abraham who had their women and not always the women of their bed, either, but strange women. But there is no other woman here for you this night, Mr McMaster, and a wife has rights as well as a husband."

He was so still that she thought she had gained her point and, emboldened, she pulled her whole body close, sought for the troubled centre of his being, believed that she had won.

Then violently he threw her off with a sweep of his arms, threw her so that she fell from the bed, landed kneeling on the ground.

And as he did so he thrust himself upward, stalked towards her, towered over her like some great, threatening steeple.

"Women!" he thundered. "Will you come between me and my God? Cursed be ye, cursed and barren and of no account. Get thee hence that Satan spawned to trouble me. Get thee hence!"

But it was he who went, turning to the doorway, standing there and challenging the ship with his gaze, all thought crystallising at last into the one, clear, undeniable knowledge of what he would do, of what he must do.

"It is the will of God," he said alone in the moonlight. "Surely this is the will of God."

Still crouched by the bed and with the silent tears now streaming down her cheeks, Dulcie saw him outlined against the light and he was like a man she had never known.

296

"I'm glad we came," said the Bogeyman contentedly. "Yes, I'm very glad we came. This will be the grand finale. I feel it in my bones. I feel it. Like a Greek tragedy. There will be some tremendous denouement. There's bound to be."

"I doubt it," sniffed the Earl of Dail. "It'll be just another of this man's ranting meetings. There aren't even many people. We should have gone and had some girls. That would have been more in my line."

It did not seem strange to either of them that they should be together, that the events at Dail Castle had not driven a wedge of fierce hatred between them. The link which bound them – curiosity, friendship, the attraction of opposite magnetic poles, whatever it might be – was not to be dissolved by any incident. The Earl had, of course, been furious over the attack on the castle but either he was so detached from real feeling as to be incapable of rancour or else he considered a continuing relationship with the Bogeyman more important than his castle or his wife.

If anything, indeed, the pair were closer now than they had ever been and the Bogeyman had a strong suspicion that Milanda Dail had conceived, though this Tony had not mentioned.

The appearance of the child would be interesting. Whose heredity would be displayed in its features? A part of the Bogeyman's mind hoped that it too might be born legless, while a greater part wished genuinely that the Earl's heir might be a true Dail – physically at least.

It was very interesting, he thought, that it was only since that night that he had met the Countess socially; that Dail had actually introduced him to Lady Milanda.

The meeting had been prosaic, a cool smile, a shake of the hand from the Countess, a formal bow from the Bogeyman.

And yet beneath surface, what an interesting pattern of cross-currents existed. The rapist and the raped – with the husband smiling complaisantly over them. The Bogeyman regretted that he had no gift for the written word to transcribe that meeting on to paper, to delve into the thoughts that churned in every head.

Also it had pleased the Bogeyman to note that there now seemed a degree of intimacy, of warmth even, between the Earl and his Countess. This was new, or he presumed it to be new from Tony's earlier words.

Thus his own statement to Dail had been borne out. He had in fact done the man a favour. And of course his own men enjoyed that night, enjoyed it in every way. They still talked about it, and there was no longer any suggestion that he had been bought by the Earl.

His position had been cemented though it seemed to matter less to him now. Some of his own enthusiasm had left him and he wondered how much of this he could attribute to the decline of Mungo McMaster's star.

They were seated in the rear of Dail's Rolls Royce which was parked in one of the side streets that abutted on Gonagal's Bit. The car was positioned to get away quickly if any violence ensued and yet to give them a good view of all that happened – or as good a view as was possible over the increasing encroachment of Council equipment; the watchman's hut, the barrows, the lorries that awaited Monday and the final stage of the work on the playground which Councillor McCullough's enmity had expedited.

Amidst the gear, the gathering members of The Movement had less than their usual space and yet there was space free even so.

"Not more than about eight hundred I would say," the Bogeyman commented. "Perhaps a thousand."

"There are more in the side streets though," answered the Earl. "I expect they're waiting for the march to start before they join. Probably they don't like to get their feet muddy."

"Before, in his other marches, there wouldn't even have been room to park the car here," the Bogeyman insisted.

He opened the cocktail cabinet and took out two glasses. He poured brandy for himself and the Earl and sank back into the soft, West Country cloth of the upholstery with a sigh of contentment. This was really rather better than the theatre. There was more comfort, better drink – and the outcome of the play was less predictable.

An opening scene was already being played.

*

"Hughie," pleaded Janey Macatammany, trotting to keep up with her husband's brisk steps. "Will you for God's sake come home? You'll kill yourself."

Wee Hughie Macatammany walked the brisker, coat tails flapping, head erect and shoulders back.

"I must go," he said. "Now stop making an eejit of yourself. Away back home and mind the baby."

She tried to pull him to a halt.

"The doctor said any excitement, anything violent, you'd be dead in a flash. He said nobody would be able to do a thing for you."

Hughie turned away his head, a light in his eyes that did not come entirely from the street lamps.

"Arise, take up thy bed and walk. That's what he toul' me, two days ago. Arise, take up thy bed and walk. Me that had been lying all those weeks and not able to as much as wipe my arse. Take up thy bed and walk . . . and I did. I walked. He made me walk, Janey, the same as he made you right in the head again. I'll do his bidding. The Movement's

299

on its way again. Now away back to the baby and don't mind me."

*

"I heard," Milligan told Levine, "that he's planning to march on the shipyard, demand Sunday closing, and that they throw out the Papishes."

"He hasn't a pup's – either way," Levine answered. "He's got a big voice but money talks louder. They've got contract dates to meet. They need Sunday working. They need the Papishes, too. But it should be interesting . . . Have you got a cameraman here?"

"Two," answered Milligan. "Damn it, it's a cold night. We'd be better snug by the fire in a nice pub than here."

"And miss a story! I'm surprised at you, Tod Milligan. I thought a little discomfort would be nothing to Belfast's ace newshawk. I want to hear you phoning 'Hold the front page! – I've got a scoop!' "

"There'll be no scoop. All the papers have got men here. Maybe there won't even be a story."

Milligan felt gloomy for no particular reason. There was something about this night which was indefinably depressing and it was not only the light, cold drizzle that had moistened the pavements.

Levine, on the other hand, was quite cheerful.

"Look, the Committee men are coming out of the Tabernacle now. I don't see your friend, the Yank. What was his name – Brek?"

"He's catching the evening boat to Glasgow. I think there's a branch of The Movement starting there."

*

In fact, with some inner and unspoken regrets, Brek was now waiting at the Liverpool shed at Belfast docks, two suitcases before him and a large hogshide briefcase held in

300

his hand. His hand was unlikely to release its grip on the case, for the contents were some two thousand three hundred and twenty-seven pounds, the sum total of the Movement's financial reserves, the Church Money, the collections which had been wheedled or bribed or bullied from members and supporters.

Brek regretted taking this step. But he had been totally unable to get any response from McMaster to his veiled suggestions that there would be even more scope for the preacher's talents in the United States and, by implication, even more money for Brek.

Even now Brek could not be sure whether or not McMaster knew about the existence of the money. It seemed incredible that it could have been gathered without his knowledge. And yet the Committee had been very insistent that it was to be a surprise, that the Church keys were to be presented to the preacher 'out of the blue.'

"He must've had some angle I just never cottoned to," Brek thought. "He must've . . . Anyway, if he didn't know about it he's not missing anything."

He went aboard then with his luggage and sought out the bar.

The drinks he downed then were not to ease any qualms about taking the money. On that score he felt his conscience was clear. The money was there. The church would never be built. So why leave the money for some other shark to grab?

Brek had felt for weeks, perhaps months, that The Movement was doomed. Certainly since McMaster's fall he had been absolutely sure of that. He had seen the mounting indifference of the members and the preacher's own growing loss of confidence. Dissolution was just around the corner. Disaster was imminent.

Prudence dictated that he get out and get what he could. He was only surprised that no other Committee member had had the same thought. Or perhaps they had. Maybe they were just waiting.

From the bar he could see the towering mass of the Big One across the river. He lifted his glass in silent valediction. But the toast was to McMaster, not the ship.

"What a waste," he thought. "What a goddam, downright waste."

*

Mungo McMaster could feel the power flow back into him as he looked down from his little mount, from the pulpit above the sea of waiting faces. He could feel the strength there again, thrilling through his body, echoing in his voice.

And even if he had not felt it in himself he would have known it was there from the reactions of the men and women facing him.

At the beginning, when he first rose at his pulpit, they had been uneasy, withdrawn. There had even been a clear space immediately beneath him. So far had the rot gone, he marvelled. In former times there had been no space, scarcely an arm's length separating him from the nearest worshipper.

They had come with reluctance, they had come because the Committee had made them come. And the Committee had made them come only because he himself had called the Committee together, overcome their hesitations and their arguments – he and Wee Hughie, the first and most faithful.

Perhaps even, it had been the presence of Wee Hughie which had carried the day. For the sight of the little man on his feet, brought to his feet by McMaster when the doctors had said he was doomed to lie forever in a bed, was proof more than anything else that McMaster was himself again; that the power and the glory which had briefly deserted him were returned.

The Committee had been convinced (save only Brek) and the Committee had brought the others.

And even if all the straying sheep were not back in the fold, McMaster thought ecstatically, after this night's doings they would surely return.

As he began to speak his gaze was on his true enemy; on the huge, towering pulpit of steel that was the stem of the great ship.

Only rarely did he look down on the sea of faces, watch with an inner exultation how soon and how close they gathered about him.

"Beware the Devil when he shakes your hand, brethren. When Satan comes with gifts held out, yea, when he offers you the fatness of the earth and the richness that is therein, then is he most dangerous of all.

"For it is said truly that Satan is the great deceiver. I tell you he steals into a man's heart when that man knoweth not and his false gifts glitter as the sun shines in the sky and the stars beyond his reaching?

"Did not this Satan take Christ to the mountain top and lay out before him the countries of the world and the cities thereof and all the riches and bid him take them and bow down? Yea, did not Satan in his cunning offer all manner of richness and good things to eat and comely damsels and every corruption?

"So does he today. So he steals into our hearts and destroys our simplicities and takes men from God's ways to his way.

"Man shall not live but by the sweat of his toiling body and whence came that body but from God? Therefore must man obey God and believe on him. And he that doth not believe he shall be cast out. He shall be cast down into that great fiery furnace that awaits and he that fornicates with false gods, shall not he be scourged?"

The great gaunt body was growing more animated and the voice gathering still more power.

"Stripped naked you will be there in the sight of the Lord, yea, the men and the women and the children, naked to your bare, shivering, frightened skins as you that have whored with the false ones and kissed the golden gods you shall feel the lash and the sting. Upon your back, upon your belly, yea upon backside and frontside and every side will the lash fall and there is no part of your body so tender and so soft it will not feel that great terrible lash fall on it. You will scream aloud and beg for mercy and you will say you did not know.

"But the Lord will hearken not. He will gather up the thunder of his brows. He will look down on you.

" 'You did know,' He will answer. 'McMaster toul' you.' "

In his Rolls the Earl of Dail tried unsuccessfully to stifle his laughter.

"Shut up, Tony!" snapped the Bogeyman. "Don't you know that this is the voice of history as it is really spoken – ludicrous, irrational, immense?"

The Earl continued to hiccup as McMaster's voice dragged his listeners into the spell it wove, a spell that, as ever, had almost nothing to do with the words it said but everything to do with how they were said.

"... And yet there is still salvation. Yea, believe on me and I will bring ye yet to eternal life. Thus saith the Lord and I speak his words. Has he not hearkened to me? Oh, ye of little faith, has he not hearkened before? Do they not live who would have died? Do ye not work who were idle?

"Therefore ye will believe and follow me and do my bidding and set again the world on its paths to righteousness and deliverance ... Ye will follow me ... *March*!"

CHAPTER FORTY

Though far from his largest, this was perhaps Mungo McMaster's most impressive march. There was no band this time, no drum majorettes flaunting their thighs. There were no banners.

There were only men marching with McMaster leading the way and a lone Lambeg drum thundering out the step behind him.

"Broo-oo-oom . . . broo-oo-oom . . . broo-oo-oom . . ."

Because of Mungo McMaster's long stride it was a slow step and the shorter-legged were taking two paces for every one of his.

The column swung out onto the Newtownards Road and turned towards the city. Almost as many followed the marchers or walked beside them on the pavements as were in the roadway. The women did not march and older men soon began to tail off. But the rest kept moving, jostling the idlers from the pavements outside the pubs and chip shops and cafes.

Behind McMaster was the drummer and behind the drummer came the Committee, Wee Hughie in their midst, his face rapt as he marched proudly. Never once did he turn as Janey continued to call him from the pavement.

> "*Onward Christian soldiers,*
> *Marching as to war,*
> *With the Cross of Jesus*
> *Going on before . . .*"

Ahead of the column were the police and more constables flanked the marchers. Afterwards difficult questions were to be put to the police. Promotion for a few officers was gravely hindered. But in fact they could scarcely be blamed. They had no advance warning of McMaster's duplicity. They got no real chance to react before it was too late.

"Hey!" said a Committee member as McMaster swung abruptly right-handed into Station Street. "Didn't he say we were for the Ormeau Road?"

And indeed the route given to the police had indicated that the march would cross the Lagan and make for the Ormeau Park. All the police control was based on this.

No one could have guessed that McMaster would turn right and head directly for the shipyard.

But where McMaster led, his people would follow again. Implacably the column swung after the tall, scarecrow figure and before the Royal Ulster Constabulary could realise they had been duped, the damage was done.

Hundreds of men had already swung from the main road. And not a policeman was ahead of them to turn back the throng. Probably it was as well. No policeman, no man save McMaster himself, could have stopped these marchers now.

They passed the County Down Railway Station and the tramping feet picked up a new rhythm, words rose over the sound of their feet:

> "*On the green, grassy slopes of the Boyne,*
> *Where the Orangemen with William did join,*
> *Where they fought for our glorious deliverance*
> *On the green, grassy slopes of the Boyne . . .*"

And then they lit torches.

*

"The last time that happened," said Milligan grimly, "the rest of the city went black. Let's hope it doesn't happen again."

"I think you've got it wrong, Tod," Levine panted. "The lights went out first – and then the torches were lit."

"Either way, they're lit. And he's making for the Yard. That's plain enough. Lit torches and a shipyard . . . The mind begins to boggle at the possibilities."

They were brought to a halt just beyond the station. Twice as many people were trying to move along the street as it could take. They funnelled in and jammed. Only the central stream, the marchers themselves with their high-held, flaring torches were still in motion as the central current of a river moves always faster than the sides.

"Damn, I hope my photographer's getting this. It would be like him to have pissed off back to the office after the meeting. Try to push on . . ."

"It's no bloody good – "

They could hear the work still in progress in the Yard, the rattle of the riveting hammers and the screech of grinders as an obligato to the Orange songs.

"He's going to try to stop them working," Milligan forecast. "And if they don't there'll be one hell of a fight. Come on, let's get forward. The gate won't last long."

The gates had splintered and vanished by the time the reporter and the solicitor reached it. The tide of men still poured remorselessly through, still singing, still carrying their torches high.

Inside the Yard, there was more room. The crowd spread out. Now it was hard to see what was happening. It was hard even to pick out McMaster's tall figure.

And still they advanced, the steady tramp of the feet, the songs bearing them onward:

"*The Protestant Boys are loyal and true*
Though fashions are changing, the loyal are few.

"*When treason was rampant and traitors were strong,*
The Protestants rallied and stood by the Crown.
The Protestant Boys are true to the last,
Though cowards belie them when danger is past . . .

> *"While over our heads the old colours still waved,*
>   *When rapiers were bristling and bullets were whistling,*
>   *The Protestant Boys still carried the day . . ."*

It was plain beyond any doubt that Mungo McMaster and his marchers were heading for the ship. Singing their song, glassy-eyes, hypnotised by the voice and the beat of the drum and perhaps not knowing where it was they were heading, they marched behind McMaster towards the Big One.

The big man, the big ship, the inevitable conjunction was at hand.

*

A Rolls Royce may go where no other car can pass. In its proud bonnet, the silver nymph on the radiator, it carries its own cachet of authority.

No policeman even tried to halt Dail and the Bogeyman as the car purred forward through the tumult-filled street and past the shattered gates.

The police met a random, vicious crowd and because this was not an organised riot with visible directors and intelligible aims the police task was made the more difficult. Almost anyone was a target for a truncheon. Almost anyone was struck and bundled aside.

And the police themselves were getting as rough a handling as they had ever received; pummelled, kicked, stoned as they tried desperately to bring some sort of order to the streets, to bar the way to the reinforcing mob that surged and circled and drove all the time for the gates.

If the police had been together and if they had been ahead of what had become a mob they could have barred the way. But they were broken up. And they were working from behind. They were like a man trying to pull an eel from a hole in a rock. There was nowhere they could get a grip.

"I never did see a riot so closely," the Earl observed with

satisfaction. "Oh, my word! Did you see that? Oh, what a terrible thing to do to a peeler! Oh, my word!"

"Can't you go any faster?" the Bogeyman demanded of the driver. "Make directly for the ship – that's where he'll be. Make for the ship."

There was a feverish hunger on his face. This was the finale, he was sure. He intended to miss no moment of it.

And yet, after all, he was to miss it.

*

The lights were now as much in Wee Hughie Macatammany's head as in his eyes. They were strange lights of all colours that looped and whirled and merged in a confusion of shapes.

And yet through them it seemed to him that he still saw McMaster.

"The steps!" he cried. "He's mounting the steps! He's going straight up the steps to Heaven."

No one heard him, for he had no breath to speak loudly. The iron band about his chest saw to that. It was tightening all the time, making his breathing shorter and still shorter.

But then, why did he need to say anything? Could they not all see that bright and shining figure rise above them, mounting higher and higher to its due place.

He was sorry now, he thought, that he had sent Janey home so brusquely. It was not every night you saw a man mount the steps and go straight the way to Heaven. But she should never have run after him that way, following and calling and making him ashamed of her.

Still and all, maybe she was better out of this throng. They were packed awful close and maybe the ones on the ship would start throwing things, rivets and bolts and what came to their hands. She was better off at home that was sure. Home, and watching the wean. That was what a woman was for and giving a man a bit of comfort in his bed.

Man dear, he thought, but Mr McMaster would be giving

the strong words out in a minute or two. Up there where he belonged and giving them their hands to suck for the breaking of the Sabbath and . . . and all those other things he had said. He wouldn't be in their shoes when the Minister started on them.

His torch had gone out and when he tried to light it from another man's he found he could not hold it properly. His hands were numb and had no strength in them. His feet were cold, too. His feet were deathly cold like the time he was playing in the snow the year of the bad winter. He would have liked the torch lit just to warm his hands and feet.

The band around his chest grew tighter still, with a cold, hard strength that had astonishingly stopped the breath entering his lungs at all. He would have marvelled at this but for the sight of McMaster, so bright and shining above him and his hand held down for Hughie to step up and join him.

"Up here – " and it was a wonder how his voice carried – " up here you'll be, Wee Hughie . . ."

He could see McMaster quite clearly as he fell.

*

"Mister. Our mate's took bad. You'll need to help us."

No one waited for agreement. They pulled open the door of the Rolls and Wee Hughie's body was laid in gently on the West Country cloth.

Dail's protests started and finished in one breath.

"Brandy, Bogey," he said.

And the Bogeyman brought out the expensive brandy and tried to pour it between the pallid lips.

Then: "He's dead," he said sombrely.

*

Janey Macatammany told herself afterwards that she had known even as the knock came to the front door. But this was not true. She thought that this was Hughie returning and she was pickling in brine the words she would say to him as she opened the door.

"Are you the Widow Macatammany?"

Within, the baby began to whimper.

CHAPTER FORTY-ONE

At the Court of Enquiry the cause of the fire was never conclusively established. A very strong body of evidence suggested that it had been started by Mungo McMaster, deliberately or by chance.

But there had been so much random fire about the Yard, so many blazing torches apart from all the normal hazards of shipbuilding, that without direct evidence of an eye witness no one could state categorically that McMaster had himself lit the fire which was to destroy him.

Metaphorically he had lit that fire in Gonagal's Bit when he stirred up the spirits of the people he led, when he marched them for the last time.

But as to the physical beginnings of the fire, not a living soul could say.

Tod Milligan was a trained observer and he could not be sure. Sidney Levine was a solicitor and schooled to the knowledge of facts. He could not be sure either. There were men who thought they were sure until they entered the courtroom and found their recollections under the close examination of skilled lawyers. Then they also were less sure.

Looking back, Milligan was inclined to doubt if that gaunt preacher would embark on a course involving his own destruction. It had not been McMaster's style.

*

"Look – there he is!"

A dozen voices called the words together. A score of hands pointed upwards to the glow of light that seemed almost to come from the sky, it was so high above them.

"Right on the stem head – McMaster. He's there . . ."

The pulpit McMaster had seen in shadow form had become a pulpit in fact. Here was truly the highest pulpit in the world.

As McMaster was seen a silence spread outwards across the crowd. The fighting ended, dwindling through scuffling to stillness.

The police could have moved in now and no one would have hindered them. But the police too had fallen under the spell of this strange occasion. They too halted and looked upwards at the man on the prow of the great ship, infinitely far above them and yet by the power of his great voice able to converse with them below.

"Verily I say unto you . . . Cast aside that which is evil. Follow the good and the sweet and the true. Go not whoring after those gods which are false. Rather you shall destroy the false gods and they that follow the false gods. Yea, these shall ye destroy, the man and the woman and the child and the manservant and the maidservant and the ox in the stall and the ass in the field. And the works of they that hunger for strange honey, these also must perish utterly from the face of the earth, so that no man shall know whither they stood.

"I shall cast them into the ever-burning fire, saith the Lord. I shall destroy and cleanse. I shall cleanse the world that is about me and beneath me and above me and behold at the last there shall be no more evil . . ."

At last the police had begun to move through the throng, heading for the ladders that scaled the scaffolding, making for the ship.

No one hampered them deliberately. But to force their way even through this passive crowd was a terrible effort. They were sweating and rumpled before the first dark uniform reached the first ladder and set the first hand to the rungs.

Of all the people there perhaps only Milligan and Levine noticed when the work stopped on the ship.

It had not stopped at the first incursion of the crowd. Riveters had hammered away even while McMaster swarmed into the ship and ran headlong through its passages and across the long spread of decks to the bows.

The riveters heard nothing beyond their own world, beyond the hammering of steel on steel, the judder of air hammers and the hot glow of rivets. They could not hear McMaster's ecstatic declamation and in their work they were too absorbed to look below at the gathering masses.

But when the white-hot rivets stopped flying up to them they could work no more. When on the ground the braziers were overset and the rivet boys no longer able to wield their tongs, then they had to stop. They had to listen.

Protestant and Catholic, drunk and sober, good men and bad, they had to listen.

"And it is written that a great fire shall strike down from the Heavens to destroy those things which are the Devil's and to cleanse the world of unrighteousness. And in that hour behold the righteous shall take the evil-doers and they shall be as dead men that lie upon battlefields.

"Fire, it is said, fire will cleanse and purge and make clean the world and the Lord's coming will be at hand . . ."

As ever, McMaster's words were less heard than his voice. The trumpet call that vibrated from his throat, magnified by the sounding-board that was a great ship seemed to those beneath to fill all the great basin between the hills that was the city of Belfast. Could the whole world not hear that voice that was less now the voice of a man than some great supernatural call that pealed from Heaven itself.

Fire . . . cleanse . . . destroy . . .

Destroy . . . cleanse . . . fire . . .

The reiterated words booming down from on high had a simple, intelligible message.

When the fire came it seemed the inevitable answer to the demanding and commanding voice.

And had McMaster lit the fire? Had his followers? Had it been lit by irked Catholics unable to endure that ranting abuse any longer?

To the watchers in the Yard the questions were irrelevant.

When the first orange glow struck upwards above the ship's deck it might have come as a direct answer from above. This could be a heavenly fire that struck the ship, fire and brimstone from God's own hand, or McMaster's.

For in those long minutes that seemed like the passage of the ages, McMaster was God or God was McMaster. It was no human figure which gestured and thundered but something transcending all normality.

God walked the shipyard and gave down his message through McMaster as once he had done through Moses.

No one doubted as the blaze rose, no one even thought of doubting, for they could still hear the voice, still see the man. Indeed, they could see him now clearer than before, gaunt and black, arms outstretched, outlined against the mounting glow of the flames that were engulfing the ship.

*

Because she was a liner, the Big One had stocks of timber, panelling and fabrics stowed untidily about for use as required. There was paint, too, great drums of paint with its linseed oil base.

The ship was of steel but within the ship there was enough to burn.

The fire rose and rose with a speed and ferocity almost beyond belief. The whole ship was lighted. Across the river in the streets of Belfast the lamps were dimmed by the burning glory of the Big One.

The cleansing fire . . . the destroying fire . . .

*

"My God!" Milligan cried. "He doesn't see the flames! If he doesn't get off there pretty damned quick – "

Levine did not answer. He was absorbed by the spectacle, taking it in, in all its terrible aspects, committing it to a memory which surely he would transmute into something rich and rare.

Police whistles were shrilling now and alarm bells beginning to clang. The Yard's own fire service worked with frantic haste to get their apparatus moving. In the city fire brigade alarm bells clanged.

A policeman smashed an office door and phoned in a frantic message to headquarters.

And yet still, beneath the ship's stern, undisturbed by all the din and all the chaos now about them, the great crowd stared upward at the figure high above.

So the Aztecs may have gazed at their king-gods whom they selected each year, feasted and lauded for a term – and then sacrificed on the pyramidal altars.

The roar of the flames now drowned the words McMaster said and surely even he must have heard them. Yet he never turned, never looked behind him to the mounting inferno.

And though the words were drowned the message was the same. Posture and gesture conveyed it as clearly as throat and lungs had conveyed it before.

Isolated on the stemhead, McMaster seemed as if he was in some way immune to heat, impervious to the flames. He was a creature of fire whom fire could not harm. This was his fire and he was its master.

The staging itself had caught now in a dozen places round the ship. Within, the Big One was a roaring inferno. Fire fighters and police were driven back, step by step. The water from the hoses was a puny trickle to fight this monster that was devouring the Big One.

Even on the ground men could see that here and there in places the shell plating of the ship was glowing red-hot.

And still McMaster stood. Still his hands and arms moved and it seemed impossible that he could live there.

The wind changed suddenly.

And from the crowd there was a sound that lay between a groan and a cry of delight, a mindless, instinctive, wondering sound.

For the flames licked McMaster, engulfed him, swept forward down the ship's deck and were all about him in a golden intensity that surely must destroy all life in its path.

And yet when the wind changed again in a moment or two the preacher was still in his place. Outspread arms carried a garment of flame now, on his head a crown of fire flickered and danced. Every part of his body made up a living, burning, impossible cross.

He could not live, and yet he did live.

And when for an instant the wind quietened the flame's roar they could hear the thunder of his voice still.

"Repent, then, I tell you. Repent . . . repent . . . for the fire shall destroy and cleanse and . . ."

Again the wind roared the flames forward and again the figure was engulfed and this time surely he must die.

Yet again they saw him standing there when the fire drew back.

And this time it seemed that even his flesh was burning in a terrible living crucifix of fire.

It was impossible. It had to be impossible. No man could be burned so and live. And yet they saw it. It was impossible and yet it happened.

Afterwards Levine rationalised: "Of course, when you get third degree burns, that is, when the skin surface itself is destroyed, you don't really feel pain. The nerve ends are destroyed and, in fact it's almost like an anaesthetic. When burning at the stake was a common punishment many a victim used to make long statements from the very heart of the flames."

That was afterwards. No one could rationalise then, not as they gazed upwards at the blazing body on the high prow of the ship.

The spell of the instant was such that no one would have

317

been more than a little surprised if McMaster had stepped over the prow and walked down through the air towards them. Or if he had taken off from the ship and leaped like a meteor into the sky.

Around the crowd the firemen hauled their hoses. Engines roared past. Water hissed as it played on the scorching plates. But not one stirred. No eye left the figure high above on the ship's bow, the blazing, living figurehead whose message now must surely last for ever.

Twice the flames had come and licked about McMaster and twice he had emerged alive.

Then a third time the wind drove the flames forward like a gargantuan blowlamp.

And when at last they fell back the gaunt figure was no longer there.

Even so, long seconds passed and the crowd did not stir, sure that there must be yet another resurrection, sure that McMaster would emerge again from the flames.

Only gradually did they return to normality, shake their heads, blink amazed eyes into seeing once more the world about them.

Now at last the police could begin to move them.

And now Milligan heard the words which were to set the city in a holocaust. McMaster had died by the fire and the fire would cleanse the city. This was what his message had been.

Now events must follow in their old inevitable pattern as soon as the words were said. McMaster was dead and McMaster had unleashed death.

"They've killed McMaster," were the words. "They've killed McMaster."

And everyone knew who 'they' were.

318

EPILOGUE

Timelessly the man sharpened his scythe. Steel blunts swiftly cutting rushes. Rushes grow as quickly as they are cut. If it was not rushes it would be heather or bracken or any other useless plant such as the Black Mountain could provide.

There had been a big fire in the city, he thought, as he rubbed the blade with the worn carborundum stone. He had seen the glow of it in the sky during the night. He had been tempted almost to get out of bed and walk up to the brow of the hill and look down at where the fire was. A good fire was a bonny sight.

But bed was snug and it would take more than a sight to get him from it. So he lay there and saw the glow in the sky and was thankful the fire was far enough from his bleak steading. It was none of his business.

Just the same, if he had not gone early to bed he would have walked up the hill to see the fire. It must have been a brave one.

Across the hill a dog fox loped easily, ignoring him. It could see he had a scythe in his hand and not a gun. The man swore mildly. The fox had had more than one chicken from him. He tested the blade's edge with his thumb and found it sharp enough.

Just before he bent to the next clump of rushes he heard the slow clip-clop of hooves. Up from the city, slowly over the brow of the hill, a donkey came walking with a woman on its back.

They came very slowly and as he looked at the woman and

319

the animal he had a vague memory of seeing them before. The woman wore a blue, faded, hooded cloak, pulled well over her forehead.

The hood did not conceal the tired lines in the face, the deadly sickness in the eyes.

For a moment the man almost laid down his scythe and went to call her to the house. For a moment he was about to offer her food and rest.

But if you started that thing once with tinkers the place would be polluted in no time. You had to have a bit of care.

Silently leaning on the scythe he watched the woman and the donkey trot past with the whole of Ireland before them.

THE END